"Kindly do as you are told, Miss Hamilton, and we will go our separate ways," Sir D'Arcy ordered.

Venetia knew she had been at fault in the near-collision between her gig and Sir D'Arcy's coach. She was also well aware that she was the one who should back down the road and turn around, but D'Arcy's imperious tone made her bridle; she was stubbornly determined to stand her ground. She averted her gaze and murmured, "I am afraid I must insist, Sir D'Arcy, that you move your coach!"

She was quite prepared for a long verbal tussle over the matter, but to her surprise, Sir D'Arcy glared at her for a moment, strode back to his carriage, reached inside it, and marched back to her. Without a word, he seized her around her slim waist, picked her up and carried her in his strong arms to a nearby silver birch tree.

"Whatever are you doing, sir?" she cried, struggling furiously. "Unhand me this instant!"

"With pleasure," he smiled setting her down, but retaining a vise-like grip on her arm as he produced a length of rope and tied her firmly to the tree. Then, laughing, he returned to her gig, and after a moment spent calming the alarmed chestnut, Sir D'Arcy slowly urged the horse and the gig back up the lane toward the crossroads.

Venetia lifted her chin and tossed her curls defiantly. He had settled the dispute by brute strength, but she was determined not to give him the satisfaction of seeing her grovel. Yet, what if he should leave her here by the road, all alone, tied up? Her heart suddenly began to pound with fear. . .

CAROLINE COURTNEY

The Romantic Rivals

WARNER BOOKS

A Warner Communications Company

WARNER BOOKS EDITION

Copyright © 1980 by Arlington Books (Publisher), Ltd.
All rights reserved.

Cover design by Gene Light

Cover art by Walter Popp

Warner Books, Inc., 75 Rockefeller Plaza, New York, N.Y. 10019

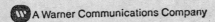 A Warner Communications Company

Printed in the United States of America

First Printing: October, 1980

10 9 8 7 6 5 4 3 2 1

One

Venetia Hamilton tossed back her golden curls and laughed for pure joy. How happy she felt today, bowling along the leafy Dorset lane in Aunt Matty's fine new gig. The sun was shining in a clear blue sky and every tree was filled with the melody of bird song.

With her blue eyes sparkling Venetia leaned forward, urging the glossy chestnut pony to quicken her pace.

"Hurry, girl, hurry!" she encouraged the pony. "I fear I dallied too long at that milliner's in Lyme Regis. I promised Aunt Matty faithfully that I'd be back by three to help her entertain the formidable Lady Leamington. My poor aunt will be in the most monstrous stew if we are late!"

She cracked her whip on the side of her burnished leather boot, and the gig raced with reckless speed along the narrow, winding lanes. Venetia felt breathless with excitement. She was proud of her ability to control the pounding chestnut, and exhilarated by the rush of warm April wind in her face.

They were approaching a crossroad. But Venetia refused to slow their pace.

"On, on!" she cried, leaning to the right as the gig careered round the corner. Instantly, the smile froze on her face. Approaching fast up the slight gradient toward her was a magnificent coach-and-four.

The large dark-blue coach filled almost the entire width of the narrow lane, and the high-spirited grays were being driven at a furious pace by a tall, elegantly dressed gentleman. But both Venetia's gig and the carriage were traveling at such a lick, there seemed no way for either to avoid a most disastrous collision.

Horrified, Venetia tugged with all her might on the reins.

"Easy, girl, easy!" she commanded desperately, terrified that the lightweight gig would overturn into the ditch.

Fortunately, the gentleman in charge of the gleaming coach proved to be both quick-witted and an excellent horseman. Observing Venetia struggling to control her pony and gig, he rose in his seat, and in a flash had brought his high-stepping grays first to a moderate pace, then to a halt. The carriage wheels screeched as the grays pulled up, barely a foot away from Venetia's quivering chestnut.

Venetia closed her eyes, feeling weak with relief. How terrible if she had wrecked Aunt Matty's new gig, on her first time out! True enough, Aunt Matty was a dear, kind soul, but Venetia divined that even the most saintly lady would have found it impossible to forgive the wrecking of a costly new gig. She thanked heaven the driver of the carriage had possessed the wit and skill to bring his horses under control. She was determined to make haste and express her gratitude.

But before she could move from the gig, she saw that the dark-haired gentleman was already striding toward her.

She gave him her most dazzling smile, saying, "Oh, I really cannot begin to thank—"

"You stupid, ignorant, reckless girl," he shouted. "What the devil d'you think you were playing at?"

6

His handsome, rugged face was grim as he waved his whip at her. "Never in all my days," he raged, "have I observed such witless behavior. Whatever possessed you to stampede round that corner at such an insane pace? Don't you realize you could have been killed!"

Shocked, Venetia drew a sharp breath, "How dare you address me in tones of such hostility!" she retorted. "I agree, I was not traveling at a snail's pace, but I was in a hurry, and I had anticipated that these back lanes would be deserted. I had certainly not expected to be confronted with a coach-and-four being driven as if you were hell-bent on putting out a fire! It is my opinion, sir, that it is *you* who were traveling at a reckless pace, not I!"

Venetia was shaking with anger. A moment ago, she had been quite prepared to shower the dark-haired stranger with her grateful thanks for the alert manner in which he had averted an accident. But now, faced with such arrogance and scorn, her fighting spirit reasserted itself. Handsome and dashing he may be, she thought, but she would not sit there and be cowed by him.

The gentleman glared at her, his gray eyes steely as he tapped his whip on the side of her gig.

"You are not only an irresponsible driver," he snapped, "you also display an appalling ignorance of the rules of the road. Are you not aware that vehicles traveling up a gradient take precedence over those coming down? As you turned round the corner to descend the hill you should have slowed, in mindful consideration of anything traveling up toward you."

Venetia bit her lip and said, "I regret, sir, I have never heard of such a rule."

He replied sarcastically, "That, my girl, is patently obvious!"

Venetia's face was flushed, and she admonished, "Since you are determined to be unpleasant, I should be glad if you would direct your scorn to me by name, and not as *my girl*. The reason I am unfamiliar with rules pertaining to gradients is that I hail from Lincolnshire. The land is flat there, and hills are rare. My father is Sir Peter Hamilton, of Boston Park."

Venetia deliberately introduced herself by mentioning her father, hoping that this aggressive stranger would be impressed by the mention of his name. Sir Peter was, after all, one of the wealthiest and most influential men in all east England.

But the stranger did not look in the least impressed. He favored Venetia with a curt bow, and declared, "I am Sir D'Arcy Rawnsley, Miss Hamilton."

Venetia inclined her head. "How do you do."

He frowned and commented, "I regret that I am making your acquaintance under such disagreeable circumstances. Is it traditional in Lincolnshire, Miss Hamilton, for young ladies to career round the countryside in gigs, and unescorted?"

Venetia flared.

"Sir D'Arcy, I am twenty-one years old, in command of my own fortune, and my own life. Unfortunately, my fiancé is in France at the moment, serving with his regiment. Were he here, I assure you he would not tolerate for one instant your overbearing, patronizing attitude towards me!"

The glimmer of a smile touched Sir D'Arcy's firm mouth. He tucked his whip under the arm of his immaculate chocolate-brown riding jacket and replied, "I am delighted to hear you are marrying a military man, Miss Hamilton. No doubt he will instill some much needed discipline into your unruly character."

Venetia gripped her seat, her knuckles white. It was all she could do to prevent herself from striking out with her whip at this thoroughly objectionable man! But that was just what he was trying to goad her to do, she realized, catching the hint of a mocking smile in his gray eyes. He was trying to provoke her into losing her temper to justify his unwarranted criticism of her character.

Venetia lifted up her head, and said frostily, "Sir D'Arcy, I am late for an urgent appointment. As you are clearly incapable of conversing in a civilized manner, perhaps you would kindly back up your coach so I may proceed along my way."

He stood with arms akimbo, making no attempt to

move. "On the contrary, Miss Hamilton. It is *you* who must back up your gig, so that *I* may proceed."

Venetia replied cuttingly, "I fear I am sadly unacquainted with southern manners, Sir D'Arcy. In Lincolnshire, it is customary for well-bred gentlemen to give way before ladies. It pains me to think that your ignorance of such courtesies is clearly going to put you at a great social disadvantage. If you care to give me your address I will glady send round my footman with a book on social etiquette which I am sure you will find invaluable."

Sir D'Arcy seemed to choke. But Venetia could not fathom whether he was reacting with rage or laughter. Then he said, with great deliberation, "Your kind consideration quite overwhelms me, Miss Hamilton. But you see, when one is on the road, then I am afraid practical considerations take precedence over social niceties. The plain fact is that if I backed my coach down the road, I should have to travel for nearly half a mile before I came to a wide enough gap for you to pass. Whereas it is only a mere ten yards or so for you to reverse to the crossroads." He tapped his foot impatiently. "Come along, now Miss Hamilton! I am tired of this charade. Kindly do as you are told, and we will go our separate ways!"

Venetia bridled at the imperious note in his voice. He was, of course, unquestionably right about which one of them should reverse their vehicle. If Sir D'Arcy had troubled to address her in a reasonable, courteous tone, Venetia would have complied at once, naturally. But his arrogant attitude made her stubbornly determined to stand her ground.

She averted her gaze and murmured, "I am afraid I must insist, Sir D'Arcy, that you move your coach!"

Venetia was quite prepared for a long verbal tussle over the matter. *I shall be late for Aunt Matty's visit from Lady Leamington*, she thought. *Well, so be it. There is a question of principle at stake here, and I am determined to win! I shall not allow this overbearing man to bully me in such an outrageous fashion!*

To her surprise, Sir D'Arcy glared at her for a moment, then turned on his heel and strode back to his carriage. Venetia felt like singing with triumph. He was going to back up his coach! Clearly, he was beginning to feel ashamed of himself, and was seeking to make amends by acting as a gentleman should. *Well,* thought Venetia, *as I ride past him in my gig I shall, naturally, be gracious. After this unfortunate episode, it will be pleasant to part on amiable terms with Sir D'Arcy.*

But Sir D'Arcy was making no move towards his horses. Instead, he reached inside his carriage, and then marched back toward Venetia.

What happened next left Venetia stunned, breathless, and speechless with rage. Grim-faced, Sir D'Arcy advanced on the gig, seized Venetia round her slim waist, and carried her in his strong arms to a nearby silver birch tree.

At last Venetia found her voice. "Whatever are you doing, Sir D'Arcy?" she cried, struggling furiously, but in vain. "Are you deranged? Unhand me this instant!"

"With pleasure," he smiled, setting her down. But he retained a vise-like hold on her arm as he produced a length of rope and proceeded to tie her firmly to the tree.

"How dare you!" protested Venetia, her blue eyes stormy. Oh, the indignity of it all! "Let me free, you scoundrel! I warn you, my father and my fiancé will have you horse-whipped for this!"

Laughing, Sir D'Arcy returned to Venetia's gig and spent a moment calming the alarmed chestnut. Then he slowly urged the horse, and the gig, back up the lane toward the crossroads.

Venetia writhed and tugged at the rope which restrained her. But Sir D'Arcy had been ruthlessly thorough when he tied the final knot.

"You do not deserve the name of gentleman!" she screamed. "I shall never forgive you for this. Never!"

He strolled past her toward his carriage, and commented mildly, "I would advise you to remain still, Miss Hamilton. If you keep pulling against that rope you will only burn your pretty wrists."

"I'd like to see you burned alive!" retorted Venetia, as Sir D'Arcy drove his carriage toward the crossroads.

Her heart suddenly began to pound with fear. Surely he was not intending to drive off in a cloud of dust, leaving her here tied to the tree? This was a remote country lane, with few passersby. She could be stranded in this place for hours, helpless, with no one to hear her cries. And when night fell, what then? What would become of her?

Venetia lifted her chin and tossed her curls defiantly. *Whatever dreadful fate Sir D'Arcy has in store for me, I will not plead with him,* she resolved. *I shall not give him the satisfaction of seeing me grovel. If he rides off now in his carriage, I shall simply look the other way and affect that I do not care a bean!*

It was with some relief, however, that Venetia noticed out of the corner of her eye that Sir D'Arcy was dismounting from his carriage. She glared at him as he strolled at an unhurried pace toward her.

"Set me loose at once, you scoundrel!" she demanded.

He smiled. "My, what a hellcat you are. Has your fiancé any idea what he's taking on, I wonder?"

Venetia replied—with as much dignity as she could muster under the circumstances—"Captain Dermot is a man of honor. He would never demean himself to behave in such a dastardly manner toward a lady."

The smile vanished from Sir D'Arcy's face. He asked gravely, "You are betrothed to Captain Dermot? Captain Drystan Dermot?"

"I have that pleasure," answered Venetia. "Though I am surprised his name is familiar to you. I cannot imagine anyone as noble as Captain Dermot lowering himself to acquaintanceship with one as ill-bred as you!"

She had anticipated a swift, sharp response to this barb. But Sir D'Arcy remained silent, and thoughtful as he untied the rope. The instant her hands were free, Venetia flew at him aiming a forceful blow at his rugged face.

He was too fast, and too powerful for her. "Oh no you don't," he said. Laughing, he lifted her into his arms and held her tight against his broad chest. Ignoring her indignant kicks, and muffled screams of protest, he carried her back up the lane and deposited her in the gig. Furious, Venetia reached for her whip.

Realizing her intention, Sir D'Arcy folded his arms, and said laconically, "I shouldn't, if I were you. Consider the facts. I am in every way your superior. I am bigger, stronger, more powerful. In addition, I am in control of my emotions, which you patently are not. If you attempted to lash out with that whip, your aim would be wild and it would be a simple matter for me to splinter the thing over my knee. I should then be so irritated at having my time wasted over such an infuriatingly trivial incident, that I should then proceed to lose my temper and you, my dear Miss Hamilton, would follow the whip over my breeches!"

"You really are the most insufferable man I have ever had the misfortune to meet!" exploded Venetia. "I assure you, when my financé hears about this, he will not rest until he has given you a thrashing which will severely deflate the size of your swollen head!"

Sir D'Arcy looked puzzled. "Tell me, Miss Hamilton. Do your parents approve of your engagement to Captain Dermot?"

Venetia flushed, crushing down the uncomfortable memory of her father's anger when she confessed her love for Drystan. She said haughtily, "My father, Sir D'Arcy, is an enlightened man. He desires only that I should be happy, and if he were here now I promise you he would severely berate me for wasting my breath on such a dastardly creature as you. Good afternoon!"

Sir D'Arcy gave a mocking, courtly bow. "Au revoir, Miss Hamilton. Lyme Regis is a small society. I am confident we shall meet again."

"I sincerely hope not," said Venetia icily, gathering up the reins and urging the chestnut forward.

As she sped away down the narrow lane, Venetia's blood was boiling. *And to think,* she reflected, *that half an hour ago I felt as if I were the happiest girl in England. I had a letter from my adored Drystan in my reticule. The sun was shining, the air was sweet with scents of spring. Oh, all was right with my world. Now that wretched man has spoiled it all. Because of him, I feel out of temper, confused and unsettled. How dare he treat me in such an overbearing manner? He is without doubt the most uncivilized, objectionable man I have ever encountered. What was it that he had the impertinence to allege?—"I am in every way your superior."—What effrontery! Did he seriously imagine that I would meekly accept such an arrogant remark as gospel truth?*

Well, Sir D'Arcy, you are right about one matter: Lyme Regis is a small place. We shall undoubtedly meet again. But be advised of one thing. You may have come off best in this, our first encounter. But from now on, Sir D'Arcy, I shall make it my business to ensure that I have the whip hand over you!

As Venetia entered the hall of Woodhouse Lodge, Aunt Matty came rushing to greet her. She was a small, finely boned woman in her middle years, with kindly brown eyes and a permanently perplexed expression on her delicate face.

"Oh, there you are at last, Venetia! I was afraid an accident had befallen you."

Venetia bent, and kissed her aunt reassuringly on the cheek. "I am sorry I'm late, Aunt Matty. I was delayed on the road by a particularly stubborn beast which refused to budge from my path."

A confused frown appeared on Aunt Matty's forehead, but she was clearly too worried about Lady Leamington's imminent visit to question Venetia further on the reason for her tardy arrival.

"Have you known Lady Leamington for long, Aunt Matty?" enquired Venetia. "I am greatly looking forward to making her acquaintance. Is she really so very formidable?"

Aunt Matty sighed as she led the way into the cozy drawing room. "Ottilia and I came out together. But even as a slip of a seventeen-year-old girl, she was still fearfully bossy and forthright. No one dared cross her. And all the young men were absolutely petrified of her."

An impish smile crossed Venetia's lovely face. "Do

tell, then, Aunt, how she managed to ensnare the Earl of Leamington. He's incredibly rich, I believe. Surely he must have been considered a monstrous good catch?"

Aunt Matty's wispy brown curls bobbed as she nodded her assent. "Oh, yes, many girls were setting their caps at him. Of course, Cedric wasn't the earl then, just the heir to the title. But he was such a difficult man. Portly and not at all handsome. And so painfully shy. At all the balls he would lurk in a corner, clearly too overcome with embarrassment to approach a lady and ask her to stand up with him."

"So what cunning ruse did Lady Leamington employ to entice the earl's heir to the altar?" asked Venetia, drawing across the screen to shield her aunt from the draft from the windows. "After all, if he was in too much of a quake to ask a girl to dance, imagine the agonies he must have endured plucking up enough courrage to ask her to marry him!"

Venetia was glad to hear her aunt laugh. Realizing that Aunt Matty was dreading this visit from Lady Leamington, Venetia had deliberately provoked a conversation about her aunt's younger years in the hope that the affectionate laughter of nostalgia would make her feel more relaxed.

Beaming, Aunt Matty recalled, "Oh, Ottilia was never the type to employ subtle tactics, Venetia! For the duration of three balls she sat with the rest of us as we pondered on the reluctance of the earl's heir to ask any of us to dance. Then at the fourth ball Ottilia could stand it no longer. She stood up, stalked across the ballroom and halted by Cedric's shoulder. She's a few inches taller than he, you know. Well, she simply glared at the poor fellow in the most menacing fashion. I blush to think of it. And what could he do? To have walked away from Ottilia would have been most dreadfully rude. On the other hand, if he didn't take some action, it was obvious that she intended to stand there, looming over him, all evening! So after an interminable pause, he finally stuttered out an invitation to her to partner him in the cotillion."

Venetia laughed. "And no doubt, from that moment

14

on she stuck to him like glue until the *ton* accepted them as an established pair."

Aunt Matty leaned forward on the sofa, her brown eyes twinkling, "They do say that it was she who proposed to him. It would be just like Ottilia to do such a thing." Aunt Matty assumed a brisk, gruff tone. "Now look here, Cedric old thing. Don't you think it's about time we took a canter up the aisle together?"

"Why Aunt," exclaimed Venetia in delight. "I had no notion you were such a wicked mimic! I insist that we have an evening of charades together soon. It will be such fun!"

Venetia paused by the window, then cried out in alarm, "Oh, here is Lady Leamington's carriage advancing up the drive, and I have not yet changed my dress! I will run and do so, directly. I assume you will be entertaining Lady Leamington in the Blue Saloon, Aunt?"

"No, no!" cried Aunt Matty, looking flustered. She twisted a lace handkerchief in her hands. "I shall receive her here, in the drawing room. It is pleasant enough in here and I . . . I . . . anticipate that Ottilia will admire the fine view across the lawns."

"As you think best, Aunt," murmured Venetia, hastily excusing herself to go and change her dress.

As her maid tied the fastenings on a gown of fresh, pale pink muslin, Venetia mused on her aunt's strange reluctance to use the Blue Saloon. Since her arrival a week ago from Lincolnshire, Venetia had only managed to glimpse briefly at the Blue Saloon. Through a half-open door she had admired its classical proportions, the marble fireplace, and the brilliant azure silk curtains. Surely such a room would have provided the most perfect setting for the nervous Aunt Matty to impress her distinguished guest? But as the maid brushed her shining golden curls, Venetia smiled in understanding.

Of course, she thought, *how foolish of me. Naturally, dear Aunt Matty has chosen to receive in the cozy drawing room because it is the place in which she feels most at home. The cool elegance of the Blue Saloon would overwhelm her. Poor Aunt Matty. I must do everything in my power to ensure that the frightening Lady Leamington does not set her all atremble!*

With her grooming completed, Venetia hurried downstairs. She was just in time to observe a large, florid-faced woman sailing like a galleon into the drawing room.

"Ah, Matilda!" boomed Lady Leamington. "Delightful to see you again after all these years. But my, how wan you look! Are you getting proper nourishment, my dear?"

Aunt Matty replied bravely, "I am perfectly well, thank you Ottilia. Oh, now here is my niece, Venetia."

As Venetia bobbed a curtsy she found herself under the scrutiny of piercing, cold-blue eyes. "Mmm," nodded Lady Leamington, "She's a very pretty girl, Matilda. Now let me get this right. Venetia is the daughter of your brother, Sir Peter Hamilton?"

"That is indeed so," smiled Aunt Matty, urging her guest toward the sofa. "Venetia heard that I had recently removed to Lyme from London, and kindly offered to come and keep me company for a while, until I settled in."

"Quite so," rasped the iron-haired lady. "And do I not recall seeing an announcement of a recent engagement between Miss Venetia Hamilton and Captain Drystan Dermot? A hussar, is he not, Matilda?"

Venetia could tolerate no longer being spoken of as if she were an inanimate portrait, hanging on the wall.

"That is correct, Lady Leamington," she said, smiling. "The Captain and I plan to be married when he is next granted leave from his regiment."

As Aunt Matty rang the bell for tea, Lady Leamington wagged a reproving finger at Venetia. "Ah! It is all coming back to me now. It was something of a whirlwind romance, was it not? And your parents do not approve of the match!"

Her cheeks burning, Venetia bit back a crushing retort. Really, she thought hotly, there must be something strange about the air of Lyme Regis which infects its inhabitants with the urge to pass comments on affairs which are no concern of theirs whatsoever! First there was that objectionable Sir D'Arcy Rawnsley this afternoon, expressing impertinent surprise that my parents allowed my betrothal to Drystan. And now Lady Leamington, having been acquainted with me for all of three minutes, is preparing to pass *her* judgment on the matter.

Venetia said with dignity, "Naturally, my parents were anxious, as no other member of my family has ever married a military man. My father feared that after my quiet upbringing in Lincolnshire, life as the wife of a captain would be too strenuous for me."

"And you know what fathers are like, Ottilia," commented Aunt Matty with a smile. "They are ever convinced that not even the most handsome, most wealthy bachelor in England is good enough for their darling daughter."

Lady Leamington slapped her knee and roared with laughter. "That's true enough! I remember my father telling me I was a damn fool for wanting to marry Cedric. *'He may be an earl's heir, Ottilia,'* roared Papa, *'but the fellow's as dumb as an ox and thick as two short planks!'* "

"Then . . . if I may enquire," Aunt Matty said hesitantly, "why did you want to marry Cedric?"

"Because I knew no one else would have me," declared Lady Leamington flatly. "When I came out, I sat in front of my glass and forced myself to face facts. I had no great fortune. I had a countenance only a horse would have fallen in love with. And I was too dashed lazy to cultivate any social graces. So when I set eyes on Cedric, I knew he was my one and only chance."

Aunt Matty smiled her thanks at Venetia as the golden-haired girl gracefully crossed the room to pour the tea. "And have you been happy, Ottilia?"

"No complaints," barked the Countess. "You see, what everyone failed to appreciate when Cedric behaved so unsociably at those stuffy London balls, is that basically, he's a country person. We're two of a kind. We both enjoy country pursuits rather than that rarefied London scene. So because we gain pleasure from the same activities, we get on like a house on fire." She rounded on

Venetia. "I'm one of the best shots in the county, you know."

"I can well believe that, Lady Leamington," murmured Venetia, handing the Countess her tea.

Lady Leamington went on, "Of course, if I'd been blessed with Venetia's pretty looks, I'd have been delighted in playing the field. I must say, Venetia, I think you're making a mistake rushing into marriage with this hussar. Should have thought you could have bagged yourself someone better than a mere captain. Who are his people? Is he one of the Bath Dermots? I know them well. Lady Dermot had the gall to tell me it was indecent of me to ride to hounds."

Determined to stand her ground in defense of the man she loved, Venetia said steadily, "I believe Captain Dermot's family hail from York. I have not yet had the pleasure of meeting them."

"York?" frowned the Countess. "I've never heard of York Dermots."

"Really, Ottilia," said Aunt Matty with surprising firmness. "It is unreasonable of you to expect to be on nodding terms with every family in the land who happen to be named Dermot. Come to that, it may be that Captain Dermot's people have never heard of Lady Leamington, either."

The Countess bridled. "Stuff, Matty! If they are unfamiliar with the Leamingtons of Lyme, then these York Dermots must be way down the social register!"

Chastened, Aunt Matty fiddled with the fringe on her shawl, and looked with mute appeal at Venetia. Taking her cue that a drastic change of subject was called for, Venetia exclaimed, "Aunt Matty, ever since I arrived I have been meaning to compliment you on that delightful portrait hanging over the mantel. How charming it looks today, with the afternoon sun streaming in upon it."

The portrait, set in an oval rosewood frame, was of a lovely dark-haired girl in the bloom of her youth. The artist had caught to perfection the radiance of her pale skin and the soft, luminous glow of her lovely brown eyes.

Lady Leamington peered at the portrait, "Why yes,

Venetia is quite right. It is indeed exquisite. And what a beautiful girl! Who is she, Matilda?"

Venetia observed a strange, distant expression clouding her aunt's eyes. Aunt Matty was blushing, and seemed incapable of answering Lady Leamington's question.

Suddenly realizing the truth, Venetia said softly, "It is you, isn't it Aunt Matty? The girl in the portrait is yourself!"

Aunt Matty's color deepened even further. But before she could reply, Lady Leamington snapped, "Nonsense. That dewy-eyed girl can't possibly be you, Matilda! I certainly have no recollection of you ever looking as lovely as that!"

"I was in love!" blurted Aunt Matty. "That portrait was commissioned by the gentleman I intended to marry. The reason I look so—well—so different from the way you knew me, Ottilia, is that during the sittings I was dreaming of the man I loved."

"The man you loved!" exploded Lady Leamington. "What fanciful notion is this, Matilda? You had plenty of beaux, admittedly, but I do not remember your forming a special attachment to any of them."

"It was all very secret," whispered Aunt Matty, her voice quivering. "If you do not mind, Ottilia, I do not wish to discuss the subject further."

Seeking to divert Lady Leamington's attention, Venetia remarked, "The portrait is exceedingly fine, Aunt Matty. It was painted by Mr. Reynolds, was it not?"

Aunt Matty nodded. "He was such a charming man. He made me feel so at ease during the sittings."

Venetia was intrigued. As she demurely bent her head to her embroidery she pondered on the secret—and presumably doomed—romance between the young Aunt Matty and her dashing admirer. *And he was no penniless rake, either,* reflected Venetia. *For it was he who had commissioned the portrait of Aunt Matty. And it was common knowledge that Mr. Reynolds commanded extremely high fees for his work. So I wonder why Aunt Matty never married her admirer. What tragic event befell to keep them apart?*

Lady Leamington, it was plain, was determined not

to be impressed that Aunt Matty had sat for the celebrated Mr. Reynolds. "Speaking for myself, I prefer the work of Mr. Romney. He can always be relied upon to produce a true likeness of his subjects."

"With respect, Lady Leamington, I fear I must disagree with you," murmured Venetia. "Mr. Romney is ruthlessly professional, I agree. But I find his approach too cold-blooded, too calculating. There is a softness about Mr. Reynolds' painting which sets him far above Mr. Romney."

Lady Leamington sniffed. "I don't know how you can bear to have that portrait hanging in your drawing room, Matilda. If I were you I could not abide to be reminded of how young and pretty I once was. You're not looking at all well, Matty."

"I confess, I was unwell for some months when I resided in London," said Aunt Matty. "I hoped the remove to Lyme, and the bracing sea breezes, would lend me renewed vigor."

Lady Leamington spread her square, large-knuckled hands in a gesture of bewilderment. "But why have you chosen to live here, at Woodhouse Lodge? Everyone knows it is one of the worst houses in the district. It is damp, crumbling, downright inconvenient, and unhealthy. Had you asked my advice, Matilda, I could have recommended a score of suitable houses for you to buy. But I fear you will regret purchasing Woodhouse Lodge."

For once, Venetia agreed with Lady Leamington. On her arrival from Lincolnshire, she had been surprised to find Aunt Matty living in such a cramped, unattractive house. And Lady Leamington was right: Woodhouse Lodge was horribly damp.

However, seeing that Aunt Matty was on the verge of tears after Lady Leamington's onslaught, Venetia hastened to her aid. "Indeed, Lady Leamington, I believe my aunt has made a most judicious choice of home. Believe me, we are so cozy here. And what need has Aunt Matty for a huge, rambling place? Besides, large houses are inevitably drafty, and my aunt feels the cold most dreadfully."

"And the view!" murmured Aunt Matty somewhat

desperately. "Is this not the most delightful aspect, Ottilia, overlooking those lovely lawns?"

"Mmm," expressed Lady Leamington, dismissing the expanse of verdant green with a scornful glance. Lady Leamington, Venetia realized with a wry smile, was simply not interested in any expanse of land which could not be galloped across.

To Venetia's relief, Lady Leamington arose. "I must take my leave, Matilda. I have enjoyed our little chat. And I was glad to have the opportunity of meeting you, Venetia."

Aunt Matty ventured nervously, "I had hoped, Ottilia, that you would bring your own niece with you today, as company for Venetia. They are of an age, are they not?" She turned to Venetia. "Ottilia has her niece, the Lady Blanche Vaisey, staying with her at Leamington Hall. I thought it would be pleasant for you to make her acquaintance."

Lady Leamington slapped her thigh. "How thoughtless of me! I should have mentioned earlier . . . Blance sends her sincere regrets . . . that is . . . she was so looking forward . . . Oh, dash it. I'm no use at expressing insincere sentiments. The truth is, Blanche wanted to spend the afternoon titivating herself up for her new beau. That's why she didn't accompany me. I hope you're not too put out, Matty."

Aunt Matty smiled. "Not at all. I can remember how it was when one was twenty-one, and the most important thing in all the world was to look pretty for the gentleman who was calling that afternoon. Who is her new beau, Ottilia?"

Lady Leamington sat down again. Venetia's spirits sank as she watched the lady settling herself on the sofa. "Now I must own, Matilida, that Blanche and I don't see eye to eye on every matter. But when it comes to beaux, she does have impeccable taste. *She* would never bother herself with anyone inferior, however dashing and handsome he may be." Her eyes flashed in reproof to Venetia.

Furious, Venetia stared challengingly back. *Say one more word in criticism of Captain Dermot, Lady Leamington, and I swear I shall remain demurely silent no longer. You will discover to your cost that you Leamingtons do not have the monopoly of blunt speech. We Lincolnshire Hamiltons are quite adept at speaking our minds, when required!*

Sensing the chilly vibrations wafting her way from Venetia's chair, Lady Leamington hurried on, "Blanche's new beau is quite the most elevated person. He is incredibly wealthy, amazingly handsome, and so charming. When we were introduced he bowed with such grace, and said to me, Lady—"

"But Ottilia!" exclaimed Aunt Matty. "Who *is* this gentleman? What is his name?

"Oh, how foolish of me not to have said. He is titled Sir D'Arcy Rawnsley. Is that not an impressive sounding name? It perfectly matches his appearance and manners, I assure you."

Venetia was thankful she had her embroidery to occupy her. Furiously, she stabbed the needle in and out of the fine linen. The stitches were ragged and uneven. Later, she would have to pull them out and restitch them. But she cared not. For each vicious stitch represented a hearty stab at the loathsome Sir D'Arch Rawnsley.

Really, she fumed, *how can Lady Leamington be so taken in by him? He is an arrogant, overbearing, totally infuriating man. Yet Lady Leamington speaks as if he is the most superior being on this earth!*

To her surprise, Aunt Matty was nodding in agreement with her guest. "Oh, Sir D'Arcy. Indeed, he is one of the most gallant gentlemen I have ever had the good fortune to encounter."

Venetia could not restrain the enquiry. "You know him, then, Aunt?"

"Very slightly. He has an imposing house in Curzon Street, you know. I recall that one day when I was returning from shopping in Bond Street, a young blade drove by at a furious pace in his gig, driving straight through a huge puddle and splashing my new pelisse so that it was quite ruined with mud. Well," Aunt Matty leaned forward, her brown eyes warm with the recollection, "Sir D'Arcy happened to be riding by. He observed my distress and chased after the young dandiprat, berating him most soundly for his lack of consideration. The young blade returned, and under Sir D'Arcy's wrathful gaze, apologized most handsomely."

Clearly, thought Venetia, *the smoky air of London must have conspired to dull Sir D'Arcy's aggressive temperament*. She said aloud, "I wonder what has caused Sir D'Arcy to abandon his fine Curzon Street house and bestow his admirable presence on Lyme Regis?"

Fortunately, Lady Leamington did not recognize the heavy irony in Venetia's tone, "Oh, but did you not know? Sir D'Arcy owned a fine country house just outside Weymouth. Such a tragedy! It was recently burned to the ground! I assume he has come to Dorset to inspect the wreckage, and see if anything could be salvaged. I imagine that my dear niece Blanche will be a great comfort to him at this time of such distress."

"I do hope we shall soon have the pleasure of meeting your niece," murmured Aunt Matty.

"Oh yes indeed. I am arranging a ball in her honor," replied Lady Leamington. "Hope to see you both there. It'll be good to see Leamington Hall gay with music and dancing again. I've felt for some time that Cedric and I are getting stuck in our stuffy old ways. We need livening up."

"A ball!" exclaimed Aunt Matty in dismay. "Oh, I fear I never attend balls nowadays, Ottilia."

"Fudge!" boomed Lady Leamington. "A spot of vigorous country dancing will bring back the roses to your cheeks. I shall expect you to be amongst the first arrivals, Matilda. After all, the entire county will be present. And it will be a delightful opportunity for you to renew your acquaintance with Sir D'Arcy Rawnsley."

"Yes, to be sure," muttered Aunt Matty, looking vastly relieved as Lady Leamington headed for the drawing room door.

During the pause in the hall while the footman fetched her pelisse, Lady Leamington rounded on Venetia.

"Come to my ball, Venetia, and study well Sir D'Arcy. I guarantee, after you set eyes on him, you'll wish you'd never hurled your cap so hastily at that hussar. Still, on the other hand, it's probably fortunate that you are engaged, for Blanche has her sights firmly set on Sir D'Arcy. But I wager you'll be kicking yourself, Venetia, for missing your chance with the most eligible man in all southern England!"

Two

"Oh, my, what an exhausting woman Ottilia is," sighed Aunt Matty as Lady Leamington's carriage disappeared down the rutted drive. "Will you excuse me, Venetia? My head is throbbing, and I feel sorely in need of a rest before dinner."

As the drawing room doors closed behind her aunt, Venetia lay full length on the sofa, and took a letter from her reticule. She was glad of the chance to be alone, for she was longing to reread the letter from her fiancé which had been forwarded by her parents at Boston Park.

For a moment she held the letter against her smooth cheek, savoring this precious link between herself and the man she loved. In truth, she still felt raw and unsettled from the strain of suffering in silence Lady Leamington's unstinted praise of the insufferable Sir D'Arcy Rawnsley.

Really, thought Venetia hotly, *if I hear that man's name just once more today, I shall scream! Why is it that neither my Aunt Matty, nor Lady Leamington, nor her niece Lady Blanche have the wit to recognize the truth about Sir D'Arcy? Oh, how cunningly he has gulled them!*

Venetia smiled wryly. *But of course, their contact with Sir D'Arcy has been in public. Naturally in the company of others, he would take care to present his best manners. I, however, encountered him on a lonely country road. I caught him unawares, before he had time to assume his mask of sociable gallantry. So to me alone has his true, peppery temperament been revealed.*

Venetia placed a velvet cushion behind her back. *Well, infuriating though it may be for me to have to listen to Lyme ladies caroling the alleged virtues of Sir D'Arcy, I must count myself fortunate that I at least know the truth about him. Who knows, had my mishap with him not taken place, I might have met him at Lady Leamington's ball and deemed him the most estimable gentleman. Why, I might even have been so foolish as to fall in love with him!*

Laughing at the absurdity of such a notion, Venetia unfolded her fiancé's letter, and with quickening heart began to read,

> *My dearest Venetia, I have just returned to camp after a hectic (and victorious!) skirmish with the French. What ruffians those frog eaters are! Their lines were in total disarray and how proud you would have been could you have seen me lead the charge which sent them scurrying into retreat.*

Venetia closed her eyes in anguish. Oh how she hated to think of her beloved Drystan endangering his life against the hateful French!

Admittedly, when they had first met, at the Assembly Ball in Boston, she had been dazzled by the dashing appearance he presented in his striking hussar's uniform. Venetia vividly recalled the flutter of excitement that ran round the girls in the Assembly Room as the handsome, fair-haired stranger strode through the doors. Every unmarried female present sat tense with anticipation, mused Venetia, willing the tall hussar to whirl her onto the dance floor.

But it was Venetia that Captain Dermot singled out

26

for the honor of the first quadrille. Aware that she was the envy of all eyes, Venetia had listened entranced as he talked to her, during the quadrille and later over supper, of the glories of war. As she listened to him, Venetia thrilled to the blare of the trumpets, the beat of the drum, the unsheathing of swords, and the breathtaking excitement of the charge! How glorious Drystan had made it all sound.

Captain Dermot was in Boston a brief seven days before he was recalled to his regiment in France. But that one week was long enough for Venetia to fall headlong in love. When she bade a tearful farewell to the fair-haired hussar, her sorrow at their parting was tempered by the knowledge that on his next leave, she would become his wife.

But now we are engaged, thought Venetia, *how differently I view his life as a military man. How senseless this war seems. Now I am in love, I fear for his life every minute of every day, and my only prayer is that soon the hostilities will be ended. What makes matters worse, is that I do not know exactly where Drystan is stationed:*

> *You will see that there is no address for you to write to on this letter, my dearest. We are not allowed to write of our position, for fear that the intelligence will fall into enemy hands. It is a cruel rule, my sweetest, for how I long to hear from you! I swear I cannot wait for the day when we are wed. My deepest regret is that your parents do not approve of our match. I do admire you for standing up to them the way you did. I only hope that by the time I am granted my next leave, you will have persuaded your father to accept me as his son.*

Venetia sighed. It was still a mystery to her why her adored father had taken so against Drystan. *Admittedly, I had known him only a short while when he proposed,* she mused. *But why could Mama and Papa not understand that it was truly love at first sight!*

"The man is nothing but a fortune hunter!" Sir

Peter had raged. "All Boston is well aware that on your twenty-first birthday you came into a sizable inheritance from your grandmother, Venetia. I am convinced that it is your wealth this Captain Dermot is in love with, not you!"

In despair, Venetia had turned to her mother. "Mama, what is your opinion? Is Drystan not the most dashing, noble gentleman? Oh Mama, I do love him so desperately!"

Lady Hamilton had taken her daughter's hand and said gently, "My dear, you know your Papa and I only desire your happiness. But we are only too well aware that you have led such a sheltered life here in Boston. You have had the opportunity to meet so few eligible young men. It is only natural that you should be swept off your feet by the first handsome stranger who crosses your path. But—"

"Oh Mama," cried Venetia, "Please do not speak as if this were a mere girlish infatuation! I am truly in love!"

Lady Hamilton gazed in dismay at her husband. "I blame myself," she murmured. "Had I been stronger in health, Venetia would have gone to London, stayed with Matilda and enjoyed a proper season when she came out."

Venetia hugged her "You must not speak like that, Mama! I promise you, I had no urge for London life. It was no hardship for me to stay here in Boston and take care of you, for London holds no lures for me. I have been there only once, but how I loathed the noise, the bustle, the artificiality of society!"

"Nevertheless," said Sir Peter, "It is a fact that a London season would have enabled you to sort the wheat from the chaff where men are concerned. Surely you appreciate, Venetia, that I cannot possibly permit you to become engaged to a man you have known for barely a week!"

"But it will be ages yet before we are able to be married, as we do not know when next Drystan will be allowed leave," Venetia explained. "Surely there is no harm in our merely becoming engaged. "Oh, I shall be utterly wretched if you do not give us your permission!"

For several hours the argument raged at Boston Park. But Sir Peter and Lady Mary had never for long been able to refuse their daughter anything upon which she had set her heart. At last, Sir Peter reluctantly gave his assent to the betrothal.

A few days later, after Captain Dermot had quit Boston, Lady Mary suggested to Venetia that she journey to Dorset, to stay with Aunt Matty.

"I'm worried about her, Venetia. I don't understand why she suddenly decided on this move to Lyme Regis. She always seemed so content in London. You would be doing me a great service if you would go and keep her company for a while, and see her well settled in Lyme."

Venetia smiled now as she gazed round Aunt Matty's drawing room. *You were only telling half the truth, Mama,* she mused. *Yes, you were concerned about Aunt Matty, but at the same time I am sure you and Papa thought that a change of scene . . . a new society . . . fresh excitements . . . would soon make me forget Drystan.*

But that I shall never do, vowed Venetia fiercely. *However many balls I attend, and eligible young men I meet, I shall remain true to Drystan. My love for him shall never waver. Oh, how I long to see his handsome face again!*

Her eyes dropped to the last paragraphs of his letter.

I am counting the hours, my sweetest Venetia, until we are together again—and united as man and wife. What a wonderful life lies before us. During the long, lonely evenings while the men sit singing round the campfires, I withdraw from them all, and plan our future! We shall of course rent a house in London for the season. But I confess that all these years of living on alien, foreign soil have made me yearn for the peace of the English countryside. We must find ourselves a summer home, Venetia. Somewhere by the sea. Would that suit you?

Oh a thousand curses, I am being called

*for the final inspection of my men. In haste
then, I remain, Your loving and devoted Drystan.*

A heavy sigh escaped from Venetia's lips as she
folded the letter and placed it safely in her reticule. *How
cruel fate was to separate two people so much in love as
she and Drystan!*

However, Venetia did not possess the type of temperament that would allow her to sit and mope. *You must
remain cheerful, Venetia,* she instructed herself, AND THINK
POSITIVELY! Her lovely blue eyes began to sparkle as she
contemplated the surprise she had in store for her fiancé.

He had said in his letter that he desired a summer
residence, by the sea. *Well what better place than Lyme
Regis,* thought Venetia. *It is utterly delightful here. And
I do believe, on my ride back from Lyme this afternoon,
that I saw the most perfect little house. It was about a
quarter of a mile, as I recall, from the banks of the River
Lym. A lovely stone built place, with Virginia creeper
climbing up the walls. The creeper was a little overgrown,
and many of the windows were shuttered. Unfortunately,
I was in a hurry to return to Aunt Matty, so I could not
linger long and gaze on the house. But I am convinced it
was untenanted. There were no carriages or grooms in
the drive, in fact, no sign of life at all.*

Venetia jumped up, her mind awhirl with exciting
plans. *Tomorrow morning, I shall take Aunt Matty's gig
and make a closer inspection of the house. And if, as I
suspect, it is for sale, then I shall buy it! How amazed
and surprised Dystan will be. And when he has recovered
from his initial shock, and delight, he will take me into
his arms and gently reprimand me.*

"*You should have waited for me to return on leave,*"
he will say, "*then I could have bought the house for you.
It is my duty to provide for you, Venetia.*"

But I have my grandmother's inheritance, thought
Venetia. *Why should I not spend it on a house for
Drystan and myself? It will give me such pleasure! Oh, of
course I recognize that it is a totally unorthodox thing to
do.* Venetia tossed her golden curls defiantly. *Who cares*

about convention! I am determined to have the whole matter of the house cut and dried whilst I am staying in Lyme. Oh, I do hope that little house with the Virginia creeper is for sale! It was quite enchanting. And it was strange, for as soon as I set eyes on it, I felt that I belonged there.

Venetia closed her eyes, picturing the stone steps that led up to the oak front door. She blushed. Would this be the threshold across which Drystan would carry her as his bride?

At ten o'clock the following morning, Venetia turned the gig out of the Woodhouse Lodge gates, and set forth on her quest. She had said nothing to Aunt Matty about her mission.

Aunt Matty is a dear, kindly soul, reflected Venetia, but she does have a tendency to gossip. It would be fatal if she let slip in a letter to my father that I was intending to invest my grandmother's inheritance in a house for Drystan and myself. Given time, I am convinced that my parents will come to hold Drystan in high esteem. But for the moment, I have to accept that they do not approve of my engagement to the Captain. And if my father received word of my intentions with regard to the house, why he would be sure to gallop down here and whisk me straight back to Lincolnshire!

No, Venetia decided, the best course will be for me to go ahead, purchase the house, and present everyone with a fait accompli! After all, Grandmother's money is mine, to do with as I wish. And once the deeds of the house are in my possession, no one will be able legally to wrest them from me.

Instead of riding directly to the house, Venetia elected to drive up to the top of Dragon's Hill, where she would be able to obtain a clear view down on the property. She only had time, yesterday, to observe the house for a very short time, and she longed to stand apart from it, and see it against the background of its grounds and the lovely surrounding countryside.

It was a beautiful ride up Dragon's Hill, with the grassy banks massed with primroses and the hedgerows beginning to be speckled with green. As she breasted the top of the rise, she was greeted with a wave from old Ben Jack, a local fisherman who lived in a quaint old folly that dominated Dragon's Hill.

"Mornin', Miss Venetia," he said with a smile, laying aside the net he was mending. "Fine day for a ride."

"It is indeed," Venetia replied. "But my, how windy it is up here!" She laughed as she descended from the gig, holding on to her plumed hat to stop it being blown away in the breeze.

"Come round to the side of the folly, miss," invited the weather-beaten fisherman. "You'll be in the lee of the wind there."

Venetia followed him round to the side of the sand-stone structure. It was three stories high, and through the open door Venetia smelled the tantalizing aroma of fresh-baked bread.

"Oh!" sighed Venetia, "how delicious that smells!"

"I'd be glad to offer you a piece, Miss Venetia," said Ben Jack, grinning. " 'Tis not often I have visitors up here. And rarer still for me to have the chance to show off my prowess at baking."

Venetia's eyebrows rose in surprise. "Do you look after yourself here, Ben? Have you no wife to care for you?"

He shook his head. "Never had time to find myself a wife, miss. Spent most of my days at sea, then when I returned I came to live here. It suits me, up on Dragon's Hill. I like the fresh air, and the smell of the sea. And like all seafarin' men, I'm good at cooking, and doin' for myself."

He bustled into the folly and emerged with a stool for Venetia to rest on. In his hands he carried his best blue china plate containing a chunk of crusty new baked bread, spread with golden butter.

"My, what a feast!" exclaimed Venetia. "Oh, Ben, it tastes wonderful. To own the truth, I was so eager to be away this morning, I had only a slice of toast for my breakfast. I hadn't realized I was so hungry!"

Ben Jack took up his net, and sat in the sun next to Venetia. He liked Miss Venetia. *Well,* he asked himself, *which other of those society ladies would you find willing to sit next to a poor fisherman, and share his bread with such obvious enjoyment?* True enough, lots of the ladies from Lyme found it pleasurable to have an outing up Dragon's Hill. But they never stopped to pass the time of day with him. He was lucky if he got so much as a regal wave of the hand as the perfumed beauties sped past his folly in a cloud of dust. But Miss Venetia now, was different.

"If I may ask," said Ben Jack, "what was so important that you rushed away without eating a proper breakfast?"

Venetia's eyes shone. "That house," she replied, "the one down in the valley, with the three chimneys, and the Virginia creeper. I came up here specially to look at it. Do you know if it is for sale?"

Ben Jack turned to regard the house, with its pretty gardens, the orchard, the shrubbery, and then the meadows leading down to the sparkling River Lym.

"Ah, you mean Virginia Lodge," he said. "Used to belong to old Lady March."

"Used to?" breathed Venetia, hardly daring to hope.

"She died six months ago, poor soul," murmured Ben Jack. "I'd assumed there'd be some kin who'd take the house over. But it seems that weren't to be. Yes, Miss Venetia, Virginia Lodge, is for sale right enough."

Venetia clasped her hands in joy. "Oh how wonderful! What a happy day this is turning out to be. I shall hurry down into the valley and ask to view the property immediately."

Ben Jack smiled as he regarded the pretty, exultant young girl. Her hands were trembling with excitement as she drew on her gloves. He said, "One word of warning, Miss Venetia, Virginia Lodge is being cared for by a Miss Renshaw, the housekeeper. She's a right sour-face and no mistake. If I were you, I should approach her with care. I've known grown men quake at the rough edge of her tongue."

"Have no fear, Mr. Jack," Venetia assured him as she ran toward her gig, "I am determined that Miss Renshaw and I shall establish an excellent relationship.

And I am quite convinced that nothing can go wrong for me today."

He grinned. "Good luck, then, Miss Venetia."

"Thank you Ben, and thank you for the delicious bread. May I come and see you again?"

"You're welcome anytime, Miss Venetia." He smiled and raised an arm in salute as the golden-haired girl sped off down the hill.

Venetia was in high spirits. Even the thought of the dour Miss Renshaw failed to dampen her enthusiasm. *After all,* Venetia reasoned, *Miss Renshaw is only the housekeeper, not the owner or even the agent of the property. She cannot refuse to allow me to inspect Virginia Lodge.*

Virginia Lodge! *What an enchanting name,* mused Venetia as the gig raced along the narrow lanes. *Oh, I can't wait to see inside!* Venetia's heart pounded with excitement as she rode for the first time up the graveled drive of the house she longed would one day be hers. *Oh, Drystan,* she thought, *if only you were here now to share this moment with me!*

As she descended the stone steps, Venetia mentally prepared her strategy: *I shall greet Miss Renshaw with my most dazzling smile. I shall frankly confess that I have fallen in love with this house, and I shall enlist her help, as a fellow woman, in all that requires to be accomplished for its purchase. After all, if Miss Renshaw served Lady March as housekeeper for many years, she will naturally be fearful that the new owners will dismiss her. I shall make a point of allaying all her worries on that score.*

Firmly, Venetia rang the bell.

But as the oak front door creaked open she was surprised to be greeted not by an imposing housekeeper, but by a flustered parlor maid.

"Oh, dear," muttered the girl, "If it's Miss Renshaw you're wantin', she's gone into Lyme."

Venetia smiled at the rosy-cheeked girl. "My name is Venetia Hamilton. I understand that this house is for sale, and so I am anxious to look round it."

The girl bit her lip. "I'm not supposed to let anyone in without Miss Renshaw's permission."

"Quite right, too." Venetia nodded. "Miss Renshaw is clearly a most responsible person. But I am sure she would not mind if I spent half an hour viewing the house. I have traveled here specially, you see."

"I really don't know, miss. I wouldn't have time to escort you round myself. I'm supposed to be sorting the linen, you see. Miss Renshaw insists that all the inventories are kept up to date, even with no mistress livin' here."

Venetia took advantage of the girl's hesitation. "Oh, I should not dream of interrupting your duties, er ... there, we have been talking for all this time and I do not even know your name!"

"Mollie, miss," the girl replied with a smile, then stood aside to admit Venetia into the spacious hall.

"Well, Mollie, you run along, and I'll drift round the house as silently as a ghost. I promise you, Miss Renshaw will find nothing disturbed, and no blame will fall on you."

"That'll make a nice change," the girl said. "She's always on at me about something. Yesterday a sparrow flew in through the drawing room window and knocked a vase off the mantel. Miss Renshaw said it was my fault for leaving the window open, and now I have to spend my day off sorting the linen!"

Quickly, Venetia untied a silken ribbon from her hair. "Here, Mollie, Why don't you take this? The green of the silk will look so pretty against your dark curls. And it will be a little memento of our guilty secret!"

Delighted, Mollie dipped a curtsy as she took the ribbon. "Oh, thank you, miss. I'll wear it tonight to the barn dance in the village. Now are you sure you don't mind looking round the house on your own? There's not too many rooms to see, mind you. It isn't a big house."

Venetia assured her that she would be quite content to wander alone round Virginia Lodge, and Mollie disappeared to attend to her inventory and try on her new ribbon.

With bated breath, Venetia began her tour of discovery. Mollie was right, it was indeed a small, compact house. But although the rooms were few, they were each of a good size and gracefully proportioned. Venetia particularly liked the green-and-gold drawing room, with its long windows looking out onto lawns, and flower borders.

The house was still furnished exactly as the late Lady March had left it. How strange, mused Venetia, wandering through the sunny morning room, that none of Lady March's kin desired to inherit the house or her possessions. It seemed a quite unnatural state of affairs.

When she had inspected the elegant dining room, with its deep red damask curtains, Venetia wandered up the carved oak staircase to view the upper rooms. She was delighted to discover that all the main bedchambers and dressing rooms were light, airy places. What a refreshing change, she thought, compared to the gloomy, sunless apartments in Aunt Matty's new house.

Venetia could not resist lingering a long while in one particular bedchamber which possessed a glorious view over the small orchard, and then to the lush hills beyond. The bedchamber was decorated in exquisite shades of pink. The window and bed curtains were of deepest rose, while the coverlet, and window seat cushions were fashioned of palest pink silk.

"How lovely it would be to awake in this room," whispered Venetia, sinking onto the bed, and resting her golden head on the lace edged pillow. "And at night, to draw the curtains, and leave one lighted candle on the window seat to illumine my beloved Drystan, my husband, as he comes to take me in his arms . . ."

Venetia closed her eyes, imagining Drystan leaning tenderly over her, stroking her hair, bending to bestow a loving kiss on her trembling lips. Oh, how warm and passionate was his mouth on hers! Kindled deep within her was the first flickering flame of desire, a flame that she knew would soon consume her in a fire of passion.

Venetia stirred on the bed. It all seemed so real! It was as if Drystan was really there, was truly kissing her! Why, she could even detect in the air the masculine smell of his leather boots and tweed riding coat.

Now you are truly dwelling in the realms of fantasy,

Venetia admonished herself, smiling as she abandoned her dream and slowly opened her eyes.

Her smile froze on her face. She stifled a scream of horror. No, she had not imagined that singular male presence. For there, standing by the bed, with a sardonic smile playing around his firm mouth, was none other than Sir D'Arcy Rawnsley!

Venetia sat up and exclaimed indignantly, "You scoundrel, Sir D'Arcy! Whilst my eyes were closed, just now, you crept up on me and kissed me, did you not! Do not attempt to deny it. You took advantage of me in the most dastardly, underhand manner!"

His gray eyes glimmered with amusement, and he remarked, "I should not dream of denying it. I am afraid it was a temptation I found myself powerless to resist. On entering the room, I find a lovely fair-haired girl, looking for all the world like a beautiful princess waiting to be wakened with a kiss. So I duly obliged." He waved a broad, strong hand. "Unfortunately, such is the nature of the world, that my princess, on awakening, was not at all grateful for my gallant action. Instead she has fixed me with the most withering stare and is calling me the most frightful names!"

Venetia hastily scrambled off the bed and glared up at Sir D'Arcy. In truth, much of her fury was directed at herself. How could she have been so foolish as to imagine that Drystan himself was kissing her! Worse, how could she, a betrothed girl, have found it within herself to respond so willingly to Sir D'Arcy's extremely passionate kiss? *Oh, Venetia, you are shameless,* she scolded herself. *Why, it is not as if you even find the man agreeable! You loathe him. Yet at the touch of his lips you ached to surrender yourself to him utterly!*

It just goes to show, thought Venetia angrily, *what a practiced charmer Sir D'Arcy is. He must be in his early thirties, and no doubt has traveled a great deal. Naturally, he will have known many women. He will have learned how to tame them and make them melt into his arms. Well, Sir D'Arcy, I own you are a dangerous man. But I can assure you, I have no intention of allowing myself to become one of your conquests! You shall never boast at White's that you tamed and subdued Miss Venetia Hamilton, only to cast her aside, of course, in the way of all your other casual affairs.*

Venetia drew herself up to her full height of five feet three, and said icily to the dark-haired man towering over her, "And may I ask what exactly you are doing, roaming so freely round this house?"

Sir D'Arcy strolled over to the window, and said nonchalantly, "Oh, I intend to buy it."

"But you can't," cried Venetia, her face pale.

"And why not, pray?" he enquired, with a lift of his dark eyebrows.

"Because I want it! *I* had planned to buy it!"

Sir D'Arcy laughed. "Oh, what a priceless situation! Tell me, Miss Hamilton, what is it about you and I that we always seem to find ourselves in contention with each other?" He smiled. "Well, nearly always."

Venetia flushed, realizing that he was referring to her warm response to his kiss. Oh, she thought desperately, if only I had not lain down on that lovely pink bed and closed my eyes, that dreadful incident would never have taken place!

Venetia said coldly, "I find it an odd conincidence that you should suddenly appear, and then declare that you, too, wish to purchase Virginia Lodge. I suspect that you called at the house on some quite different business, and heard me talking to Mollie, the parlor maid. From my eagerness to inspect the house, you ascertained my purpose . . . and now you are merely seeking to make mischief by challenging me over the purchase."

Sir D'Arcy shook his head in bewilderment. "I assure you, Miss Hamilton, I could never in a hundred years have devised such a devious scheme as that. My, what an ingenious brain lurks inside that pretty head. No, I promise you, I am genuinely seeking a small summer residence. My previous house burned down recently and I shall not trouble having it rebuilt. In truth I never much liked its position. But Virginia Lodge has the most delightful aspect, I am quite determined to own it."

Venetia turned away from him, her hands clenched in fury. Of course, she remembered now Lady Leamington commenting that Sir D'Arcy's Weymouth home had been destroyed by fire. So he was telling the truth.

Venetia glanced round the room, noting the way the sun glanced off the deep pink curtains, the inviting little window seat, the delicate rosettes in each corner of the ceiling. She remembered the other rooms, so graceful and light, so perfect for herself and Drystan. No, she thought fiercely, I shall not give up Virginia Lodge without a fight! Sir D'Arcy shall not have it. Just because he is a man, he is accustomed to having his own way. He regards opposition from a mere woman as totally insignificant. Well I'll teach him not to underestimate me!

She whirled round to face him, and declared firmly, "I must advise you, Sir D'Arcy, that I regard Virginia Lodge as the ideal place for my fiancé Captain Dermot and me to start our married life."

At the mention of Captain Dermot's name, Sir D'Arcy's face darkened. "You little fool," he muttered, almost to himself.

Venetia's chin rose defiantly, "So what are we to do, Sir D'Arcy? Leap on our horses and race one another to the offices of the late Lady March's agent?"

"It's an amusing notion, is it not?" he smiled. "But it is an adventure I freely confess I should be chary of attempting. Knowing your inventive turn of mind, Miss Hamilton, I should not put it past you to devise fiendish delays for me . . . a trip rope across the road, perhaps?"

Venetia's eyes danced at the thought. *Oh, what a joy it would be to see this arrogant man tumble in the dust! Yes,* she mused, *you are right Sir D'Arcy. I would employ any means to prevent you having this house. I should have no shame, either, in selecting my methods, for it would merely be tit for tat: you, after all, were underhand enough to sneak into this room and catch me unawares with your kiss.*

A blush tinged her cheeks. Why, oh why, did her thoughts keep dwelling on that kiss?

Sir d'Arcy went on, "However, I fear that where the

matter of the purchase of Virginia Lodge is concerned, there is no question of either one of us being permitted to buy it outright."

I do not understand," said Venetia. "The house is for sale, is it not?"

Sir D'Arcy paced the room. "It is indeed. But I understand from the late Lady March's agent, that in her will she attached a rather unusual condition to the sale of the house. It is all extremely complicated."

Venetia was suddenly aware that she had been closeted for the best part of half an hour in a strange bedchamber, with a man with whom she was barely acquainted. She could well imagine the shocked reaction of Aunt Matty, her parents, her fiancé, if they ever discovered that she had behaved thus.

She said quickly, "Sir D'Arcy, I feel this is hardly the proper place for us to conduct such a discussion. Shall we take a stroll in the gardens, and together attempt to unravel this mysterious condition surrounding the sale of Virginia Lodge?"

Sir D'Arcy laughed mockingly, "Why, my dear Miss Hamilton, I do believe you are afraid for your reputaton! Do you imagine that I will spread the word round Lyme that I ravished you in the Rose bedchamber at Virginia Lodge?"

"On the contrary," flared Venetia, "it is your reputation I fear for, Sir D'Arcy. It will, I imagine, sink to an all-time low when the blades of Lyme discover that *despite* being alone with an unchaperoned girl for a full half hour, you were still unable to have your way with her!"

Sir D'Arcy shook his head in amazement. "My, what a low opinion you have of me, Miss Hamilton." He strode to the door, flung it open, and gave an elaborate bow. "Never let it be said that I detained a lady against her will. After you, Miss Hamilton!"

Feeling faintly foolish in the face of his mockery, Venetia swept from the room. "We would be best to leave by the garden door," she remarked. "The housekeeper, Miss Renshaw, is due back at any moment. She is evidently the most fearsome creature, and to be frank, I am not in the mood to cross swords with her just at the moment." She could have added, *for it is a hard enough task, Sir D'Arcy, keeping my wits about me in my tussles with you!*

Venetia and Sir D'Arcy slipped out of the garden door, and made their way into the seclusion of the small orchard.

"We are safe from prying eyes here," said Sir D'Arcy courteously pulling aside an overhanging branch to allow Venetia a free passage. "Unless of course, the terrible Miss Renshaw possesses the ability to see through trees."

"I do believe poor little Mollie, the parlor maid, would believe Miss Renshaw capable of any sorcery," Venetia remarked, laughing. "Now, Sir D'Arcy. Pray tell me what strange condition I have to fulfill in order that I may own Virginia Lodge."

He took a step back, and stood with hands on hips. "Dash me! You certainly believe in positive thinking, Miss Hamilton! I was under the impression that I, too, had an interest in purchasing the house."

Venetia's blue eyes sparkled. It afforded her immense pleasure to observe Sir D'Arcy so put out.

"It seems to me," she said, "that since there is some mystery to be solved to decide who is to have the house, then the whole matter hinges on which of us possesses the greater wit, and flexibility of mind. You have already confessed, Sir D'Arcy, that you are impressed by my ingenuity. Therefore it seems likely that I shall confound you, and solve the mystery first!"

He leaned back against an apple tree, and remarked laconically, "Ah. But you are overlooking the fact that I know the details of Lady March's condition. I could refuse to tell you."

"In which case," retorted Venetia, "I should go straight to the agent and obtain the facts from him. Besides," she gazed artlessly up at the dark-haired man from beneath her long lashes, "it is obvious that you have no notion how to set about solving the mystery. Otherwise, you would have had the deed to Virginia Lodge in your hands by now. You would certainly not be wasting precious minutes by passing the time of day with me."

Sir D'Arcy sighed. "Once again I find myself defeated by your fine intelligence, Miss Hamilton. I confess, you see before you a broken man!"

"Will you kindly stop laughing at me in that patronizing manner, Sir D'Arcy," flared Venetia furiously, "and tell me about Lady March's will!"

Sir D'Arcy nodded. "Very well. I understand from Lady March's agent, who is Mr. Plumb, of the attorneys Plumb, Silson and Cartwright, that Lord and Lady March were blessed with an extremely happy marriage. When Lord John March died, his wife was so overcome that she simply pined away, following him to the grave a bare six months later."

Venetia tapped her foot impatiently, "Yes, yes. But what has this to do with the sale of the house?"

Sir D'Arcy raised a hand. "Patience, Miss Hamilton. I am coming to that. Lady March was born here in Lyme, and lived all her married life in Virginia Lodge. She was so much enamored of the house, that she was reluctant to leave it even to attend a neighboring ball or assembly."

"Ah, I am beginning to understand," smiled Venetia. "She loved the house so much, because it held so many happy memories for her, that when she knew she was dying she determined to ensure that the next owner would be someone who would cherish it as much as she did."

"Exactly," said Sir D'Arcy. "Accordingly, she instructed her lawyers to draw up a will whereby anyone wishing to purchase Virginia Lodge must prove their genuine interest and concern for the property."

A soft smile illumined Venetia's lovely face. "Of course," she whispered, "Mere possession of the purchase price would not be enough. Virginia Lodge *is* an extraordinary house. There is a special atmosphere about it . . . something which sets it apart from ordinary houses. I can well understand Lady March's anxiety that it should always be properly loved and care for. But what method has Lady March employed to ensure the future owner's true sincerity?"

"Ah, now here she was rather cunning," explained Sir D'Arcy. "Somewhere in Lyme Regis, she has hidden her husband's family standard. The only person who is entitled to buy Virginia Lodge, is the one who takes the trouble to unearth that flag."

"That is uncommonly clever," said Venetia, idly fanning her face with a spray of apple leaves. "For only someone with a genuine love for the house would go to all the trouble of searching out a tattered old family standard."

"My thoughts precisely," said Sir D'Arcy. "I suppose she could have chosen to hide something valuable, like a piece of the March family plate. But by selecting an item of purely sentimental value, like the standard, there is no risk of anyone regarding the quest in the spirit of a lowly treasure hunt."

"But . . . but . . . " Venetia's agile mind was racing, "did you say that she had hidden the standard *somewhere* in Lyme? Are we given no more details, no more clues to its whereabouts?"

Sir D'Arcy shook his hard head. "None."

Venetia threw up her hands in despair. "But . . . well . . . Lyme Regis is not a large town, but there must be a million hiding places for something as small as a flag! Surely Lady March must have given some further hint?"

"I am afraid not," said Sir D'Arcy.

Venetia regarded him through narrowed eyes. She was convinced he knew more than he was prepared to admit. *Well,* she reasoned, *that was perfectly understandable. If I were in his boots, with my sights firmly set on owning Virginia Lodge, I'm sure I would not reveal all I knew to my opponent for the house.* Realizing that there was nothing further to be gained from Sir D'Arcy, she said lightly,

"Well, I must confess myself completely foxed, Sir D'Arcy. To own the truth, I am beginning to wonder if Virginia Lodge is worth all the bother of such a tedious search for a mere flag. However, I wish you well in your quest, if you have the time and inclination to try and unravel the mystery."

He nodded. "You are most gracious, Miss Hamilton! I confess, the idea of a challenge appeals to me. But if you are seriously abandoning your interest in the house, why do we not join forces in the search for the standard? I should appreciate the benefit of your keen intelligence."

Was he mocking her again? Venetia could not be sure. It was impossible to fathom the expression in those glittering gray eyes.

She affected a yawn. "I fear I have many demands on my time, Sir D'Arcy. My aunt, Miss Matilda Hamilton, is of a nervous disposition. It would distress her greatly to think of my roaming around the Lyme countryside in a fruitless search for a tattered piece of cloth. Now if you will excuse me, I must be on my way. I have tarried here long enough."

"Allow me to escort you to your gig," said Sir D'Arcy. As they strolled toward the drive, he remarked, "I had not realized that you were the niece of Miss Matilda Hamilton. I was fortunate enough to make her acquaintance in London. She is a most charming lady. I should be most grateful if you would mention my name to her, and present my compliments."

"Of course," said Venetia chillingly as he assisted her into her gig, "it is just possible that she may remember you."

Sir D'Arcy handed her the reins. "And are you quite sure you will not change your mind about Virginia Lodge?"

"Oh, I am quite positive," asserted Venetia airily. "The house has no interest for me now. I shall look elsewhere for a residence for Captain Dermot and myself. Good day, Sir D'Arcy."

With that, she set off at a cracking pace down the drive. Had she glanced back, she would have been surprised at the expression of rage on Sir D'Arcy's handsome face, as he stood staring after her.

But Venetia's pretty face was set firmly in the direction of the town of Lyme Regis. Her thoughts were centered on a certain Mr. Plumb, of the attorneys Plumb, Silson and Cartwright.

Venetia's eyes sparkled as she sped on. *I must persuade Mr. Plumb to show me Lady March's will,* she resolved. *The will must contain more clues to the where-*

abouts of that standard. And once I have the facts in my possession, I shall not rest until I find that flag.

I give you fair warning, Sir D'Arcy. On our first encounter, you bested me. Today, in the Rose bedchamber, you took unfair advantage of me. But you shall not defeat me over the purchase of Virginia Lodge. For I have fallen in love with that house. And I am determined that it shall be mine!

Three

Venetia's heart lifted as she drove down Sherbourne Lane into bustling Broad Street, the main thoroughfare of the pretty town of Lyme Regis. It was not only the elegant houses and wide variety of shops that Venetia loved about Broad Street. What fascinated her was the manner in which the cobbled street sloped downward to the sea. It is almost as if, she thought, the street was quietly well aware of Lyme's reputation as a fashionable resort, and was proudly urging people down the hill to gain the benefit of the fresh sea breezes!

But much though Venetia longed to wander down to the Cobb pier and gaze at the sailing ships, she knew she must concentrate her attention on finding the chambers of the august Messrs. Plumb, Silson and Cartwright. Hurrying past the elegantly dressed ladies of society busy completing their morning's shopping, Venetia at last found the attorneys' chambers tucked away in nearby Coombe Street. This was a narrow thoroughfare with steps, here and there, leading down to the stream which flowed past the old mill.

She was greeted at the musty chambers by a bespectacled clerk. Venetia gave her name, and stated briefly the nature of her business. She was then taken straight through into the offices of Mr. Plumb himself.

He was a rotund, fresh-faced gentleman in his middle years, who presided behind an imposing mahogany desk. Lining the walls of his chambers were rows of dusty ledgers, legal reference books, and sealed parchment.

"It is indeed a pleasure to make your acquaintance, Miss Hamilton," Mr. Plumb said with a smile. "My clerk informs me that you have an interest in Virginia Lodge?"

"That is correct, Mr. Plumb," replied Venetia. "I am particularly interested in the terms of Lady March's will, and the condition that the house may only be sold to the person who finds her husband's standard. Would it be at all possible for me to have a sight of the will?"

He nodded. "I have it here, Miss Hamilton. But if you hope to find a hint in it of where the standard is hidden, I must warn you that you are doomed to disappointment. It simply states that the standard of Lord March is concealed somewhere in Lyme Regis or its immediate vicinity. No more, and no less."

Crestfallen, Venetia sat back in her chair. "But surely Lady March must have realized she was setting an impossible task. It seems so unreasonable not to have left a single clue as to where one should start looking."

Mr. Plumb gazed at Venetia over steepled fingers. "I quite agree, Miss Hamilton. My only regret is that I was not here personally to attend to the drawing up of the will. Unfortunately, when Lady March sent word that she wished me to call on her, I was delayed in Weymouth, and my junior partner undertook the duty of going to Virginia Lodge. By the time I returned, the will was drawn up, signed, and witnessed. On reading it, I was so alarmed by this strange condition of the standard, that I set forth for Virginia Lodge with the intention of persuading Lady March to insert a few more clues to the flags's whereabouts." He looked grave. "Unfortunately, by the time I arrived, Lady March had passed away."

"So legally, the will must stand exactly as it was written," murmured Venetia. "Oh dear!" She thought for a moment, and then enquired, "Were you well acquainted with Lady March, Mr. Plumb? Is there anything you can tell me about her character, her temperament, that may give me some hint of where she is likely to have hidden the standard?"

He shook his head and said ruefully, "I fear I only had the pleasure of meeting the lady on a few occasions. She ventured out only rarely from Virginia Lodge, you see. She appeared to me to be a quiet, meek, extremely amiable person. More than that I cannot tell you."

"I see." Venetia stood up. "Well, thank you for giving me your time, Mr. Plumb. I can see I have a long and difficult task ahead of me!"

He smiled. "Don't hesitate to come back if I can be of any further assistance, Miss Hamilton. Virginia Lodge is a delightful house. It is shameful for it to remain empty. I hope most sincerely that you will be mistress of it one day."

So do I, Mr. Plumb, thought Venetia as she took her leave. *Oh, with all my heart so do I!*

Venetia emerged into the bright sunlight, and deep in thought, retraced her steps to Broad Street. What a daunting task confronted her now over the purchase of Virginia Lodge! It appeared, then, that Sir D'Arcy had been telling the truth after all. The infuriating Lady March had left no further clue to the whereabouts of Lord John's standard. It could be hidden anywhere in the town of Lyme itself . . . or secreted in any one of a thousand hiding places along the shore, on the cliffs, or in the surrounding hills.

It is as well, Venetia reflected wryly, *that I do not possess a pessimistic disposition. Otherwise I should be plunged into the blackest depths of despair at this moment. But fortunately, it is not in my nature to remain dismayed by anything for long. For I do firmly believe that where there is a will there is a way. And I certainly possess the will to own lovely Virginia Lodge!*

Besides, reasoned Venetia with a smile, *Lyme Regis is such an attractive town. I feel so happy, so at home here. I can sense some deep instinct assuring me that fate has led me to Lyme, because it is here that my destiny lies. Somehow, I am convinced I shall be shown the way forward . . . to the standard, and to proud ownership of Virginia Lodge.*

Venetia suddenly gasped for breath as a strong hand slapped her hard on the back. The impact was so great that it almost sent her reeling into the path of a passing carriage.

"Good heavens, girl!" boomed Lady Leamington, "what a fragile little thing you are! No substance to you at all. You and your Aunt Matilda are one as bad as the other. Pecking at your food and getting no proper nourishment! No wonder you're both so weak."

With an effort, Venetia recovered her poise, and at the same time crushed down a fearful urge to laugh. *What a priceless character Lady Leamington was! So long as one refrained from taking her remarks personally, she was really one of the most droll women in Lyme.*

Lady Leamington was standing in the middle of the Broad Street pavement, completely blocking the way of all the other pedestrians. Behind her, at a discreet few paces, stood Lady Leamington's footman. His face was just visible over the mountain of packages he held in his arms.

"I promise you, Lady Leamington," said the smiling Venetia, "that my aunt and I are not at all weak, or undernourished. We both possess small bones and small appetites, that is all." She glanced at the footman. "Have you had a successful morning's shopping, Lady Leamington?"

"Indeed not!" snapped the Countess, taking Venetia's arm and sweeping her down Broad Street. "That impertinent modiste of mine had the gall to protest that the reason my new ball dress does not fit as it should is that my waistline has thickened!"

"Oh how shocking!" murmured Venetia, deliberately averting her gaze from Lady Leamington's ample girth. Venetia felt deeply in sympathy with the modiste.

"I told the little madam! What do you mean, *thickened*? Are you aware that I hunt and walk and row? I get more exercise than any other woman in this county, damn it! How dare she use my waistline as an excuse for her bad workmanship?"

Venetia dutifully tut-tutted. She murmured, "I am so excited at the thought of your forthcoming ball, Countess. I brought no formal gowns with me from Lincolnshire. I thought I'd have some new dresses made here in Lyme. Your ball will be the perfect excuse for me to indulge myself!"

The Countess nodded her approval. "You're young and pretty, Venetia, it is only natural that you should love fine things. Would you like me to introduce you to my dressmaker? Admittedly, we had that little contretemps today, but usually she is most reliable."

Venetia was filled with horror at the notion of Lady Leamington's modiste making her precious ballgown. With her keen eye, Venetia had already noted that the waistline of Lady Leamington's muslin dress was appallingly crooked. And the hemline dipped so much, Venetia wondered if the modiste had been under the influence of alcohol when she stitched it. No, it was obvious that Lady Leamington's dressmaker was a poor seamstress. Venetia determined to avoid her at all costs.

She said tactfully, "It is most kind of you, Lady Leamington, but my aunt has already instructed her modiste to call at the house, so I may interview her."

As she spoke, Venetia crossed her fingers, for this was a blatant untruth. In fact, thought Venetia, Aunt Matty could well do with an expert dressmaker at her command. For Venetia had noticed that her aunt's clothes, though of excellent quality, were all many years old, and considerably worn.

With this thought in her mind, Venetia observed riding down the street, a striking red-haired girl, dressed in an elegant sage green riding habit. Her plumed hat was set at a jaunty angle atop her coppery curls and at her neck and wrists frothed precisely the most fashionable width of creamy lace.

It is unfortunate, mused Venetia, that the exquisite ensemble of the lady in green is somewhat marred by her overproud expression. But her attire, certainly, is of the first quality. I wonder who she is? And, more to the point, which modiste she favors?

As if reading Venetia's thoughts, Lady Leamington lifted a broad hand and waved at the girl as she rode past.

"That was my niece, the Lady Blanche Vaisey," Lady Leamington informed Venetia. "Is she not the most attractive girl? Ah! I suspected as much. There is the handsome Sir D'Arcy Rawnsley rounding the corner on his gray, to accompany her. Such a fine couple, are they not?"

"Indeed yes. They seem extremely well matched," murmured Venetia. The arrogant Sir D'Arcy and the coldly beautiful Lady Blanche. *Yes, they made an excellent pair!*

Nevertheless, Venetia could not restrain a feeling of pique that Sir D'Arcy rode by without appearing to notice her. He seemed only intent on hurrying to draw level with the Lady Blanche. Venetia consoled herself that Sir D'Arcy had ignored her simply because he had been occupied guiding his gray round an awkwardly parked carriage in Broad Street.

In any event, she thought, turning her back on the mounted pair, *what concern is it of mine whether or not Sir D'Arcy says good day to me? In fact, the less I associate with him, the better. I hope, after our conversation in the orchard at Virginia Lodge, that he has been lulled into believing I have abandoned my hope of purchasing the house. It would be fatal for me now to let slip in idle conversation that I am still very much interested in buying the property.*

It suddenly occurred to Venetia that Lady Leamington, who was acquainted with everyone of note in Lyme, might be in a position to furnish her with more information about the temperament and habits of Lady March.

Accordingly, as the Countess paused to inspect the milliner's window, Venetia enquired, "Lady Leamington, I believe you have lived all your life in Lyme. Were you at all intimate with the late Lady March?"

The Countess wrinkled her long nose. "Hardly what you'd call intimate, you know, my dear. Georgina, Lady

March, hardly ever came out into society, and that husband of hers wasn't at all partial to hunting, so our paths very rarely crossed. Why do you ask?"

"Oh, I had just heard Lady March spoken of, that is all," said Venetia lightly. "I merely wondered what nature of woman she was."

"Well as I say, I had very little to do with her," remarked Lady Leamington, casting a disapproving eye at a frivolous pink beribboned creation in the milliner's window. "Though I do recall meeting her on the clifftop path one day. My horse had gone lame, and I was walking him home. Georgina was struggling along, all alone, carrying a basketful of damn-fool stones of all things. Seems she was partial to collecting them from the beach and putting them in bottles. I told her straight out that in my opinion that was a pretty paltry sort of pastime."

"And how did she react to that?" enquired Venetia, her eyes dancing as she imagined the clifftop confrontation between the two ladies.

The Countess shrugged. "Oh she just gave me a very amiable smile, muttered, *'chacun a son gout,'* and wandered on. That episode was typical of her nature. She was simply a meek woman, who quietly pursued her own interests and never intruded herself on anyone. If I were being uncharitable, I'd call her dull. But of course, I'd never speak ill of the dead."

Venetia restrained a sigh of frustration. She had been so positive that Lady Leamington would have been able to provide some rewarding revelations about Lady March. But in truth, all the Countess had done was confirm what Venetia had been told by Mr. Plumb: that the late Lady March had been an amiable, quiet, unassuming lady.

And neither Mr. Plumb nor Lady Leamington have given me any further notion on where Lady March might have hidden the standard, thought Venetia. *I must face the fact that I have drawn a total blank this morning!*

But unexpectedly, Lady Leamington had a further remark to make about the former occupants of Virginia Lodge. "It's a great pity Georgina never bore him any children," the Countess boomed, in a voice loud enough to be heard half across Lyme. "Women are no different from mares, after all. I know if my mares are incapable of breeding they develop silly, nervous habits. That would probably account for Georgina's shyness of society, and this ridiculous business of arranging sea stones in bottles!"

The Countess marched on, oblivious to the amazed stares from the respectable citizens of Lyme at this astounding intelligence.

Venetia quickened her pace to keep up with Lady Leamington, and murmured, "So there are no sons or daughters, no kin at all, to inherit Virginia Lodge?" Venetia was anxious to have this point straight in her mind. *How terrible it would be,* she thought, *if I did find the standard, only to be informed that the house could not be mine because a mysterious cousin had surfaced to contest the will and claim the property as his own!*

Lady Leamington shook her head vigorously, "There are various cousins and nieces lurking somewhere in England. But they're all well enough set up, I believe. And all town dwellers too. None of them are interested in taking on such a small house on the depths of Dorset."

Venetia breathed a sigh of relief, and sent up a prayer of thanks to these unknown relatives of Lady March. *Virginia Lodge may be a small insignificant house to you,* she thought, *but to me it means everything!*

As they approached Buddle Bridge, Lady Leamington called to her footman and ordered her carriage to be brought. "I must confess, Venetia, I am anxious to return home and quiz Blanche on her outing with Sir D'Arcy!"

"For how long is your niece fixed to stay with you?"

The Countess snorted, "She's been here three weeks already and frankly, for most of the time she was bored out of her mind. I suspect she was on the point of making her excuses and hightailing it back to London. Then, however, her pretty green eyes alighted on Sir D'Arcy! Now wild horses couldn't drag her back to the capital."

Venetia thought of Lady March's expression, *'chacun a son gout!'* and decided that the beautiful Lady

Blanche must be soft in the head to set her cap at the insufferable Sir D'Arcy.

But she could not resist the mischievous enquiry, "And is Sir D'Arcy, do you think, as enamored of Lady Blanche as she is of him?"

The Countess roared with laughter as she entered her carriage. "I have not the faintest notion, Venetia! But one thing's for sure. Blanche is a girl who knows how to get her own way. If she's set her sights on Sir D'Arcy, then he'll be powerless to resist her. You mark my words!"

For some unaccountable reason, for the rest of the day Venetia was unable to shake from her mind those last confident words of Lady Leamington's. She devoted the afternoon to writing a long letter to her parents in Boston. After dinner, she enjoyed a quiet game of whist with Aunt Matty. But throughout it all, she could still heard the Countess declaring in ringing tones, *If she's set her sights on Sir D'Arcy, then he'll be powerless to resist her!*

Before she blew out her bedchamber candle that night, Venetia reread Drystan's last loving letter to her. She paid particular attention to the lines in which he expressed the desire that they should live in a house by the sea.

Smiling, she fell asleep, and dreamed of a little stone house, covered in Virginia creeper. She saw herself sitting in the morning room attending to her correspondence. Everything about the scene was golden. The sun streamed in past the pale yellow curtains, and glinted on the band of gold on her wedding finger. She felt supremely content. The door opened, and with joy in her heart she turned, stretching out her hand to welcome Drystan, her husband.

But the smile froze on her face. For the man standing in the doorway was not her beloved fair-haired Drystan. This man was tall, and dark, and the sound of his mocking laughter shattered the air of sunny tranquility Venetia had cherished so much.

She awoke with a start in her bed at Woodhouse Lodge. Venetia found she was shivering, and her forehead was damp with perspiration. Shakily, she left the bed, and drew the heavy damask curtains to let in the early morning light.

She refused to accept that her infuriating dream involving Sir D'Arcy at Virginia Lodge had caused her to feel so feverish and unwell. It would be ridiculous to imagine that he had *that* much influence over her, Venetia reasoned. *How amused he would be to think he had the power to induce me to sleep so fitfully!*

No, she thought, *the real reason I feel so out of sorts is that this bedchamber is most certainly damp. Lady Leamington commented on the fact, I recall, and she was right. There is a distinct musty aroma to the entire house. Perhaps it would be wise for me tactfully to broach the matter with Aunt Matty. She should certainly have the dampness attended to without delay, or her health will suffer.*

There was no opportunity for Venetia to mention the subject at breakfast, however, for Tucker, Aunt Matty's maid, informed her that Miss Hamilton was suffering from a slight headache, and would rest in bed that morning.

"Oh, I am so sorry my aunt is unwell," said Venetia anxiously. "Would it help, you think, if I mixed her one of my special powders, and took it up to her?"

Tucker pushed back a strand of graying hair under her cap. "That's kind of you, Miss Venetia. But in all the twenty years I've served Miss Hamilton, I've never known her react well to a headache powder. What she needs is a cool lavender compress on her forehead, and later on I'll ask Cook to heat her up some nice chicken broth. That'll do the trick."

As Tucker left the breakfast room, Venetia reflected that Aunt Matty was indeed fortunate to have such a devoted maid as Tucker. With no husband, sons, or daughters to care for her, it must be comforting for Aunt Matty to know that there was one person in the house who possessed an intimate knowledge of all her daily needs. Someone who understood all her little foibles. Who knew that headache powders disagreed with her, that in spring, the smell of cut grass made her sneeze, and that she had a secret weakness for a tot of cherry brandy in her after-dinner coffee.

What a pity my letter to Mama and Papa is already sealed, thought Venetia. *Next time I write, I will reassure Papa that his sister is being well cared for. I wonder if I should also mention the matter of the damp? For to be sure, if it is not attended to soon, it will only get worse. There is no question of damp quietly curing itself. Fortunately, I do not believe Virginia Lodge suffers from a similar affliction. As I walked through the rooms, I was particularly struck by their sweet, fresh air.*

Nevertheless, resolved Venetia, *I would do well to take another look at the house, just to satisfy myself that it is of really sound construction. And whilst I am there, I will make a point of getting on the right side of Miss Renshaw, the housekeeper.*

After all, if she had served Lady March for many years it is likely that she, like Tucker with Aunt Matty, would have a close knowledge of her mistress's temperament. Naturally, it would not be seemly for me to appear to be questioning the housekeeper too keenly about her late mistress. But a carefully worded question slipped into the conversation might bring forth just the lead I am looking for concerning the whereabouts of that standard!

Before Venetia left the house, she went upstairs to reassure herself that Aunt Matty had not taken a turn for the worse. She found the faithful Tucker sitting on a stool outside her mistress's bedchamber.

"Your aunt is sleeping, Miss Venetia," said Tucker, looking up from the stocking she was darning.

"Oh, well in that case I won't disturb her," said Venetia, feeling a trifle nonplussed at the sight of Tucker seated so staunchly outside the door. It was almost, thought Venetia, as if the maid was guarding Aunt Matty's bedchamber against an army of possible intruders!

She went on, "It is such a lovely day, I intend to take full advantage of it, and explore some more of the countryside. But I shall not be taking the gig. It occurred to me that Aunt Matty may feel in need of fresh air to blow away her headache. A spin in the gig along the coastal path would do her a power——"

Venetia broke off, as from within Aunt Matty's room there issued a clattering noise, followed by a muffled curse.

"What . . . what was that?" asked Venetia anxiously.

Tucker's faded blue eyes regarded her blandly. "What was what, miss?"

"That noise, from Aunt Matty's room! We must enter at once, Tucker, and see what is wrong!"

As she spoke, Venetia stretched out a hand toward the door handle. But Tucker implacably barred the way. "There is no cause to fret yourself, Miss Hamilton. I assure you I heard nothing."

Venetia was beginning to feel as if she was in the middle of a bad dream. Whatever was going in Aunt Matty's room? And why was Tucker behaving in such a suspicious fashion?

Venetia said firmly, "Tucker, with respect, my ears are a great deal younger and sharper than yours. If I say I heard a noise, then depend on it, a noise there surely was! It made a kind of clattering sound. And then I am positive I heard Aunt Matty's voice."

"Ah, I know what that must have been," Tucker said calmly. "The window sash must have come loose again, and be banging against the glass. As for the voice, well you know Miss Hamilton often talks in her sleep. It's nothing to be alarmed about."

Venetia wondered if she was making a ridiculous fuss about nothing. Had she not already established to her full satisfaction that Tucker was the most loyal and devoted servant? Surely, if there was the remotest likelihood of anything ailing Aunt Matty, Tucker would be by her side in an instant. The very fact that she was still positioned outside the door would appear to prove that Aunt Matty was indeed sleeping peacefully and should be left undisturbed.

Gracefully, Venetia murmured, "I shall be on my way, then. When Aunt Matty awakes, would you kindly tell her I was asking after her. And do urge her to take a ride by the sea."

"I'll do that, miss, don't you worry," smiled Tucker.

Venetia retired to her own apartments, where she put on her walking boots, and a light pelisse. Then she set off at a brisk pace to cover the three miles which separated Woodhouse Lodge from Virginia Lodge. An April shower had freshed the hedgerows, the droplets of water sparkled like diamonds on the spiders' webs strung across the bushes.

But for once, Venetia scarcely noticed the charm of the Dorset countryside. Continually, her thoughts strayed back to Woodhouse Lodge, and that strange scene she had enacted with Tucker outside Aunt Matty's bedchamber. Try as she might, Venetia could not rid herself of the notion that all was not well in Woodhouse Lodge.

I must not tarry long at Virginia Lodge, Venetia resolved. I must hurry back in case Aunt Matty needs me.

Venetia was so absorbed in her thoughts that she did not at first notice the man and the woman riding toward her up the drive of Virginia Lodge.

"Good morning, Miss Venetia!" exclaimed Sir D'Arcy, sweeping off his hat.

She politely returned his greeting, and there then followed a tense silence as Venetia and the lady on horseback took stock of one another. Venetia had recognized the fiery red curls of Lady Blanche Vaisey, who was looking exceptionally attractive today in a bold riding habit of bright peacock blue.

Lady Blanche's green eyes gazed coldly down on Venetia. They appraised her pelisse, which though plain blue, and unadorned, was excellently cut and clearly of first quality. They regarded her flawless complexion, her golden curls, her lustrous blue eyes. A frown creased Lady Blanche's forehead as she contemplated the slight smile tilting the corners of Venetia's generous mouth.

Her curiosity aroused, Lady Blanche murmured silkily, "Pray introduce us, D'Arcy!"

"Oh, are you not acquainted?" said the dark-haired man who had been observing this silent confrontation between the two ladies with not inconsiderable amusement.

"Miss Venetia Hamilton, the Lady Blanche Vaisey."

He turned to the lady in peacock blue. "Miss Venetia has traveled down from Lincolnshire to stay with her aunt, Miss Matilda Hamilton."

Lady Blanche's eyebrows lifted. "Oh," she murmured disdainfully, "Lincolnshire! No doubt you are glad to escape from it, Miss Hamilton. It is a dull, flat county, to be sure. There is no flair or style about Lincolnshire!"

Venetia opened her mouth to voice a hot denial of this condemnation, but Sir D'Arcy was there before her. "What nonsense, Blanche," he laughed. "You must not allow yourself to be so blinded by prejudice. Lincolnshire has few hills, to be sure, but nowhere else in England will you see such magnificent skies. And I can vouch for the fact that Lincolnshire people are far from dull! In my experience, their ladies, in particular, are possessed of the most headstrong natures!"

Aware that he was taunting her, in memory of their first clash when her gig had almost collided with his carriage, Venetia resolved not to rise to his bait. She said, with dignity, "If you will excuse me, I will continue with my walk. Despite the sun, there is a chill wind this morning."

She made to move on, but Sir D'Arcy restrained her. "In case you have it in mind to call at Virginia Lodge and interview the housekeeper, I should warn you that you will meet with a frosty reception. I have just *attempted* and I use the word advisedly, a dialogue with her myself."

Lady Blanche tossed her red curls. "She is the most rude, insolent woman! Really, D'Arcy, when you are master of Virginia Lodge, I shall insist that you dismiss Miss Renshaw. I was most surprised that you continued to be so courteous to her after the shrewish manner in which she addressed us. Had I been in your boots I should have taken my whip to her!"

Venetia repressed a smile. Her heart warmed toward the housekeeper of Virginia Lodge. How she wished she had been there to see Sir D'Arcy flinching under the rough edge of her tongue!

Sir D'Arcy looked thoughtful. "Mmm . . . I believe it would be unwise to judge Miss Renshaw too hastily,

Blanche. She is clearly a very worried—even frightened—woman. Now, I wonder why?"

Lady Blanche sniffed. "Well if she ever has the impudence to speak to me again in that hostile tone, I'll do more than frighten her, I'll make her fear for her very life!"

"In that case, Blanche," said Sir D'Arcy, in a tone that, though pleasant, held a steely undernote, "you would be well advised not to accompany me further in my quest for Lord March's standard. I am convinced that Miss Renshaw holds the key to this mystery, and I intend to make it my business to establish a good rapport with her. I should be extremely angry to find my plans dashed by any rash action on your part!"

Venetia had the pleasure of seeing the Lady Blanche flush with embarrassment. "Naturally, D'Arcy, I should not dream of interfering," she squirmed. "Perhaps I was a little hasty. But I have no doubt that *together,* we shall soon gain Miss Renshaw's confidence." She rounded on Venetia. "Am I to understand, then, that you too are interested in purchasing Virginia Lodge? Because if so, I fear your quest will be fruitless. D'Arcy is determined to have it, you know. And I shall do all in my power to assist him."

Venetia waved her hands in what she hoped was a convincing gesture of denial. "Fear not, Lady Blanche, I am merely walking up to Virginia Lodge to request permission of Miss Renshaw to pick a few blooms from the conservatory. My aunt is afflicted with a headache and I hoped to cheer her with a posy of her favorite anemones."

Sir D'Arcy nodded. "Well, we will detain you no longer, Miss Venetia. The wind is indeed keen, and I should not like you to take a chill. Come, Blanche, will you ride with me along the coastal path? The views are quite spectacular from there, I promise you."

"I fear it will not be possible for me to accompany you this morning, D'Arcy," demurred Lady Blanche. "I must go into Lyme and give my dressmaker instructions for my new gowns. Miss Millford is an excellent modiste, but she does require constant supervision."

As they rode away, Venetia heard Lady Blanche continue, "You are engaged to dine with us, are you not D'Arcy? I shall look forward to the pleasure of your company tonight, then, at Leamington Hall."

As Venetia strode on up the drive, she was oblivious to the cold wind. Her encounter with Sir D'Arcy and Lady Blanche had left her burning with fury. So the arrogant Sir D'Arcy was utterly confident that he would succeed in becoming the eventual owner of Virginia Lodge!

How patronizing was his manner when he warned me about Miss Renshaw, raged Venetia. *Just because the mighty Sir D'Arcy Rawnsley had his fingers burned by the housekeeper, then naturally it follows that a mere girl like me could not possibly triumph where he has failed! And as for Lady Blanche, my what a supercilious creature she is. How dare she presume to look down on me because I hail from Lincolnshire! She is quite insufferable.*

But Lady Leamington was perfectly correct in her surmise that Lady Blanche is in full cry after Sir D'Arcy. Well, she has my blessing. I hope with all my heart that he does marry her. She will make him desperately unhappy, and it will serve him right for his high-handed attitude. Yes, thought Venetia wryly, *if ever a couple truly deserved one another, it is Sir D'Arcy and Lady Blanche!*

Fearing that she might still be within the sights of the mounted pair, Venetia directed her steps not to the front door of Virginia Lodge, but to the domed conservatory. She could see little from the outside, for the steamed-up glass was framed by fronds of vigorous, green plants.

Opening the conservatory door, she was assailed by a pleasantly warm, flowery scent, and a shriek of alarm from Mollie the parlormaid, who was taking her ease in one of the wicker chairs.

"Ooh, miss, it's you!" exclaimed Mollie, jumping up, her rosy face a picture of guilt. "For an awful moment I thought it was Miss Renshaw. She's already caught me napping once this week. And she's in a terrible temper this morning, what with that lady in blue demanding to see round the house."

Venetia was longing to hear details of the acrimonious exchange between Lady Blanche and the housekeeper, but she knew it would not be seemly for her to question a servant about the incident.

Instead she said ruefully, "Oh dear. I was hoping Miss Renshaw would be in a good humor. For I too would like her to show me round the lodge."

Mollie absently broke off some withered foliage from a fern. "Oh, I'm sure, if she was here, Miss Renshaw wouldn't object to showing you round, Miss Hamilton. But that Lady Blanche just swept in, and tried to seize all Miss Renshaw's keys. There was a fearful tussle between the two ladies, and then the gentleman intervened, trying to quieten them down. But by this time Miss Renshaw was in such a state, she just stood on the doorstep, barring the way, screaming the most dreadful abuse at both of them!"

"Heavens!" murmured Venetia. "But did I understand you to say that Miss Renshaw has now gone out?"

Mollie grinned. "Just down to the summerhouse on the river, to calm her nerves I suppose. Was there anything special you wanted to see in the house, miss? I've served here five years, so I can answer any questions just as well as *her*."

Delighted, Venetia declared, "Then you shall be my guide today, Mollie. Come, let us delay no longer!"

They went first into the sunny morning room, where Venetia admired the elegant walnut writing table and the framed silhouettes gracing the walls.

"What excellent taste Lady March had," she murmured. "Were you happy in her employ, Mollie?"

The parlor maid nodded, "Oh, yes. It was a happy household for the most part. Except of course, when her ladyship was ill."

"Ill?" queried Venetia. "Was this a serious ailment, Mollie?"

"I don't rightly know, Miss. It always seemed to happen when I was out on an errand for Miss Renshaw.

I'd get back, and find that Lady March was confined to her apartments, and would allow no one in to see her except Miss Renshaw. 'Course, I was only an under parlormaid then, so none of the other staff would ever bother to explain anything to me."

"But how often did Lady March suffer these . . . attacks? And how long did they last?" asked Venetia.

Mollie wrinkled her snub nose as she pondered. "Oh, they happened once every three months or so. Only lasted a day, though. After that she was her usual smiling, kind self."

"It must have been dreadfully worrying for Lord March," commented Venetia, making a mental note that when she was mistress of this house, she would have the fringing on the gold curtains replaced.

"Oh, he was never there when she was ill," remarked Mollie. "He always went out."

"Heavens, how callous!" exclaimed Venetia.

"No, it wasn't like that," said Mollie. "Miss Renshaw told me that Lady March couldn't bear him anywhere near her when she was ill, because she thought her ailment made her look so ugly. Evidently she was the one who insisted that he should go right away until she was better."

"And she was cared for by Miss Renshaw?"

"Always, Miss Renshaw has a secret book of herbal remedies. They work, too. I had a dreadful cough last winter, but she gave me a potion that cured it in no time."

They left the morning room, with Venetia feeling increasingly bewildered and intrigued. *What was this mysterious ailment of Lady March's?*

Between the morning room and the dining room, Venetia noticed a narrow oak door. "What is in there, Mollie?"

"That's the china room, Miss," said Mollie, not pausing but walking on towards the dining room.

"Wait, Mollie. I should love to see Lady March's collection of china. With her excellent taste I suspect that many of her pieces must be exquisite."

"I wouldn't know, Miss. The china room is kept locked. Only Miss Renshaw is allowed in there."

"But isn't it one of your duties to wash and dust the china?" asked Venetia.

"In any other household yes, it is the duty of the parlormaid. But here at Virginia Lodge, Miss Renshaw insists on doing it herself. I suppose she's afraid I'll break something valuable."

In the dining room, the red damask curtains were flapping in the breeze. "Mercy me!" cried Mollie. "I've left the window open again. Miss Renshaw will skin me alive if she finds out!"

As she spoke, the girl ran to the window and hastily slammed it shut. In her anxiety, she must have employed more force than she intended. The glass shook in the panes, a vase on the mantel wobbled, and then to Venetia's horror, a gilt framed mirror on the wall near the window crashed to the floor, splintering into a hundred fragments.

Mollie stood with her hand to her mouth, staring at the shattered glass with stunned disbelief. Venetia took a step forward. But before she could speak an icy voice cut through the silence.

"Just what is the meaning of all this! Mollie, you stupid, careless girl! I shall deduct the price of that mirror, week by week, out of your wages. It will take you years to pay off the debt, and perhaps that will teach you to be more careful." The woman directed her frosty gaze at Venetia. "And who are you? What are you doing snooping round Virginia Lodge?"

At last Venetia found herself face to face with the awesome Miss Renshaw!

Four

Miss Renshaw was indeed a daunting looking woman. She stood almost six feet tall, and was dressed from top to toe in unrelieved black. Her iron-gray hair was scraped back into a knot beneath her cap, and her long bony hands rested protectively on the large bunch of keys at her waist.

Venetia repressed a shiver as she stared into the housekeeper's stony gray eyes. Was it her imagination, or was there something sinister lurking in the woman's thin, unyielding face? Venetia suddenly remembered what Sir D'Arcy had told Lady Blanche: *She is clearly a very worried—even frightened—woman.*

Venetia thought Sir D'Arcy was guilty of a serious error of judgement. Certainly at this moment, Miss Renshaw looked anything but frightened. It was poor Mollie, in fact, whose big brown eyes were filled with terror.

Well, I shall not be cowed, decided Venetia firmly. *Somewhere, buried deep within that hostile exterior, there must exist some human warmth. I must use all my skill to try and melt the iceberg!*

Venetia straightened her shoulders, and calmly addressed the woman in black. "Good day to you. I believe you must be Miss Renshaw. My name is Venetia Hamilton and—"

"Ah, yes!" rasped Miss Renshaw. "Mr. Plumb, the attorney, advised me you had taken an interest in the house. Well you shall not have it, Miss Hamilton! Neither you, nor that couple who tried to gain admittance earlier. None of you shall ever own Virginia Lodge!"

The housekeeper's face was contorted with fury. She pushed past Venetia and seized the trembling Mollie by the arm. "And as for you! You'll go and fetch a brush and sweep all this glass up. And you'll pay for it. Penny by penny I'll make you pay! Haven't I told you over and over not to be so careless with Lady March's things? If she were here now—"

"Miss Renshaw," said Venetia firmly, as Mollie dissolved into tears, "there has clearly been an unfortunate misunderstanding. Mollie did not break that mirror. I am afraid the fault was entirely mine."

"But miss!" blurted Mollie.

Venetia silenced her with a warning look. "I regret to say that in admiring the view from the window, I brushed against the mirror and dislodged it. Naturally, I shall be happy to make full recompense for the loss."

Miss Renshaw glared at Venetia. Then she released Mollie's arm, and snapped, "Well don't just stand there, girl, staring! Go and fetch a brush."

Pausing only to shoot a grateful glance at Venetia, Mollie thankfully escaped from the room.

Miss Renshaw's mouth twisted. "No doubt you believe it does not signify what you break in this house, since you imagine you are destined to become mistress of it?"

"Miss Renshaw," said Venetia gently, "do you not feel that you are making things harder for yourself by taking this attitude? It is inevitable that eventually someone will come along who will solve the mystery of the hidden standard. Virginia Lodge cannot remain empty forever. I fear you must accept that someday it must have a new mistress. I understand that you have many happy memories of the house under Lady March, but—"

"Understand?" whispered Miss Rendshaw hoarsely, "You understand nothing! Which is all to the good. Because whilst you remain in ignorance, it means you will never find that standard!"

"Do you know where it is?" Venetia could not resist asking the question.

The gray eyes gleamed in triumph. "Of course I know! But wild horses would never drag the secret from me."

Venetia walked to the window, and tried a different tack, "Miss Renshaw, I am deeply puzzled by your distress. After all, if Lord and Lady March had been blessed with an heir, the house would have passed to him. In time, there would inevitably have been a new mistress for you to serve under."

"I would have been happy then!" flared the house-keeper.

Venetia smiled in sympathy. "You mean because then the house would have remained in the family, and not been invaded by strangers?"

"Oh, you are stupid, stupid!" muttered Miss Renshaw. "No, that is not the point at all. I blame myself. Some months after Lord March died, Lady March insisted that I go to visit my sick sister in Bath. When I returned she had drawn up her will, and was herself on her deathbed. Oh, if only she had not made that fateful condition about the standard!"

There at least, you and I are in full accord, thought Venetia with a sigh. Realizing that there was nothing more to be gained from her discussion with Miss Renshaw, Venetia declared, "I fear I am keeping you from your household duties, Miss Renshaw. And I must hurry back to Woodhouse Lodge. My poor aunt is afflicted with a headache, so I do not care to leave her too long."

Miss Renshaw rustled to the dining room door. "Kindly wait a moment, if you please, Miss Hamilton."

Thoroughly nonplussed, Venetia lingered in the dining room, and was joined a moment later by Mollie.

"Oh Miss Hamilton, I can't thank you enough for what you did," exclaimed the parlor maid as she bent to sweep up the broken glass. "She would have made my life unbearable. I'm so grateful, I—"

She broke off as Miss Renshaw returned. The housekeeper presented Venetia with a closely written piece of paper. "Take this," she said abruptly. "It may be of some help."

For a moment, Venetia was filled with a wild elation. Had Miss Renshaw, for some mysterious reason, relented? Did this note in Venetia's hand contain the vital information which would lead her to the whereabouts of the standard?

Hardly daring to hope, Venetia lowered her eyes and read:

> *Take a bowlful of lime flowers and brew into a tisane, by pouring on boiling water and allowing to steep for three to five minutes. Strain, and serve sweetened with honey.*

"It is a cure for headaches," said the housekeeper. "I pride myself on my knowledge of herbal remedies. Perhaps the potion will be of some assistance to your aunt."

"How . . . how kind of you!" cried Venetia brightly. "How very thoughtful. I am sure my aunt will be deeply touched at your concern."

At that moment, Venetia remembered that she had told Sir D'Arcy she was calling on Miss Renshaw for the sole purpose of requesting permission to pick some anemones for Aunt Matty from the conservatory. Oh dear, thought Venetia ruefully. How foolish of me to have uttered such an untruth. It would be typical of Sir D'Arcy to quiz my aunt on her pleasure at receiving the blooms . . . and then I should be in hot water with everyone!

Well, there is nothing for it, but that I must take some flowers back to Aunt Matty.

Accordingly, Venetia said hesitantly, "Miss Renshaw, I wonder if I could trouble you for one further favor."

Miss Renshaw pursed her lips and sighed. "No doubt you have it in mind to see round the house. I cannot refuse to accompany you, of course, it is my duty as housekeeper. But it is such a trial, as I have many other things to do today. And it would be a waste of your time as well as mine, for I assure you, you will never be mistress of so much as a single floorboard in Virginia Lodge!"

With a considerable effort of will, Venetia forced herself to keep her expression sweet and demure. But what a tiresome woman she found Miss Renshaw to be. And *so* repetitive!

Venetia said gently, "No, no, I should not dream of taking up so much of your valuable time, Miss Renshaw. There is really no need for me to inspect the rest of the house." Mollie, completing her sweeping up of the shattered mirror, uttered a stifled giggle at this point. Venetia shot her a swift, conspiratorial glance, recalling the morning when Mollie had admitted her for a secret tour of Virginia Lodge.

Venetia went on blandly, "It is merely that I happened to notice an abundance of fine anemones in the conservatory. As they are my aunt's favorite flower, I wondered . . . "

"Oh is *that* all?" Miss Renshaw remarked with obvious relief. "Come, I will cut you the blooms myself."

Yes, you will attend to the flowers, and then you will stand by the conservatory door, watching me until I am safely out of the grounds, an amused Venetia thought.

When the jewel-bright anemones were cut, tied, and safely in Venetia's hands, Miss Renshaw accompanied her to the conservatory door.

Then she said, unexpectedly, "I will tell you this, Miss Hamilton. Lord March's standard lies not within this house, or anywhere in the grounds of Virginia Lodge." She paused, her hands entwined round the large bunch of keys at her waist. She looked across the lawns, and murmured, as if speaking to herself, "I went down to the summerhouse this morning. Lady March's boat is still there. She was a keen fisherwoman, you know. She liked nothing better than to row herself to a quiet inlet on the

River Lym, and while away a few hours casting her line."

Venetia was in a bouyant mood as she arrived back at Woodhouse Lodge. For had not Miss Renshaw unbent sufficiently to give her a clue to the whereabouts of the standard? Clearly, Lady March had hidden it somewhere down on the river.

So, thought Venetia, *her eyes sparkling, I now have the advantage over you, Sir D'Arcy! You may be possessed with the most overbearing confidence that you will be the one to own Virginia Lodge. But it is I who will be on the river tomorrow morning, searching the banks, and every nook and cranny for Lord March's flag.*

As she entered the house, Venetia was greeted by Aunt Matty's maid. "Good afternoon, Tucker. Isn't it a glorious day!" exclaimed Venetia cheerfully.

Tucker cast a dubious glance out of the window, where dark rain clouds were gathering. "If you say so, miss," she murmured. "To my mind the weather seems to have taken a turn for the worse. I hope Miss Hamilton doesn't stay out too long. She took your advice, Miss Venetia, and went for a spin in the gig."

"Oh I am so glad," smiled Venetia. "See, I have brought her these pretty anemones. I will take them upstairs and arrange them in her bedchamber as a surprise!"

"No!" cried Tucker sharply, grasping Venetia's arm. As Venetia's eyes widened in surprise, the maid went on, in a calmer tone, "That is . . . Miss Hamilton isn't partial to fresh flowers in her bedchamber. They make her sneeze in the night. Why not put the anemones in the drawing room instead? They would look so pretty arranged in a bowl on the mantel."

"Very well," agreed Venetia. She hurried upstairs to remove her pelisse and change from her walking dress into a light afternoon gown of palest green muslin. Then she collected an attractively shaped fluted vase from the china room, and was on her way to fill it with water, when she chanced to glance through the open door of the Blue Saloon.

That is where I shall place Aunt Matty's bouquet, decided Venetia. She sauntered into the lovely room, wondering why Aunt Matty was always so reluctant to use it. It was by far the most elegant room in Woodhouse Lodge, and afforded a delightful view of the cherry tree in the garden.

Observing the fire was laid, Venetia bent and quickly put a light to it. *When Aunt Matty returns from her ride,* Venetia resolved, *she shall be greeted by a glowing fire, tea, buttered crumpets, and my pretty flowers in that fluted vase. I shall insist that she put her feet up on the sofa, and she shall tell me whom she has encountered this afternoon during her ride by the sea.*

As the flames began to lick up the chimney, Venetia moved the sofa nearer the fire. As she did so, she noticed that some of the stuffing was beginning to burst through the sofa's dark-blue velvet cover. And the stretch of carpet where the sofa had stood was badly frayed.

Curiously, Venetia crossed to the window and examined the beautiful sapphire-colored curtains. To her dismay, she found that the delicate silk had been faded at the edges by the sun. How strange, thought Venetia, wondering why Aunt Matty had allowed the furnishings in here to become so shabby.

She then glanced out of the window, and was surprised to see that the cherry tree was almost completely obscured by black smoke. It must be the gardener, she realized, taking advantage of Aunt Matty's absence to burn a pile of rubbish. She hoped he would complete his task quickly; the smell of the smoke was distinctly acrid.

At that moment, Venetia was suddenly conscious of a loud roaring noise behind her. She whirled round, and with a cry of horror ran toward the chimney. The logs and coal in the grate were not merely burning merrily as she had intended. Instead, the bright flames were leaping ferociously up the chimney, as if drawn by some powerful, evil force. Still the frightening, roaring sound continued. And still the black sooty smoke billowed round the garden.

Panic-stricken, Venetia dashed into the hall, and

screamed, "Tucker! Fetch help quickly! The Blue Saloon chimney is on fire!" As Tucker led the rush of servants into the hall, Venetia quickly took command. "We must form a human chain, and pass buckets of water hand to hand. Hurry now!"

While the buckets were being filled, Venetia ran back into the Blue Saloon and seized a linen cloth from a side table. Gritting her teeth against the searing heat from the fire, she laid the cloth along the carpet edging the grate. Tucker staggered in with the first container of water.

"Oh thank heavens!" cried Venetia.

She took one side of the bucket, and together the two women hurled the water onto the blaze. They recoiled, choking, as the smoke filled their eyes and the steaming logs fell from the fire basket and rolled onto the linen cloth Venetia had prepared.

"At least the cloth will protect some of the carpet from the mess," gasped Venetia, wiping her streaming eyes with a grimy hand. "Quickly, Tucker. We must throw the next bucketful up the chimney. Oh, I do wish that frightful roaring would stop! The heat is so intense, it is like a furnace up there. I am terrified the entire chimney breast will crack, and the house will split in two!"

For the next ten minutes, Venetia and Tucker worked feverishly, hurling water with all their might as far as they could up the chimney. At last, Venetia stood back from the charred and blackened grate, and whispered, "I think we've beaten it, Tucker. The flames have stopped roaring up the chimney."

All that could be heard now was the hissing of the wet coals, and the soft thud of damp soot as it fell into the hearth.

"Lucky you raised the alarm as soon as you did, miss," said Tucker, taking out a handkerchief and wiping her blackened eyes. "Otherwise the whole house might have gone up."

"Whatever has been happening?" quavered a distressed voice from the door. "Venetia. Tucker! What is the meaning of all this?"

74

Dry mouthed, Venetia ran toward her agitated aunt. "I can explain, Aunt Matty. But have no fear. Everything is under control. I lit a fire in here, you see, but the chimney caught slightly. I am truly sorry about all the mess, but nothing has been damaged. Not even the carpet, for see, I covered it with a tablecoth."

Aunt Matty threw down her gloves and bonnet on the sofa. "But whatever possessed you to light a fire in this room, Venetia? You know I never use the Blue Saloon." She turned to Tucker. "Why did you not explain to Miss Venetia that the fire was never lit in here?"

"I'm afraid I was occupied elsewhere, Miss Hamilton. *Upstairs*," said Tucker, with heavy emphasis.

"Oh, yes. I see," murmured Aunt Matty.

"Do not look so distressed, Aunt," pleaded Venetia. "There is no harm done. And my intentions were only for the best. I so wanted to make everything cheeerful and welcoming for you!"

Aunt Matty's face softened, "Of course, my dear. I'm sorry I snapped at you. I was simply so shocked. I had such a peaceful ride along the coastal path. But then to return home to find servants shouting, and passing buckets of water, and all this confusion and chaos—"

Venetia suddenly remembered the anemones which were still lying on the hall table, near the fluted vase. She ran and fetched them, and presented them to her aunt. "I hope these cheer you, Aunt. I thought they might raise your spirits after your headache this morning. Though after the shock of this chimney fire, I fear your poor head must be beginning to throb worse than ever!"

"No, I feel perfectly well," said Aunt Matty thoughtfully. "Run and change your dress, and cleanse that dreadful soot from your hands and face, my dear. Then we shall take tea together in the drawing room. There is something important I wish to divulge to you. I think the time has come when I must take you into my confidence!"

Intrigued, Venetia hurried upstairs and flung off her streaked pale-green dress. While her maid fetched a fresh gown from the dressing room, Venetia cleansed the sticky grime from her skin, and pondered on what revelations were to come from Aunt Matty.

My, what an eventful day it has been, thought Venetia. *I have endured difficult encounters with Sir D'Arcy, Lady Blanche, and Miss Renshaw. And now it appears that Aunt Matty is possessed of a strange secret. I wonder what it can be? But one thing is certain. I was right when I suspected earlier on that all was not well at Woodhouse Lodge.*

It was over half an hour before Venetia entered the drawing room.

"I am so sorry to have kept you waiting, Aunt," she murmured, crossing to the sofa. "But I discovered that half the contents of the chimney appeared to have fallen on my hair! It was in the most dreadful state. I was compelled to ask my maid to wash it, and though she toweled it vigorously, it is still not dry."

Aunt Matty smiled, reflecting that Venetia presented a most charming appearance in her white muslin dress, with damp curls fronding her delicate face.

"Take that little stool and sit by the fire," said Aunt Matty, pouring the tea. "Your hair will soon dry."

"Thank you," replied Venetia a trifle nervously, "But I think I will not sit too near the chimney. I have had quite enough of fires to last me a lifetime!" She sighed. "Oh Aunt Matty, I am mortified that I should be the cause of such an upset."

Aunt Matty handed her a cup of tea, and said gravely, "Now Venetia, I will not have you feeling guilty over what happened in the Blue Room. If anyone is to blame it is myself. I should have made you acquainted with . . . with certain facts as soon as you set foot in this house. But due to my own foolish pride, I had hoped to conceal the truth from you."

Venetia enquired, with deep concern, "What is it, Aunt Matty?"

For a moment, Aunt Matty gazed helplessly into the fire. Then she lifted her chin, and told Venetia, "I am afraid I am in severe financial difficulties, Niece. At one

76

time, as you may know, I was in possession of a not in-considerable fortune, which ensured that I could live quite comfortably."

Venetia nodded. "Your London house was extremely elegant, as I recall."

"Unfortunately," whispered Aunt Matty, her eyes misting, "I was forced to sell my London home. I was badly advised over my investments, you see. Most of my fortune disappeared overnight, and I suddenly found myself heavily in debt. The tradesmen would no longer give me credit. Even my faithful milliner came banging at the door, dunning me for money. Oh, it was such a nightmare!"

Venetia left her stool and rushed to the sofa to embrace her aunt. "Dearest Aunt Matty, I am horrified to hear of your distress. But why did you not advise my father of this turn of events? He would gladly give you financial assistance!"

Aunt Matty took out a lace handerchief and dabbed her eyes. "No my dear. I could never ask my brother for common charity."

"It is not common charity for a wealthy man to make over some of his funds to his only sister!" protested Venetia. "Why it would simply be an act of Christian and brotherly kindness. I shall write to him this very evening, and implore—"

"No, no!" cried Aunt Matty. "You must do no such thing, Venetia. I could not bear it. You see . . . oh dear, you will think me a very silly woman, Venetia. But some years ago, I regret to say that I found myself in similar financial difficulties. I trusted my advisers, and they let me down. Your father immediately came to my aid, and replenished my funds once more. Whatever would he say if he discovered that I had not learned my lesson—that I have made the same dreadful mistake a second time!"

"I am convinced he would instantly forgive you and make generous provision for you out of his estate," said Venetia stoutly.

Aunt Matty shook her head. "My pride would not allow me to approach him for help again. I should feel so ashamed. Please, Venetia, you must give me your solemn word that you will not breathe a word of this matter to your father!"

"But Aunt Matty——"

"Please, Venetia!"

Venetia sighed. "Oh . . . very well, Aunt. I promise. But wait! I have money of my own, inherited from my grandmother. You shall have that, Aunt! It will be a simple matter for me to contact my bankers, and arrange a draft."

"I would not dream of allowing you to do such a thing," said Aunt Matty firmly. "That fortune was left to you by your mother's mother, Lady Clarkeson. It is not, strictly speaking, Hamilton money at all. I should feel the most fearful fraud if I allowed myself to touch a penny of it. Besides you may have plans of your own for spending that fortune. It may be important for your future. I should be distraught if, for my sake, you broke into your inheritance and deprived yourself of something you had set your heart on."

Without a moment's pause, Venetia resolutely abandoned her dreams of Drystan and herself at Virginia Lodge. "Aunt Matty, there is nothing in the world that I desire to spend my inheritance on," she lied gallantly. "I assure you, it would give me the greatest comfort if you would allow me to give immediate instructions to my bankers."

Aunt Matty stroked Venetia's golden hair, and murmured, "You have a sweet, generous nature, Niece. But I insist that your fortune remain untouched. This unfortunate situation is all of my own making. All my own fault. It is up to me to find my own solution to my problems. But I am so glad you are staying here with me, Venetia. It is delightful for me to hear a young girl's happy laughter in the house. And I often stand at the window, you know, and watch you bowling off in the gig. How bright and vibrant you look in the sunshine! The sight of you never fails to raise my spirits."

Venetia poured her aunt some more tea, and remarked, "But Aunt Matty, the gig! You see, had I been more observant, and less involved with my own affairs, I would have noticed that you were effecting certain economies around the house. But that fine gig threw a complete smoke screen over your financial difficulties."

"Oh, dear," muttered her aunt, sipping her tea. "I freely own that the purchase of the gig was a foolish extravagance. But when your dear mama wrote and asked if you may visit me, I fell into a state of alarm. What would my niece think, I fretted, coming to a house which did not possess its own carriage? It was all so vexing. I knew you would be invited to many balls and assemblies. Yet how were you to travel? So I elected to throw caution to the winds, and purchase a new gig for us. I should have liked a carriage, of course, but they are prohibitively expensive!"

Venetia's pretty face was etched with despair. "You should not have *spent all that money on a gig just for me! You should not.*"

"It was not just for your convenience," asserted Aunt Matty. "After all, I am not getting any younger, I too prefer the comfort of the gig to riding sidesaddle on my mare."

Venetia played with the silken fringe on the sofa, and commented, "I am so glad you have confided in me, Aunt. Otherwise I might inadvertently have made the most dreadful gaffs . . . like inviting Lady Leamington to view the Blue Saloon!"

Aunt Matty rolled her eyes in horror. "Oh Venetia, she must never, ever be allowed in there. I am so ashamed of those faded curtains, and the threadbare carpet. I ordered the fire to be kept laid in there, just for appearances' sake. But I could not afford to have that chimney cleaned, so I had told Tucker to ensure that no one ever lit the fire."

"Well, smiled Venetia wryly, "they say a chimney fire is just as effective as calling in the sweep. I am convinced all the soot has been removed now. Most of it fell on my hair! No doubt my father would term that rough justice!" She paused as a thought struck her. "Am I to understand Aunt, that Tucker is also completely in your confidence?"

Aunt Matty nodded. "Yes, Tucker is completely

trustworthy, and discreet. She was a tower of strength when I was selling the London house, and moving here."

Now Venetia understood why Aunt Matty decided to purchase damp, gloomy Woodhouse Lodge. It was all she could afford!

She took her aunt's hand. "A trouble shared is a trouble halved, so they say. Fear not, Aunt Matty. I shall put my mind to the problem. I am sure there must be some way we can make you solvent again."

"My income is sufficient to allow me to live very modestly," Aunt Matty said, sighing. "But there is nothing left over for the luxuries of life. That's why I was so delighted by the anemones you brought me, Venetia. As you may have noticed, the garden here at Woodhouse Lodge is somewhat wild and unkempt. I can only afford to engage a part-time gardener. And unfortunately, my limited budget does not permit me to indulge in buying my favorite plants. It's so long since I had my favorite anemones in the house. Thank you, my dear!"

That night, Venetia lay awake long after midnight had chimed. She was filled with feelings of dismay and compassion for Aunt Matty. *If only,* Venetia thought, *she would allow my father to help her. He is not an ogre. I am convinced he would be horrified to learn of his sister's plight. Oh, why, why did I give my promise to Aunt Matty that I would not tell him the true facts about her financial difficulties?*

And she is quite determined not to take any of my fortune. What, then, is to become of her? Surely she cannot remain forever in this small, unhealthy house? It is plain that she has not the money to spend on having the damp attended to. It will get progressively worse over the years, creeping up through the brickwork, and into the wood. Gradually, the curtains, the sofa covers, and the linen will come to have that unpleasantly moist feel about them. And vigilant though Tucker may be with her hot stone bottles, if Aunt Matty comes to sleep between damp sheets, she will surely catch the most lethal chill.

Venetia's eyes flew open in horror as she anticipated Aunt Matty's future. *If only she had married,* mused Venetia. *I wonder why she did not? Judging by that*

Joshua Reynolds portrait hanging in the drawing room, she was extremely pretty in her youth. She came from a good family. She appeared to have every advantage in life. And did she not tell me, that when she sat for that portrait, she was in love? What happened, then, to separate her from the man she loved?

My, thought Venetia, what a long, long day this has been. One filled with incident, and mysteries. Oh, how reassuring it would be if there were only someone in Lyme in whom I could confide. I should love to discuss the strange behavior of Miss Renshaw this morning. One minute she was coldly antagonistic toward me. The next, she was offering me the recipe for a potion for my aunt, and advising me where to look for Lady March's standard. Inconsistent behavior indeed!

And then, how dearly I long for advice on Aunt Matty's problem. She cannot be allowed to remain in this sorry state. I must urgently direct my thoughts to finding a solution.

Perhaps I shall be inspired by the beautiful tranquility of the River Lym tomorrow. For I intend to take Miss Renshaw's advice and follow Lady March's route along the river bank. If Lady Luck is with me, I shall by midday have the precious standard safely in my hands!

Five

The water of the River Lym shimmered with the light of the morning sun. Venetia rested her oars for a moment, and reveled in the peace which surrounded her. A water vole slithered down the bank and streaked into the water. A mother duck proudly led her family of ducklings into the seclusion of a reeded inlet. Overhead, a bright blue sky was visible through the new delicate green leaves of the willow trees lining the bank.

Venetia sighed with content. No wonder Lady March had spent so much time on this river. It was truly delightful here. And heaven knows, thought Venetia, she herself needed tranquility after that disturbance at Woodhouse Lodge this morning!

Everything had started to go wrong for Venetia when Tucker entered the breakfast room and announced that Miss Hamilton would not be joining her.

"I am afraid she is afflicted with another headache," said Tucker. "She will rest in bed this morning."

Venetia laid down her napkin. "Now, Tucker. There

83

is no longer any need for us to play games with one another. My aunt acquainted me with details of her present difficulties."

"Yes, Miss Venetia," replied Tucker. "It is probably thinking over all her worries which has brought on this new headache."

Venetia sighed. "I must confess, Tucker, I was frankly suspicious yesterday when you were reluctant to allow me to enter my aunt's bedchamber to enquire after the first headache. Now you are alleging that she is similarly afflicted once again! Two headaches, two mornings running. That is hard to believe, is it not?"

Tucker reddened, but insisted implacably, "Nevertheless, miss, it is a fact that Miss Hamilton is in severe pain today."

"Come, Tucker. You may own the truth to me! Is this another of my aunt's attempts at economy? Is she hiding in her room each morning, in an attempt to save on the cost of her breakfast? If so, she is being extremely foolish. She eats little enough at the best of times, but a good breakfast is essential if she is to remain in good health."

"It is nothing like that, Miss Venetia," declared Tucker. "It is simply that when Miss Hamilton has a headache, she becomes nauseated at the sight or smell of food."

Venetia stood up and said firmly, "I shall call on my aunt forthwith."

Tucker rushed after her. "Oh Miss Venetia, I assure you, she desires to see no one. She merely wishes to lie quietly in a darkened room."

Venetia ignored her and marched purposefully up the stairs. She was quite convinced that Aunt Matty was not suffering from a headache. Really, Tucker must regard herself as a complete woodenhead, Venetia fumed. *Something strange is going on behind Aunt Matty's bedchamber door. I am sure of it. Well, Aunt Matty has taken me into her confidence, and I have committed myself to helping her out of her financial difficulties. But I cannot even begin to think of a solution unless I am in possession of all the facts. Tucker must be made to appreciate that she is not helping her mistress by these evasions about headaches. I must know the truth!*

And what happened? Venetia closed her eyes at the awful memory. *I swept in, and found the curtains drawn, and Aunt Matty curled up in bed, massaging her poor forehead to ease the pain. That will teach me to act so impulsively! How absurd I felt!*

Fortunately, Venetia had remembered the recipe for lime flower tisane given to her by Miss Renshaw. She had handed it to Tucker, who had promised to have it made up for Miss Hamilton to sip without delay.

As Venetia opened her eyes, she caught a flash of bright blue in the air above the water. A kingfisher! *No doubt the water is teeming with carp and trout,* thought Venetia. *I wonder if he caught his prey?*

Well, she resolved, *I must follow the kingfisher's example. To be sure, it is pleasant sitting here idly in the sun, letting the boat float gently downstream. But now I must concentrate my thoughts. I must imagine that I am Lady March, searching for a hiding place for Lord John's standard. Now where would be the best place to put it?*

Somewhere dry—obviously—though she could have wrapped it in an oilcloth. I gave the summerhouse a thorough search when I took out the boat, I am sure the flag is not hidden there. So where else could it be, along this river bank?

Venetia decided that the best course would be for her to begin by rowing as far as she could up the river, to familiarize herself with its individual nooks and crannies. *It may be,* she thought, taking up her oars, *that round the next bend there is a secret little hut, or perhaps a tree house. Yes, a tree house would make an ideal hiding place! I must remember then, to look up into the trees, and not just direct my attention to the river bank.*

Despite her delicate frame, Venetia was an accomplished oarswoman. As her oars dipped rhythmically in and out of the water, she reflected that when she had arrived in Lyme from Lincolnshire, she had never expected her stay in Dorset to be so eventful. *Life was never as exciting as this in Boston,* she mused. *Except, of course, during that wonderful time when Drystan came into my life. My, how he lit up the world for me! Whenever I was with him, everything seemed so much gayer, and brighter. And how dull and drab life seemed when he departed to rejoin his regiment. I am so glad Mama persuaded me to visit Aunt Matty. Of course, I am missing Drystan dreadfully—at least, I am sure I would be missing him, if only I were permitted more time to think about my fiancé. But somehow, life in Lyme has so far proved somewhat hectic. I am afforded little opportunity to indulge in quiet reflection.*

However, although Drystan and I are parted, at least I am not wasting my time, sitting moping over his portrait. Not, of course, that I possess a picture of him to weep over. Even so, I am glad that by my quest to purchase Virginia Lodge, I am doing something positive for Drystan and myself. Oh, how I long to see his face when I take him to see the house for the first time!

I shall take him on a ride with me up to Jack's folly. There, Drystan shall look down on Virginia Lodge, just as I did. He is sure to fall in love with it. But I shall say nothing to him about who owns it! Instead, we shall return to the valley, and I shall lead him up the drive. Then when we mount the front steps, and stand before the oak door, I shall dip him a graceful curtsy, and present him with the keys. How amazed and delighted he will be!

Absorbed in her delightful daydream, Venetia was at first only distantly conscious of the rushing noise, as she approached the bend in the river. She was still rowing strongly, pleased that she had sufficient stamina to enable the boat to glide so swiftly through the water.

Even so, she was shaken by the speed with which the boat shot round the bend. Suddenly, the air seemed to be filled with the sound of rushing water. Glancing round, Venetia's eyes widened with fear. She was approaching a weir which served the old mill!

The torrent of water foamed as it cascaded over the weir and crashed onto the rocks below. Panic-stricken, Venetia realized that in another minute, two at the most, she too would be swept over the weir, and dashed onto the sharp rocks!

For a moment, she felt numb with shock and horror.

Her oars slipped from her frozen fingers. The instant they touched the water, they were borne off by the strong current and hurled over the frothing weir. Venetia screamed as she heard them splintering on the cruel, jagged rocks.

The sound of her scream jerked Venetia out of her stunned lethargy. *I must not just sit here, accepting that in thirty seconds I shall be dead,* she thought. *I must act! And quickly!*

But what to do. She had lost her oars. The bank was out of her reach. She was a fair swimmer, but knew she would never have the strength to strike out for the bank against that vicious current. And still she was rushing, with terrifying speed, toward the weir!

Through the black wave of panic that threatened to envelop her, Venetia realized that there was one slim ray of hope. In desperation, she gazed at the willow trees on the bank. The tree nearest the weir was old and immense, with its branches reaching far out into the water.

If only, thought Venetia, her heart pounding, *I can grasp the willow branch as the boat sweeps past. But will it be strong enough to hold me? The branch looks so fragile!* Venetia knew little about willows, but dimly remembered that the wood is very resilient.

Well, Venetia realized, *I really have no choice. It is the willow or nothing.*

As the boat sped toward the terrifying weir, Venetia forced herself to stand up. For a moment, the boat rocked dangerously, almost causing her to lose her balance and tumble into the water.

Don't look at the weir, Venetia ordered herself. *Keep your eyes up, on the willow bough.*

She tensed, trying to block from her ears the deafening roar of water. Just five yards from the weir, there was the willow branch, swaying above and to the right of her.

Taking a deep breath, Venetia reached up, flinging out her arms to grasp the willow. She almost sobbed with relief as her hands closed safely round the wood. Frantically, she clung on as the bough bent under her weight, and she was plunged up to her waist into the river.

Venetia was impervious to the chill shock of water or the sound of her boat crashing onto the rocks below the weir. She was inflamed with fear as the strong current dragged at her legs under the water. *How long,* she wondered feverishly, *can I hang on to this bough? Already my arms are beginning to weaken under the strain. In another few minutes they will grow numb, and release the branch. Then for sure the current, and the river will claim me!*

"Hold on, Venetia!" The voice was masculine, firm and authoritative. "Be brave and hold on for just a minute longer!"

Venetia hardly dared believe her ears. Was that really the voice of Sir D'Arcy Rawnsley? Or was her fevered mind deluding her?

With a great effort of will, she twisted her head and gazed toward the bank. Yes, there was Sir D'Arcy's tall, commanding figure! But her relief at his unexpected arrival swiftly turned to dismay as she observed that he was running not toward her, but away, in the opposite direction to the weir!

Where is he going? she wondered frantically. *Oh, how long will he be? My plight is desperate. I am so afraid that I shall shortly lose my grasp on this branch!*

After what seemed years, but was in fact only a couple of minutes, Sir D'Arcy came into sight again. He was sprinting down the bank toward her, and in each arm he carried a long oar.

Venetia was bewildered. What is he intending to do, she pondered. Surely he is not going to attempt to row out to save me? For surely the current would sweep us both over the weir.

Suddenly overcome with exhaustion and fatigue, she closed her eyes. The cold water was swirling round her waist, pulling, tugging, urging her to release the bough and plunge toward the weir.

"Venetia!" shouted Sir D'Arcy. "Can you hear me? *Venetia!*"

Such was the commanding note of his voice, that Venetia's eyes flew open, and she stuttered, "Yes, I hear you Sir D'Arcy. But I am so tired!"

"You will be safe in a very short space of time," he called. "I propose to hold out these two oars to you. One hand at a time, you must let go of the willow, and allow the oars to support you, under your arms. Come now, quickly!"

Venetia saw that he was standing right on the edge of the bank, with the narrow end of the oars tucked under his muscular arms. The two oars were extended, in parallel, toward her. They were her lifeline.

But still she hesitated. *Admittedly, I am only lightly built,* she thought. *Even so, is it not asking too much for Sir D'Arcy to support my weight on the oars? Is there not a danger that he too will be pulled into the river, and dragged over the weir?*

"Sir D'Arcy!" she shouted, "Are you quite sure——"

"Will you stop arguing with me!" he yelled furiously. "Just do as I say, damn you!"

His aggressive tone shocked Venetia into instant action. Swiftly, she took her right hand off the willow branch and allowed the right oar to take her weight. The she repeated the procedure with her left hand.

Immediately, Sir D'Arcy began to walk backward, slowly pulling Venetia through the water toward the bank. Venetia marveled at the strength he must possess in his powerful arms to be able to hold the oars so steadily and securely. Not once did he waver, or show any signs of weakness.

To assist him, Venetia had the good sense to tread water, so she was not a dead weight being hauled to the bank. Gradually, she felt the menacing tug of the current receding. The water grew shallow. And at last, she experienced the blessed relief of feeling firm, if muddy, ground beneath her feet.

Sir D'Arcy stretched out a hand and hauled her up onto the grassy bank. "Are you all right?" he enquired anxiously. "That was the most dreadful ordeal for you!"

"I . . . am perfectly well, thanks to . . . to you," said Venetia, her teeth chattering with cold. She was acutely conscious that her thin muslin dress, wet through, was clinging to her legs in the most unseemly fashion. Her mama, she knew, would be speechless with horror if she could see her daughter in such a situation, with an un-married gentleman!

But Sir D'Arcy appeared oblivious to her embar-rassment. "We must get you into some dry things," he said, "before you catch your death of cold. My curricle is only a short distance away. Come!"

So saying, he swept Venetia into his arms, and began to stride back up the river bank.

"Sir D'Arcy," protested Venetia. "I am quite capable of walking, I assure you!"

"Yes, but not fast enough," he replied shortly, quickening his pace. "You have undergone a terrifying experience this morning. Now you are safe, it would be only natural for you to go into a state of shock. You will soon begin to feel weak and trembly. It is perfectly normal. But such a condition would have seriously de-layed us in getting you a change of clothes. And dry garments are essential, I feel, if you are not to catch a chill."

He marched purposefully on, through the willow trees, toward the lane which ran adjacent to the River Lym.

"I have no intention of relapsing into shock!" de-clared Venetia stoutly, wriggling in his arms. She had to admit, there was something remarkably exciting about Sir D'Arcy's mastery over every situation. Even, so, she thought, he sometimes carried his strong will too far. This is the second time he has picked me up and carried me to where he thought I ought to be. It is definitely a habit of his that I must set about breaking. Clearly, he has the im-pression that his word is law, wherever he happens to be. It never seems to occur to him that some people, and in particular, one Venetia Hamilton, might possess a will and a mind of their own!

But Sir D'Arcy clearly had no intention of allowing Venetia to assert her independence. Silently, he placed her in his curricle, and tucked a rug across her knees. Then they set off at a spanking pace. But not, Venetia realized, toward Woodhouse Lodge. To her amazement, Sir D'Arcy was directing the horses in the direction of Lyme!

"Sir D'Arcy," she murmured, "I fear you are taking the wrong direction. Woodhouse Lodge lies the other way."

"I am well aware of that," he replied, "I am taking you back to my house where I shall instruct my housekeeper to find you a change of clothes. If I take you back to Woodhouse Lodge in your present sopping state, I fear your Aunt Matilda will never recover from the shock."

"Oh, yes . . . yes, you are absolutely right," said Venetia. "To own the truth, Aunt Matty is in something of a delicate state just at the moment. If she learned of my adventure she would surely fall into a swoon. Besides," Venetia gave a little laugh, "she might forbid me to leave the house in future without a chaperone. And that I could not abide"

Sir D'Arcy, however, did not laugh. His expression was grim as he responded. "In my opinion, Venetia, an escort is just what you do require! Why, you are always landing yourself in the most impossible scrapes. I tell you plain, if I were your guardian I should make sure there was a long steel leash tied round your dainty waist!"

Venetia flared, "What nonsense you talk! I am not *always* involved in scrapes. I assure you, many of my hours are spent in gentle pursuits . . . I shop in Lyme, I walk along the country lanes, I play the harp, I attend on my aunt. It is all quite uneventful. It is just most unfortunate, that on the rare occasions that I find myself precipitated into a dangerous situation, *you* are always here to witness it!"

"It is fortunate I was there on the river today," Sir D'Arcy, "or you would have surely drowned."

Venetia bit her lip. "That is perfectly true," she said gravely. "I owe you a great debt. I cannot believe the coincidence that you should happen to be walking by that stretch of the river, just when I was in such dire situation!"

"Of course it was not an accident that I was on the scene," snapped Sir D'Arcy, slowing his horses to a trot as they descended the long hill which led into Lyme. "I had called at Virginia Lodge early this morning for a further discussion with the housekeeper. I thought I might find her in a more rational mood if I visited her alone."

Venetia hid a smile. So he *had* recognized that the presence of Lady Blanche was a severe handicap when it came to dealing with the strange Miss Renshaw!

Sir D'Arcy went on, "At first, Miss Renshaw was extremely hostile. Then to my surprise, she appeared to soften. She advised me that Lady March had been extremely fond of fishing, and spent many hours on the Lym."

"Oh, no!" groaned Venetia softly.

"Yes," said Sir D'Arcy cryptically. "I gather she gave you the same intelligence!"

"Yet you had more sense than to take her at her word," mourned Venetia. "You were not so rash as to take a boat and row down the river toward the weir!"

"Fortunately, I had heard from Lady Leamington about that dangerous weir," remarked Sir D'Arcy. "Evidently, there used to be a sign up, advising rowers not to proceed beyond a safe point in the river, but for some months now that sign has been missing."

"Lady March, of course, would have known not to proceed too far down the river," Venetia said. "Oh dear. So despite giving myself a fright, and a dreadful soaking, I am still no nearer to finding the standard."

Dismayed, her hand flew to her mouth. Oh, what have I done, she thought. Now I have revealed to Sir D'Arcy that I am still interested in owning Virginia Lodge! After all my attempts to keep the truth from him, I have foolishly let slip the truth in an unguarded moment.

She glanced up at him, and was annoyed to notice a smile lifting the corner of his firm lips. "You have not gulled me for an instant, Venetia," he informed her. "I have always been conscious that you are my rival for Virginia Lodge. Despite all your protests to the contrary, I knew you would not give up the house without a struggle. You are not the type to relinquish easily anything on which you have set your heart."

Taken aback that he could so easily read her innermost thoughts and character, Venetia could not resist the enquiry, "Did you . . . were you fortunate enough to catch sight of the standard during your riverside walk?"

"Fear not," said Sir D'Arcy, with a laugh, sensing her anxiety. "My first notion was to search the summerhouse. But you, of course, had been there before me and, I suspect, found nothing."

"How did you know I had looked there?" demanded Venetia, thoroughly intrigued.

He smiled, "Your perfume. It is most distinctive, I assure you. As soon as I pushed open the creaking summerhouse door, I was assailed by the scent of roses and amber. Quite bewitching! Miss Venetia Hamilton, I thought, has been here before me!"

Venetia smoothed the rug over her knees. What a contradictory man he was. One minute so overbearing, yet the next he was talking to her almost romantically!

"I began to stroll down the river bank," he continued, "And then I heard you scream. I am only sorry you were obliged to hold on to that willow branch for so long while I ran back to the summerhouse for the oars. It must have seemed a lifetime to you before I returned!"

"It did indeed!" said Venetia fervently, as they drew up outside the imposing house Sir D'Arcy had rented in Broad Street.

As Sir D'Arcy assisted Venetia from the curricle, a light, high voice interrupted them, "Ah, there you are D'Arcy! You have not forgotten you agreed to accompany me to the goldsmith? I would so value your advice on whether to choose the gold locket or the silver. The gold is so pretty, and would look well against my fair skin. But the silver locket has such intricate engraving. I am fair torn between them."

"Yes, yes, Blanche," said Sir D'Arcy impatiently. "In fifteen minutes I shall be yours to command. But for the present, I must devote my attention to preventing Miss Venetia from catching a chill."

Lady Blanche's eyebrows rose disdainfully as she regarded Venetia. "Really, D'Arcy," she sniffed, "I knew you were a keen fisherman, but I had no idea you made a practice of landing drowned Lincolnshire rats in your net!"

"Be silent, Blanche!" instructed Sir D'Arcy curtly. "If you have not the good manners to wait for me patiently, then I suggest you take yourself off to the the coffee shop, and I will join you there."

Blanche tossed her head. "Just as you please! Pray do not hurry yourself on my account!"

With that, she turned on her heel and sauntered away, her pretty nose tilted up to the sky.

Thoroughly exasperated, Sir D'Arcy turned back to Venetia. But she had gone. Bewildered, Sir D'Arcy glanced into his curricle. It was empty. He pushed open the door of his house, and addressed his steward, who was standing in the hall.

"A pretty, golden-haired young lady, Brewster! She was here with me a moment ago. But now she's disappeared! She didn't by chance run straight into the house?"

Brewster shook his head. "No, sir. Whilst you were engaged in conversation with Lady Blanche, the fair-haired lady you brought in your curricle suddenly rushed off down the street."

Thoroughly out of temper, Sir D'Arcy threw down his whip with a resounding crack on the hall table. "Really," he muttered through clenched teeth, "Miss Venetia Hamilton is getting out of hand! Why should she take it into her head to run off, just when I was about to take her into my house and see that she was clad in dry clothes! To be sure, next time I encounter that young lady, I shall give her my opinion of her astounding behavior. And I shall most certainly not mince my words!"

Venetia, meanwhile was seated next to Tucker in Aunt Matty's gig. Tucker had control of the reins, and was urging the pony on to an impossible turn of speed.

"Faster, Tucker! Oh, Woodhouse Lodge still seems miles away! Do you think we shall arrive in time?" demanded Venetia, her face flooded with anxiety.

"I don't know, Miss," replied Tucker grimly, leaning forward in her seat. "We can only hope. And pray!"

While Sir D'Arcy was engaged in his altercation with Lady Blanche, Venetia had espied Tucker riding at a sedate pace up Broad Street. Venetia had remembered Aunt Matty's headache, and how she had given Tucker the recipe for lime flower tisane which Miss Renshaw had written out for her.

Miss Renshaw! Venetia had stood on the steps of Sir D'Arcy's house feeling as if she had suddenly been stabbed. Impulsively, she had raced off up the road, to catch Tucker up in the gig.

Quickly, she had explained to the amazed maid that she feared Miss Renshaw was a crazed, sick woman.

"That recipe may have been designed to poison Aunt Matty, not cure her!" Venetia gasped. "We must return immediately to Woodhouse Lodge. Perhaps my aunt might not yet have drunk the liquid!"

Tucker shook her head. "I made it up for her myself, and left it by her bed. As I departed, she was already lifting the cup to her lips."

"Oh dear," moaned Venetia as they came in sight of Woodhouse Lodge gates. "I am so afraid that we might be too late."

"I am sure you are worrying unnecessarily, Miss Hamilton," said Tucker soothingly. "That recipe contained only herbs. I should have been instantly alerted if there had been anything poisonous about it."

"Miss Renshaw is an extremely devious and clever woman," Venetia told her. "It may be that certain herbs by themselves are harmless, but when mixed together, they produce an adverse reaction."

Tucker shook her tead. "But why should Miss Renshaw seek to harm Miss Hamilton? You know what a meek, kind soul your aunt is. Why, she has not an enemy in the whole wide world."

"I confess, Miss Renshaw's motives are a mystery to me," said Venetia, gripping the edge of the gig as they approached the front door. "But if I find that she is responsible for harming Aunt Matty, I shall personally seek out Miss Renshaw, and wring her scrawny neck!"

The gig wheels screeched to a halt. With hammering heart, Venetia flung herself through the Woodhouse Lodge door, and took the stairs two at a time. "Aunt Matty! Aunt Matty!" she called frantically. "Are you well? Oh dear, dear, aunt! Please show yourself! Please speak to me!"

"Why Venetia, whatever is the matter?"

Almost dizzy with relief, Venetia turned on the stairs. Aunt Matty was standing at the bottom of the flight, looking understandably bemused.

Venetia rushed down and embraced her aunt. "Oh, how wonderful to see you!"

"Venetia, I am of course delighted to have such an affectionate niece," murmured Aunt Matty. "But are you aware that your dress is dripping wet? Your hair is dishevelled. And just look at the filthy state of your hands!"

"I—I—unfortunately slipped into the river," said Venetia.

Aunt Matty shook her head indulgently, "Goodness knows what your dear papa would say if he could see the state of you. Run upstairs and change, then. We shall have luncheon together, and you shall tell me about your adventures!"

But to her dismay and amazement, Venetia found she could not walk a step. She felt ridiculously weak. She was trembling. Her knees threatened to buckle under her.

Heavens, she thought, Sir D'Arcy was right after all, I am suffering from delayed shock!

She clutched her aunt's arm. "Could you assist me into the drawing room, Aunt? I must sit down for a moment."

She was aware of a warning glance passed between her aunt and Tucker.

"The morning room!" declared Tucker. "You'll be more comfortable in there, Miss Venetia."

"But that's absurd," murmured Venetia weakly. "There is no sofa in the morning room. And all I require is to sit quietly for a few moments."

Thoroughly flustered, Aunt Matty pulled at her niece's arm, "Perhaps you should go straight upstairs and rest, my dear. Come, I will help you."

This is ridiculous, thought Venetia. Why here is Tucker trying to drag me to the morning room, and my *aunt urging me upstairs. In a moment I shall split in two!*

With what little strength she still possessed, Venetia shook off both her aunt and the maid, and turned into the drawing room. *If I can just reach the sofa,* she told herself, *I shall soon recover.*

But the drawing room sofa, she discovered, was completely hidden by pieces of deep rose silk. A sewing basket stood nearby. Closer examination revealed to Venetia that several of the silk shapes had been tacked, very inexpertly together.

Venetia sank onto a stool. "Why, aunt," she declared in surprise. "I had no notion you were a needle-woman!"

Aunt Matty closed the drawing room doors, and confessed with a rueful smile, "I am no needlewoman at all, Venetia! That is what is so vexing. I've tried and tried to sew those pieces of silk together, but they are so slippery to handle! And then my stitches are so ragged, and I grow impatient and stab myself with the needle, and then the edges of the silk get spotted with blood!"

Faced with this fresh drama, Venetia completely forgot the overwhelming sensation of weakness which had assailed her a few minutes ago. She slipped out of her wet clothes and drew round her the light robe brought in by Tucker.

Venetia held up two shield-shaped pieces of silk. "Aunt, with respect . . . may I ask what it is you are attempting to sew? What is to be the end result?"

"Oh dear," muttered Aunt Matty, wringing her hands. "I had hoped to keep this from you. I am endeavoring to sew myself a dress to wear to Lady Leamington's ball. The pieces you hold in your hands are supposed to be part of the bodice. But it does not look quite right, does it?"

Venetia said gently, "That is because, Aunt, you have placed one of the pieces—I think it is intended to be the back of the bodice—the wrong way up."

"Why yes! How clever of you to notice that, Venetia. What a foolish woman I am. I've been struggling with that wretched bodice for days. No wonder I couldn't get it right. And Tucker was no help. She's even more ham-fisted with a needle than I am."

Venetia laid down the crumpled pieces of silk, and said, "I suppose, Aunt, that making your own dress for the ball is another of your little economies?"

Aunt Matty nodded. "I felt I should try and dispense with my dressmaker. A ball gown costs the earth, you know Venetia. I simply cannot afford it. It seems such a brilliant notion, to sew one myself. But I am finding it such a hard task, I am sure if I ever do finish it I shall abhor the sight of the wretched thing! It will give me no pleasure whatsoever."

A thought struck Venetia. "I do believe, Aunt, you have been sewing this gown in secret in your bedchamber! You did not have a headache yesterday at all!"

"Oh, dear! Tucker told me she had the most fearful job preventing you from entering the room! If you had come in, you would have found me kneeling on the floor, surrounded by pieces of pink silk. At one point I knocked my scissors off the table. I was terrified you might have heard!"

Venetia took her aunt's hand. "And I suppose fretting over the dress yesterday, was the cause of your genuine headache today!"

"Fortunately," said Aunt Matty, "the pain disappeared very swiftly today, after I took that lime flower tisane."

Venetia felt highly relieved. Miss Renshaw, it was plain, would spare no efforts to keep either Sir D'Arcy or herself from securing Virginia Lodge. But at least she bore no malice against Aunt Matty. At one point on her nightmare ride back from Lyme with Tucker, Venetia had feared that the crazed Miss Renshaw might just be insane enough to want to set about poisoning the entire county!

Venetia gathered up all the pieces of silk, and laid them in a tidy heap on top of the sewing basket. "Aunt Matty, there is no cause for you to distress yourself attempting to fashion a dress. The solution is simple. We shall both have new ballgowns made in Lyme, and I shall have the bill sent to me. No," she raised a hand as Aunt

Matty began to protest. "I will tolerate no arguments, Aunt! After all, you are kindly entertaining me here as your guest. I know my mama would be greatly displeased if I did not show my gratitude by buying you a little gift as a token of my thanks for your generosity, and warm hospitality."

Aunt Matty's eyes were shining. "Oh, Venetia! I should dearly love a new gown. For so long now, it has been a case of make do and mend, I am afraid. But a new ball dress! Why, I feel as excited as a young girl at the prospect!"

At this mention of her youth, Venetia found her eyes drawn to the magnificent Reynolds portrait of Aunt Matty, which hung over the mantel. Observing Aunt Matty's present animation as she contemplated her new gown, Venetia could well imagine her as a young, pretty girl, enjoying her first London season.

Venetia could not resist the hesitant enquiry, "Aunt Matty, I do hope you will not think I am prying into that what does not concern me. But I remember you mentioning that when you sat for that lovely portrait, you were in love. Why, then, did you never marry?"

For a full minute Aunt Matty gazed at the vision of herself as she was twenty-five years ago. Venetia sat quite still, hardly daring to breathe. She wondered anxiously if Aunt Matty was angry with her, for introducing such a delicate, and perhaps painful subject.

Venetia said quickly, "Of course, Aunt. I quite understand if it is something you would rather not discuss. It was tactless of me to ask."

"No, no!" Aunt Matty smiled, her brown eyes warm with sentiment and nostalgia. "It is simply that I have never confided the truth in anyone before. But I am extremely fond of you, Venetia. I should like you to know what happened."

Venetia waited as her aunt crossed to the sofa, and made herself comfortable, with a cushion tucked into the small of her back. "We were both very young," she began. "I just had my coming out, and he was barely twenty years old. His name was Charles Maitland. Such a noble sounding name, I always thought. It suited him."

"Maitland?" queried Venetia. "Are they not a distinguished Norfolk family? I seem to recall that Sir William Maitland was killed in a hunting accident some years ago."

Aunt Matty nodded. "Sir William was Charles's father. They are indeed an old established family . . . but I fear that at the time I became enamored of Charles, the family fortunes were suffering a drastic decline. Sir William gambled, and drank, you see. It was all supposed to be hushed up, but everyone across two counties knew of it."

Venetia sat rapt as Aunt Matty continued, "But I never imagined that Sir William's dissolute ways would in any way influence my future. Charles and I were childhood sweethearts, you see. We loved each other dearly, and it was an understood thing that when I was old enough, we would marry and live happily ever after. So, on my seventeenth birthday, Charles approached my father and asked for my hand in marriage. To my horror and dismay, my father refused his permission!"

"Oh but why!" exclaimed Venetia. "Did your father have a low opinion of Charles's character? Or did he consider you both to be too young for the responsibility of marriage?"

"Oh, no! My father had nothing aginst Charles personally," said Aunt Matty, pushing back a strand of brown hair. "The difficulty was that my father had quarreled with Sir William. It was, I believe, over money. Sir William had borrowed a large sum from my father, and neglected to pay it back. Sir William had been in his cups when the loan was made, and when he sobered up he stoutly maintained that he had no recollection of the transaction."

"But surely," protested Venetia, "it was unfair of your father to punish yourself and Charles for the sins of Sir William?"

"My father feared," said Aunt Matty, "that Charles might inherit, in time, the bad character traits of Sir William. He insisted that Charles and I should wait a full year before we became engaged, so he could ensure that

Charles was steadfast and mature enough to make me a good, reliable husband."

"I suppose, if you view it from your father's point of view, he was only trying to act in your best interests," murmured Venetia.

"I was furious with him at the time," confessed Aunt Matty, "but Charles prevailed upon me to obey my father. He had no doubt that our love would stand the test of time. Accordingly, my family removed to London, and I was whirled into my first London season. On the surface, it was all very gay and exciting. But inwardly, I was wretched, for my parents steadfastly refused to allow Charles to call on me. Oh, how I pined for him."

Venetia completedly understood the depths of her aunt's suffering. Was she not enduring the same pain now that she and Drystan were so cruelly separated?

Aunt Matty brightened. "Then one day, I came home from riding in the park, to find my mother sparkling with excitement. Sir Joshua Reynolds had called on her! He had, it appeared, noticed me at the opera and declared himself in a fever to paint my portrait. He insisted that I would be doing him a great favor by agreeing to sit for him, and he was determined to waive his usual considerably high fee. Naturally, there was no question of my mother refusing the celebrated Sir Joshua's request, and it was fixed that I should visit his studio the following afternoon."

"My, how surprised and flattered you must have been, Aunt. For Sir Joshua to single you out, from all the girls in London! What a wonderful compliment."

Aunt Matty gave a wry smile. "I was a little puzzled, Venetia. For I was well aware that I was by no means the prettiest girl coming out that year. But what amazed me even more, was that my mother declined to accompany me to Sir Joshua's, for my sitting. He had told her that he wished the final portrait to be a surprise for her. He was anxious that she should not see the work at any stage before it was completed. So it was, that I arrived at Sir Joshua's London house with only my maid, Tucker, as chaperone."

Aunt Matty sat forward on the sofa, her hands clasped tightly together. "Imagine my feelings, Venetia! I walked, somewhat nervously, I admit, into the airy studio, and there, standing beside Sir Joshua was my own dear Charles!"

Venetia's blue eyes widened. "You mean, Charles was in collusion with Sir Joshua?"

"He it was who had commissioned Sir Joshua to paint my portrait," Aunt Matty said, smiling. "Sir Joshua was quite a romantic at heart, you know, and he willingly agreed to be a part to the conspiracy. The one fact I did not discover until much much later, was that in order to pay Sir Joshua's fee, Charles had sold his gold timepiece. It was a family treasure, too. I felt dreadful about it. But as I say, when I greeted Charles that fateful morning, I had no notion of the price he had paid for my portrait."

"He must have loved you very much," murmured Venetia.

"Yes," Aunt Matty said, and sighed. "He was indeed devoted to me. So for three wonderful weeks, that spring, Charles and I met secretly at Sir Joshua's. While Sir Joshua sat behind his easel, Charles and I conversed happily with one another. And then after the sitting, we strolled together in the garden. Oh, Venetia! Those stolen hours in the May sunshine with Charles were the happiest I have ever known. How often I think about them now!"

Venetia said thoughtfully, "And how fortunate that you were able to rely on the discretion of your maid."

"Yes," agreed Aunt Matty, "Tucker was but a young girl herself then of course, but she has always been completely faithful to me. I knew no word of my meetings with Charles would ever be relayed by Tucker to my mother."

Venetia gazed once more at the radiant young girl in the portrait. *Now I understand,* she thought, *how Sir Joshua was able to capture that soft, luminous expression in Aunt Matty's eyes. For during her sitting she was blessed with the company of the man she loved so passionately.*

"Was your mother pleased with the final portrait?" she enquired.

"Oh, Mama was quite overcome. She was utterly delighted with it. But unfortunately, it was seen by very few of London society, as at that juncture my brother— your father, Venetia—fell ill with a fever and we all hurried back to Boston Park to attend to him. Fortunately, the danger was soon past, and he fully recovered. But no sooner was he restored to health, than a fresh disaster befell our family."

"Would that be when my grandfather's banker absconded with most of the family fortune?" asked Venetia. "I have heard my father speak of the event."

Aunt Matty said ruefully, "I freely confess, Venetia, that I am a foolish woman where finance is concerned. But I do believe my stupidity with money, and my choice of advisers, is inherited from my poor father. He did his best, dear man, but he seemed to have a perverse talent for entrusting his fortune to the most unreliable people! The upshot of it all was, that although my parents were far from destitute, it suddenly became imperative that your father and I should marry into wealthy families."

"Oh dear," Venetia said sighing, "That did not augur well for you and Charles!"

"My brother Peter was more fortunate than I. He was already in love with Mary Clarkeson, younger daughter of the immensely rich Lord and Lady Clarkeson. In time, of course, Lady Clarkeson became your grandmother, Venetia, and it is her fortune which you have inherited. Mary Clarkeson brought with her a fabulous dowry to her marriage, and so your father has always been extremely comfortably off."

Venetia nodded. She knew that by wise management, her father had increased his wealth, to such an extent that Sir Peter Hamilton was now one of the wealthiest men in all eastern England.

Aunt Matty's voice was flat. "So that left me. Inevitably, when Charles once more approached my father for my hand, he was refused persmission. For days and days I argued, pleaded, begged to be allowed to marry Charles.

But my father was adamant. So Charles and I took the only course left open to us. We decided to elope."

"My!" exclaimed Venetia. "What an eventful life you led as a girl, Aunt Matty! Tell me quickly, what happened?"

Aunt Matty spread her hands. "Charles and I arranged that he would be waiting for me, with horses, by the garden door of the house at midnight. We were going to ride night and day to Gretna Green. I made all my preparations, and then went down to join my parents for what I knew would be our last dinner together, with me as an unmarried daughter under their roof."

"What a bittersweet occasion for you," murmured Venetia. "I can well imagine how you must have felt. So sad at leaving your parents, yet so filled with joy at the prospect of your union with Charles."

"I could scarcely eat a morsel of food," admitted Aunt Matty. "But then tragedy struck! Unbeknown to me, my loyal Tucker had taken a chill, and had been discovered by my mother in a faint on the stairs. My mother had Tucker taken to her room, and gave instructions that she was to stay in bed until morning, when the physician would call. Meanwhile, she assigned one of the parlor maids to the task of turning down my bed, and laying out my nightclothes. Of course, the maid entered my bedchamber, saw my traveling cloak, and my riding boots laid out ready, and immediately alerted my mother."

"Oh no!" cried Venetia. "What a dreadful misfortune! I can well imagine the rest of the story."

"Yes," sighed Aunt Matty. "I was locked in my room. And when Charles arrived at midnight, he was greeted by my furious father. But my father did not tell Charles the true facts. Instead, he maintained that I had commissioned him to speak for me. He declared that I had decided, of my own free will, to marry Lord Wilston, who was the Earl of Westley's heir. My father told Charles that I was too nervous to tell him the facts to his face . . . but that he must accept that I never wished to set eyes on him again!"

"But surely Charles would not believe such an untruth!" exclaimed Venetia. "He knew you were deeply in love with him. Did he not suspect that something was seriously wrong?"

"Ah . . . this was where my father was very clever in picking on Lord Wilston," said Aunt Matty. "You see, he had been one of my frequent escorts in London. He was a pleasant enough gentleman, but I was never attached to him. And he had certainly never proposed to me! But Charles had confessed himself jealous of Lord Wilston, and we had quarreled over the matter. Just a foolish lovers' tiff you know. It was quickly made up. But when my father stood outside the garden door, and told Charles that I was to marry Lord Wilston, the very mention of the name was enough to enrage Charles. He turned away, and galloped off into the night."

"Oh Aunt Matty!" Venetia's eyes were moist. "And what then?"

"I lay in my bedchamber, listening to the sound of his horse's hooves receding down the drive. Then I wept. Oh, how I wept."

"But surely, when you next met, you were able to explain—"

Venetia's voice trailed away at the sight of the sorrowful expression on her aunt's delicate face. "I never saw him again," she said softly. "He joined the navy, and set sail immediately for the East Indies. For all I know he could be still there, or drowned, or married."

"Did he not write? Was there no message, no word at all from him for you?"

"None," whispered Aunt Matty. "All I have to remind me of him, is the Reynolds portrait he commissioned."

"It must be very dear to you," breathed Venetia.

"Yes, it is my most treasured possession. For you see, I have never stopped loving Charles. Whenever I glance at that portrait, I remember those hours we had together in Sir Joshua's garden. We were so happy!" She smiled at Venetia through her tears. "Now you must not look so dejected on my account, Niece. For at least I have my memories. That is something to be grateful for, is it not?"

Six

"Oh, Venetia! Just look at all these fine silks and muslins! I simply cannot make up my mind which to choose!"

Venetia smiled as Aunt Matty whirled round the dressmaker's workshop, delightedly fingering the bales of beautiful fabrics which were stacked against the walls. Miss Millford, a small birdlike woman, simply dressed in gray, stood quietly in one corner, her brown eyes twinkling as she observed Miss Hamilton's delicious agony of indecision.

Aunt Matty chattered happily on, "My, I do adore this pink jaconet, but perhaps it is not elaborate enough for a ball dress. And these spotted muslins are pretty, but perhaps a little young for me. Would this blue silk be more suitable?"

Venetia saw Miss Millford wince as Aunt Matty hovered by the bale of bright blue silk. Hastily, the petite dressmaker intervened.

"I fear that a blue as brilliant as that one would overwhelm you, Miss Hamilton. You have such delicate features, such fragile coloring. Here, let me try this length of soft pink sarcenet against your skin." She held up the length of gossamer fine silk against Aunt Matty's pale face. "There! That is indeed the best color for you! Do you not agree, Miss Venetia?"

Venetia was standing by Miss Millford's long cutting out table, which was spread with patterns for ballgowns. Glancing up, she smiled in agreement, "Why yes! Aunt Matty, that pink is such a pretty color for you! Why not come and look at the patterns here. See, the sarcenet would look delightful made up into this simple, flowing style."

Venetia observed Miss Millford sigh with relief as she pushed the roll of brilliant blue silk back against the wall. *Yes,* thought Venetia, *I am glad I chose you as my Lyme Regis modiste, Miss Millford. You are not only a skilled dressmaker, but you are adept at ensuring that your clients choose only the style and fabric which really suits them. It was interesting that the blue silk favored by Aunt Matty cost considerably more than the pink sarcenet.* Venetia was impressed that Miss Millford had not sought merely to increase her profit by urging Aunt Matty to select a fabric which would have drained all the color from her skin.

Yes, decided Venetia, *I admire Miss Millford's artistry with a needle, and I also respect her sound business acumen. For if her clients select materials and styles which flatter them, they will surely return for more gowns. And by word of mouth, Miss Millford's reputation will grow.*

Which is exactly how I came to hear of her, reasoned Venetia. *From my short acquaintance with Lady Blanche Vaisey, I have found little about her that is commendable. But it has to be owned that her fashion sense is superb. She has an excellent understanding of the clothes which truly suit her. How glad I am that she happened to mention the name of her modiste when she was in conversation with Sir D'Arcy Rawnsley. Otherwise I should have found myself under heavy pressure from Lady Leamington to patronize her modiste. And as Lady Leamington's garments look as if they are held together by nails and glue, I fear her modiste and I would not have got along at all!*

Looking up, Venetia found that Miss Millford was smiling at her. "Now, Miss Venetia, what about your ballgown? Had you any particular material, or style in mind?"

Venetia replied, "I am quite undecided, Miss Millford. I am happy to be guided by your good taste and judgment."

Miss Millford nodded. She took a pace back, and appraised Venetia through narrowed eyes. "But you have the most perfect figure," she murmured. "So trim. And what a brilliant complexion! If you have a fault at all, it is your lack of height. We must choose a style which does not overwhelm you. We must emphasize your delicate features . . . make a feature of them, so that beside you, all the tall girls will feel as ungainly as beanpoles!"

Venetia laughed. "I can see you enjoy your work, Miss Millford!"

The woman took up a piece of charcoal and began to fashion a rough sketch of Venetia's gown. "It is so wonderful to be independent," she said. "I trained in Paris, you see. Oh, it was excellent experience. But the hours were long, and the work hard. By the end of the day my poor fingers were bleeding."

"Oh how dreadful," murmured Aunt Matty.

Miss Millford shrugged. "Ah, it is all the past. Now, I have my own shop, and I am in control. After all those years in those dark Parisian backrooms, being shouted at if my seams were crooked, forced to work until midnight to finish my quota of hems, oh, the freedom of having my own business is indescribable!"

"But you are much in demand amongst the ladies of Lyme," remarked Aunt Matty.

"So you must still be working very long hours." Venetia said.

"Oh, yes! Apart from your gowns, I have ten others to finish in time for Lady Leamington's ball. I shall take on extra staff, of course, but even so it will mean many nights of toil into the small hours. But I do not mind!" Her smile was brilliant. "I am working for my own pleasure, satisfaction, and profit. Not for some old crone who pays me a pittance and takes all the credit for herself!"

Venetia said anxiously, "Miss Millford, I should not like to overburden you. As there is such a heavy demand on your time, and talents, would you prefer me to have my gown made elsewhere?"

"No, no!" cried the dark-haired woman. "I am very busy, yes. But it will be a pleasure for me to make a gown for someone as lovely as you. It will be easy, you see, for you have no figure faults to disguise."

Aunt Matty could not resist asking, "Oh, Miss Millford, whatever do you mean? Who in Lyme—?"

"I can mention no names," said Miss Millford firmly. She added with a twinkle, "But I can assure you, there are certain young ladies in Lyme whom I do not dress—I camouflage! They have shoulders as broad as a farm laborer's, or thick waists, unsightly bulges, and scrawny arms. So you see," she smiled at Venetia, "it will be delightful for me to fashion a gown for your perfect figure."

She showed Venetia her sketch. "Here, I do believe this is the most elegant style for you."

Venetia's eyes glowed with delight as she viewed the sketch. It depicted a classical, high-waisted style dress, with its graceful folds enhanced by the most delicate embroidery.

"Why, it is quite lovely," she whispered. "Have you a particular material in mind for it, Miss Millford?"

"I have indeed, but I do not keep it here on display," said the modiste, in lowered tones. "It is something special I have had in reserve. Frankly, I had no mind to waste this wonderful material on some lumpy girl who merely desired me to disguise her bulges!"

The dressmaker disappeared into a small back room, and emerged a moment later carrying in her arms a length of white silk. She held it up against Venetia, and turned the golden-haired girl toward the long mirror.

"You see," said the dressmaker, "the material is plain at the top, to allow you to enhance the style with some pretty jewelry. Then, from the waist, the dress will fall in soft folds. You will note that here the silk is most beautifully embroidered with pale gold fleurs-de-lis. And at the hem, as a final touch, you have a scattering of pearls."

"Imagine it, under the chandeliers in the ballroom at Leamington Hall," Aunt Matty said, sighing. "Oh, you will look enchanting, Venetia."

Delighted, Venetia felt the soft silk, and admired the exquisite workmanship of the embroidery. "Yes, it is lovely," she agreed. "It is French silk, is it not, Miss Millford?"

Miss Millford raised a warning finger to her lips. "Shh! I dare not tell you how I came by it!"

Venetia smiled. She was coming to like Miss Millford more and more. Not only did the little dressmaker run her own highly successful business, she engaged in smuggling as well! Miss Millford was certainly an enterprising woman.

Venetia nodded. "This has been an extremely fruitful visit, Miss Millford. I should be more than pleased if you will undertake to make me a ballgown in this beautiful material."

"That is settled, then," smiled the modiste.

"No, it is not settled at all!" exclaimed a furious voice from the doorway. It was Lady Blanche Vaisey. She was wearing a scarlet pelisse, and a straw bonnet decorated with silk poppies. Unfortunately, the red of the poppies and her pelisse was clashing violently now with her lividly pink face.

"How dare you offer that embroidered white silk to this person!" she stormed at Miss Millford. "You know perfectly well you promised it to me!"

Miss Millford stood her ground. She replied calmly, "No, Lady Blanche, what you state is not the entire truth. Last Tuesday I showed you the white silk and offered to make it up for you. You, if you recall, were undecided. I asked you kindly to let me have your decision on the matter by Monday."

"And here I am!" flared Lady Blanche, her green

eyes glittering, "I have come into Lyme specially to tell you that I do desire you to make me a ballgown in that white silk. The decision has been made.".

"But too late, I fear," said Miss Millford. "Today is Wednesday, Lady Blanche."

Lady Blanche snapped her fingers. "Oh, what do a couple of days signify! The fact is that you promised me that material." She smiled triumphantly at Venetia. "I regret, you will have to choose some other fabric. Miss Millford has an excellent selection. You are bound to find something to suit."

Before Venetia could reply, Miss Millford interposed firmly, "Lady Blanche, I must insist that *you* be the one to choose another material. You are two days late informing me of your decision. I have now promised the white silk to Miss Venetia, and there is an end to the matter!"

Lady Blanche looked taken aback at the steely note in the dressmaker's voice. As she stood recovering her breath, Venetia decided it was time to effect a graceful withdrawal from the scene.

"Thank you so much for all your trouble, Miss Millford. Are you quite sure, now that Miss Hamilton and I are not taxing you too much? I should not like to think of you toiling far into the night to finish our gowns in time for the ball."

"You are not to give the matter another thought," said Miss Millford. "The ball is a week tomorrow, is it not? Well, I shall have Miss Hamilton's gown finished over the weekend. But yours, Miss Venetia, may take a little longer. With this fine fabric, it is essential that I make exactly the right calculatons for the cut of the skirt. Otherwise it will not hang properly. I will have it sent up to you on the morning of the ball."

"No, pray do not put your staff to such extra work," said Venetia. "I am aware that you will all be busy on that Thursday morning, making last minute alternations and rushing dresses hither and thither all over Lyme. With my aunt's permission, I will send my maid in on the Thursday to collect my dress."

Miss Millford expressed her thanks at Venetia's

thoughtfulness, and after arranging a convenient time for the Hamilton ladies to return for a fitting, the dressmaker escorted them to her door.

"My!" exclaimed Venetia as they stepped into Pound Street, "I do believe we effected our departure at exactly the right time, Aunt Matty. From the expression on Lady Blanche's face, I thought she was intending to pull down every bale of silk and strangle us with it!"

"What a thoroughly spoiled, petulant young lady," declared Aunt Matty, taking Venetia's arm as they stepped carefully down the steep path of Pound Street. "She was, I presume, Lady Leamington's niece?"

"Oh Aunt Matty, how remiss of me not to have introduced you! Yes, that was the celebrated Lady Blanche Vaisey."

"I assure you, I was not at all sorry to remain quietly in the background," remarked Aunt Matty. "I am surprised that Ottilia can bear her under the Leamington Hall roof. I do not imagine that she and Lady Blanche can see eye to eye over many things."

Venetia shook her head. "Perhaps Lady Leamington admires her niece's strong will. After all, one cannot imagine the Countess being able to tolerate a milk-and-water niece, with nothing to say for herself."

Aunt Matty muttered, as she settled herself in the gig, "Hmm, well no one could accuse *that* little lady of being a blushing violet." She smiled as Venetia took up the reins. "However, she had her nose put severely out of joint over her ballgown. I am so glad you won over the white silk, Venetia. It will look enchanting!"

"I confess I rather admired Miss Millford for standing no nonsense from Lady Blanche," said Venetia. "It is interesting that although she trained in Paris, she does not affect, as do many other dressmakers, to call herself Madame or Mademoiselle Millford."

"No, she is obviously English and proud of it," declared Aunt Matty. She went on thoughtfully, "It must be wonderful to possess a skill which can earn one an income. If only I were not so useless at everything!"

Venetia pressed her hand. "Come now, Aunt. I will not allow you to indulge in melancholy! It is a lovely day.

The sun is shining. The spring flowers are coming into bloom—"

"And I am going to a ball in a beautiful new dress!" exalted Aunt Matty. "Thank you so much for organizing it all, Venetia. I am so very grateful!"

"Not at all. It gives me pleasure to make you happy, Aunt," replied Venetia, lifting her head as the warm breeze ruffled her golden curls.

What Venetia said was true. She had been distressed beyond measure at the story of her aunt's tragic love affair with Charles Maitland . . . her financial catastrophe . . . and her present poverty. Venetia had lain awake for hours trying to find a solution to her aunt's problem.

If only she would allow me to inform my father of her difficulties, thought Venetia. *Or failing that, if she would but permit me to give her some of my inheritance! That I would do gladly.*

But Aunt Matty is so stubborn. So full of pride. Whenever we discuss the matter, she insists that her present unfortunate situation is all her own doing, so it is up to her to find a solution.

What a brave, courageous woman she is, realized Venetia. *To have the man she loved snatched away from her . . . to be reduced to desperate financial straits . . . yet still to retain a straight back, and a warm smile that contains not the least hint of bitterness. With her tragic past, anyone would forgive her for wallowing in self-pity. It would be easy for her to become warped and twisted by her own unhappiness. Yet she remains a tenderhearted, laughing woman. It is almost as if,* thought Venetia, *the misfortunes she has suffered have lent her a kind of strength.*

I wonder if I, too, will find myself similarly ennobled through enduring this parting from Drystan? Of course, my pain is as nothing compared with that of Aunt Matty. I know my parting is only temporary. And I am secure in the knowledge of Drystan's love. The moment he is granted leave, his one thought will be to fly to my arms. Of that I am convinced.

Yet surely, because he and I have been torn apart in this fashion, it will form an everlasting bond between us.

For we shall have proved our love and loyalty to one another.

Yes, my future is bright and rosy, reflected Venetia. *But what are we to do about poor Aunt Matty? If only she had married, she would now have someone to take care of her. But she told me that after Charles, she had found it impossible to love any other man. She had many offers, but rejected them all, much to the fury of her parents.*

When they died, Aunt inherited all her mother's jewelry. The sale of this provided her with sufficient funds to live in modest, though stylish elegance in London. But now that fortune has been squandered by Aunt Matty's callous, so-called advisers, so what is to become of her? It is dreadful to imagine her living for the rest of her days in gloomy, damp, Woodhouse Lodge.

Another distressing factor to be considered, realized Venetia, was that Tucker cannot be expected to serve her Aunt Matty forever. Devoted though she is, Tucker is no longer a young woman. If anything should happen to her, what would become of the older lady?

When Drystan returns from France, resolved Venetia, *I must speak to him without delay. Perhaps Aunt Matty could remove to Virginia Lodge, and live with us? I am sure she and Drystan would establish an excellent rapport. Admittedly, Virginia Lodge is somewhat small, but we should manage somehow.*

Venetia sighed. Virginia Lodge! How tempting it was to imagine herself living there. To plan the life she and Drystan would lead once they were married, and living in the house she loved so much.

I shall persuade him that we must stay on in Lyme after the summer, thought Venetia. For how beautiful the Virginia creeper will be in the autumn. Why, it will look as if the very house is on fire, as the red and gold tints blaze against the stone walls.

And how lovely it will be, on a crisp October morning, to stand together in the Rose bedchamber, and look out on the orchard. We shall open a window, and breathe in the scent of fruitwood, apples, and turning leaves.

The Rose bedchamber! She and Drystan together,

embracing. His hands in her hair, his mouth on hers, his gray eyes—

No! Drystan had blue eyes, not gray! Furious, Venetia lashed her whip against the side of the gig. Why, oh why did she find it impossible to rid herself of the memory of Sir D'Arcy standing over her by the bedcurtains in the Rose room? Why did that one solitary damnable kiss still refuse to extinguish itself from her mind?

"Venetia, dear," said Aunt Matty mildly, clinging desperately to the door of the speeding gig, "I thought you said we were to try and be happy on such a lovely sunny day?"

"I am happy, Aunt," said Venetia through gritted teeth. "I was thinking of my fiancé."

How strange these modern girls are, reflected Aunt Matty. To be sure, when I was Venetia's age, and I daydreamed about Charles, it never used to put me in the kind of lashing temper Venetia is currently displaying!

My Dearest Venetia,
How glad your papa and I were to receive your letter, and the welcome intelligence that you are so happily settled in Lyme. Your Aunt Matty is such a dear, kind soul. I knew I could rely on her to look after you.

A wry smile touched the corners of Venetia's mouth. Oh Mama, if only you knew the true facts. That in fact it is I who is taking care of my poor aunt!

In reply to your kind enquiry, rest assured that your father and I are in excellent health. Your papa would disagree with this statement, as he complains he is much troubled by gout. It is my belief that this is just an excuse to sit in his library all day, with his foot resting on a stool, and footmen running hither and thither with medicinal brandy. I am now quickly rereading your delightfully long letter to see if there is any question I have left unanswered . . .
Oh yes—my dear, I am afraid there has

*been no further letter for you from France. Had
one arrived, I should, natually, have forwarded
it to you without delay.*

Venetia sighed. It was now nearly three weeks since she
had last heard from Drystan. Of course, common sense
told her that a mere twenty-one days was nothing when
you considered that Drystan was in a foreign land, engaged in fighting for his country. And then it was common knowledge that the mails across sea and land were
unbearably slow.

Venetia sat on the drawing room window seat, twisting her lace handkerchief in her hands. *I know I am being
unreasonable in expecting a further letter from Drystan so
soon,* she thought. *But he promised to write to me every
single day! They were his very last words to me. I
remember the scene so vividly.*

*We were walking together through the shrubbery at
Boston Park. He kissed me for the last time, and took my
hands in his. And oh, what depths of sadness were in his
blue eyes as he said to me,*

*"My dearest, the regiment requires us to keep our
military position a secret. So it will be impossible for you
to write to me. But every night, Venetia, before I go to
sleep, I shall devote a half hour to composing a letter to
you. Believe me, throughout all the turmoil and confusion
of my days at war, I shall look forward so much to those
cherished thirty minutes when I shall pour out onto paper
all the love that is in my heart for you."*

But he had not kept his word, thought Venetia
sadly. He had not written.

Restlessly, she shifted her position on the window
seat. *Now, Venetia,* she admonished herself, *we'll have
less of that self-pitying attitude, if you please! It is all very
well for you to sit here, looking out onto the peace and
quiet of a rain-rinsed English garden, and complain that
your fiancé has been remiss over his correspondence. But
Drystan is embroiled in the heated fury of a war! Every
day, he is risking his life for your sake, and the safety of
every other woman in England.*

There are a thousand possible reasons why a letter

117

has not reached you. The courier might have been struck down on his way from the camp to the mail boat. The boat itself might have foundered on rocks, and sunk. Then again, at the end of the day, Drystan might simply be too battle weary to write letters. Or he might be wounded!

Venetia waited for the familiar thump of fear as she considered the prospect of her fiancé being injured. To her surprise, she found she was able to view the matter remarkably calmly. Somehow, it was impossible to imagine such a gay, cavalier spirit as Drystan being seriously maimed because he would take every necessary precaution to avoid placing himself in too much immediate danger, Venetia realized.

Yes, beneath that laughing exterior, there is something rather cool and calculating about Drystan. It is strange that I never realized it at the time, when we were together. But then, I was so carried away with his wit and charm. Yet now there is this distance between us, I feel I can observe his character more objectively.

Not, she hastened to assure herself, that I am in any respect the less in love with Drystan! Indeed, I do believe, it shows an admirable maturity of mind that I can admit his faults yet still regard him as the most wonderful man in the world.

She returned to her mother's letter.

Nonetheless, I do hope you are now allowing the matter of Captain Dermot's missing correspondence to cast a pall over your stay in Lyme. I appreciate that Aunt Matty has always preferred to live very quietly, but I trust you are becoming acquainted with Lyme society, and that Lyme is not too dull for you.

Venetia laughed out loud. *No, Mama, I think I can safely assure you that life is far from tedious in Dorset! Indeed, when I do return home to Boston Park, I believe I shall feel inclined to join my father in the library, and indulge in a well earned rest!*

And tonight, she thought, there was Lady Leamington's ball. How excited Aunt Matty was at the prospect! Why for the last week she has tortured herself every night, by strapping on a forehead piece to help smooth out the furrows from her brow.

Although Venetia too was looking forward to a night of merrymaking and dancing, she could not restrain the whisper that it would all be so much more delightful if only Drystan were home to accompany her. How proud she would be, entering the ballroom with a dashing hussar at her side!

But it is pointless to fret because your fiancé is not here to escort you, Venetia told herself. *After all, when you are married you will have Drystan with you every single day! And meanwhile, you have the exciting prospect of wearing your new ballgown tonight.*

Observing Tucker arriving back from Lyme with a large striped dressmaker's box under her arm, Venetia arose from the window seat and hurried to greet her. She was in a fever of impatience to try on the gown. Why, even at the first fitting when the white satin was merely tacked and pinned together, the gown had promised to be the most special she had ever owned.

Before Venetia could reach the drawing room doors, they were flung open by an agitated Tucker. The maid's bonnet was awry, and her pelisse, boots, and gloves were splattered with mud.

"Oh Miss Venetia!" gasped Tucker. "The most terrible thing has happened! But it wasn't my fault, truly it wasn't!"

Aunt Matty came hurrying downstairs. "Now, Tucker, come and sit down in the drawing room. That's right. Now just get your breath back, and then tell us calmly what has happened to bring you to this state. I—"

A gasp of dismay from Venetia interrupted her. Venetia had taken the box from Tucker and laid out her ballgown on the sofa. But the bodice, instead of shimmering pure and white, was streaked with thick clots of mud.

Tucker sat forlornly on a chair. Her face was drawn and pinched. "I went to the dressmaker's, Miss Venetia, and whilst I was waiting for the dress to be boxed up,

Miss Millford and I had a little chat. Then as I collected the box, who should emerge from a fitting room but Lady Blanche Vaisey. I hadn't realized she was there."

Venetia felt suddenly chilled. I might have known, she thought, that the name of Lady Blanche would appear somewhere in this episode!

"Lady Blanche and I left the shop at the same time," went on Tucker. "Her horse was tethered outside, but I'd left the gig at the bottom of Pound Street. Well, you know how steep Pound Street is. I was making my way along, stepping carefully because the cobbles were slippery after the rain, when suddenly, the Lady Blanche came galloping down the hill after me."

"Galloping!" cried Venetia. "What a dangerous thing to do down such a sharp incline!"

Tucker shook her head. "She may be a fine lady, Miss Venetia, but I can assure you she's no horsewoman. She had no control over the animal at all. The poor beast was thoroughly confused, and was rearing about all over the road. Which is how it happened—"

"Go on," urged Venetia gently.

"Yes," murmured Aunt Matty. "Let us hear the worst!"

"It was all over in a couple of seconds," wailed Tucker. "The horse shied against me, knocking me against the wall. Lady Blanche was shrieking at the top of her voice, and laying about her with her whip. In all the confusion, as the horse banged against me, I dropped the dressmaker's box. The lid flew off and mud from the horse's hooves fell onto the bodice. I'm so sorry, Miss Venetia!"

"Now you must not concern yourself," said Venetia firmly. "It was not your fault. Tell me," she said thoughtfully, "when you were having your little chat with Miss Millford, what was the topic under discussion?"

"Why, I just happened to mention how pleased you were, Miss Venetia, to have found such an excellent modiste in Lyme. For you had brought no ballgown with you from Lincolnshire."

"No," agreed Venetia, "I was tired of all my dresses. Rather than bring with me a trunkful of gowns I was not really inclined to wear any more, I thought it sensible to seek out a good dressmaker in Lyme and have some fresh styles made."

"I hope I was not speaking out of turn by talking thus with Miss Millford," said Tucker anxiously.

"Not at all," Venetia reassured her. *So,* she thought, *Lady Blanche overheard your remarks. Realizing that the white satin dress was all I had to wear to the ball, she deliberately set about spoiling it.*

Am I being too harsh on Lady Blanche, wondered Venetia. *After all, it would have been an accident. It is well known all round Lyme that Lady Blanche is a poor horsewoman. It might have been pure coincidence that her horse happened to be out of control just at the moment when Tucker was passing with my dress.*

And yet, mused Venetia, *all my instincts tell me that this was no accident. It is not just that Lady Blanche was foiled in her attempt to have that length of white silk made up into her own dress. Right from the start, she and I have not seen eye to eye. There has always been a tenseness in the air, a sense of friction whenever we have met.*

For my part, I regard her as a spoiled, petulant girl. But why has she so clearly taken against me? What have I done of offend her? True, in her eyes, I "stole" the white silk from her. But her hostility towards me goes further back than that. I recall when Sir D'Arcy first introduced us, in the drive of Virginia Lodge, she sat imperiously on her horse and was deliberately and unnecessarily offensive.

Aunt Matty's tearful voice broke into Venetia's thoughts. "Oh dear, your lovely dress! It is quite ruined!"

Tucker said mournfully, "Even with careful cleaning, the white silk will still look stained. Oh, what a dreadful thing to happen!"

But Venetia, meanwhile, had made a more careful examination of the dress. "No," she declared, "The gown is not totally ruined. See, the mud had only fallen above the seamline of the high waist. It should be possible for Miss Millford to detach the stained part, cut out another white silk bodice, and sew it to the skirt."

"Why yes, that is the solution," cried Aunt Matty with relief. "Quickly, Tucker. You must take the gig and speed into Lyme. Explain the unfortunate circumstances to Miss Millford, and ask her to set to work without delay! She is a skilled needlewoman. Surely she can effect the repair in time for tonight's ball?"

Sorrowfully, Venetia shook her head. "Take off your bonnet and gloves, Tucker. I fear there is no possibility of my being able to wear this gown to the ball. You see, when I was being fitted for the dress, Miss Millford told me that this was her very last length of this particular white silk. She is awaiting fresh supplies, but she cannot be certain when, if at all, they will arrive."

It all depended, reflected Venetia, on the quick wits of the dressmaker's mysterious smuggler friends. Like the letters from Drystan, so much could go wrong. If the smugglers missed the tide from France or their boat capsized, or the watch was unusually vigilant, then no more of the exquisite embroidered white silk would fall into Miss Millford's nimble fingers.

"Then what are we to do?" wailed Aunt Matty, wringing her hands. "For you have nothing to wear to the ball, Venetia!" She swallowed hard, and then declared stoutly, "But of course! I have the answer. You shall wear my new dress to the ball, niece And I shall gown myself in my tried and trusty gray velvet. With a touch of fresh lace sewn round the neck it will look as good as new."

Venetia was touched at her aunt's generous offer. "No, Aunt, that will not do at all! First, I should not dream of depriving you of the pleasure of wearing your lovely pink dress. And second, we are not at all the same shape, you know! You are an inch shorter than I, and whereas you have very little length of waist, I am a long waisted person. It is extremely kind of you, but you must go to the ball in your own pretty new dress."

"But Venetia," protested Aunt Matty, "without a proper gown, you will be unable to attend the ball at all. And I shall most certainly not go without you." She turned to her maid and said resolutely, "Tucker, kindly fetch me quill, ink, and paper. There is nothing for it. I shall send a note to Lady Leamington, making our excuses. Neither of the Miss Hamiltons will, I fear, be dancing at her ball tonight!"

"Nonsense!" cried Venetia, her eyes blazing. "Do you think I am prepared to admit defeat as easily as that, Aunt? Of course we shall go to the ball!"

"That's the spirit, miss!" beamed Tucker approvingly.

Aunt Matty looked bewildered. "But Venetia, dear. How can we go when we have nothing suitable for you to wear? Surely you are not intending to grace the Leamington Hall ballroom in your muslin afternoon dress?"

"Naturally not," said Venetia with a smile. "I have had an idea. Come with me, aunt. And Tucker, would you kindly bring that chair with you?"

Venetia swept out of the drawing room, followed by a mystified Aunt Matty, and Tucker carrying the straightbacked chair. With a purposeful air, Venetia threw open the doors of the Blue Saloon, and led the way over to the window.

"Tucker, would you please put the chair down here, in the bay."

Tucker did as she was bid. By now she had a glimmer of understanding about what was fermenting in Venetia's fertile mind. She held out her hand to the golden-haired girl. "Here, let me assist you, miss."

"Thank you," smiled Venetia, and climbed gracefully up onto the chair. She faced the window, extended her arm, and with one long dramatic gesture swept the blue silk curtains off their rail and onto the floor.

Then she turned to the two women who were staring up at her. "A blue silk dress would suit me very well, think you not? The color is a perfect match for my eyes."

"Oh Venetia!" cried an aghast Aunt Matty as her niece jumped down from the chair, "you cannot mean to use the curtains for a dress! Why, everyone would know! And in any event, those curtains are dreadfully faded in places."

Venetia knelt and examined the curtains. "I assure you, Aunt, no one will have the first notion from where my dress material originated. For have you not been at great pains to prevent your guests from entering this Blue Saloon? No one in Lyme will have set eyes on these curtains. And as for the fading, why it is only at the sides, where the sun has bleached them. I intend to cut the material most carefully, to make use of only the pure, bright blue parts."

Aunt Matty's brown eyes widened. "You are going to make the dress yourself? But Venetia, this is a mammoth task to undertake in a single afternoon! And it is not as if Tucker or I will be able to give you any assistance. I fear we are both complete dunderheads with a needle!"

"Do not fret, Aunt," smiled Venetia, "I freely confess, I am far from being as expert a seamstress as Miss Millford. But I am a quick, neat worker. I also have the advantage of an inventive mind, and a great determination to succeed!" She turned to Tucker. "There is no time to lose. If you would arrange to have the curtains pressed, Tucker, I shall set about making some sketches for my ballgown!"

Venetia's mind worked quickly as she considered the style of her dress. No sleeves, she decided, to reduce considerably the amount of sewing required. And a single length of material, cut on the bias, could be draped to form a soft, off the shoulder neckline. The bodice and skirt would be simple, unadorned, and not too full. Venetia had no intention of falling into the trap of finding herself with what seemed like a mile of hem to sew up.

The afternoon passed in a flash. Every so often, Aunt Matty poked her worried face round the drawing room door, and enquired, "Is everything progressing well, dear? It is three o'clock . . . .half past four . . . almost five-thirty . . . six o'clock!" And they were due at the ball at seven!

Venetia's thimbled fingers flashed to and fro over the blue silk. "Do not fret, Aunt. Concentrate on your own toilette. I shall be ready in time!"

At six-fifteen she snipped the last thread, threw down her needle, gathered up the soft blue garment, and hurried upstairs. Half an hour later, she drifted down the staircase, to the main hall where Aunt Matty was anxiously waiting.

"Oh, Venetia!" cried Aunt Matty ecstatically as she regarded the vision in blue. "How lovely you look! What a triumph, my dear,"

"I am rather pleased with the soft set of the neckline," said Venetia breathlessly, "but I was running out of time when I came to sew the hem. The stitches on the wrong side of the material are at least two inches long!"

"No one will notice that," Aunt Matty assured her. "They will be transfixed both by the dress, and those amazing sapphires. How well that brilliant blue becomes you!"

"My mother presented me with the sapphires just before I left for my visit here. I never dreamed I would have an opportunity to wear them so soon." Venetia smiled at her aunt. "And you, too, look so handsome in that pink dress, Aunt."

"Yes," nodded Aunt Matty, her head held high and proud, "we shall not disgrace the name of Hamilton tonight, niece. Come, the gig is at the door. Oh, how I *am* looking forward to the ball!"

Venetia smiled, but there was the glint of battle in her lustrous eyes. *And I,* she thought, *cannot wait to witness the expression of confusion, dismay, and horror on the face of a certain red-headed lady as I make my entrance into the ballroom!*

Seven

"Sir Patrick and Lady Flynt . . . The Duke and Duchess of Marchester . . . Sir D'Arcy Rawnsley . . . "

As the bewigged footman loudly announced the names and titles of the distinguished guests entering the ballroom of Leamington Hall, a dazzling smile illuminated the face of Lady Blanche Vaisey. Standing in the receiving line with her aunt and uncle, she was aware that in her embroidered ice-green silk dress, with emeralds sparkling at her white throat, she was by far the most beautiful girl in the room.

The admiration glimmering in the eyes of the handsome Sir D'Arcy Rawnsley confirmed her high opinion of her appearance. As she dipped him a graceful curtsy, he murmured, "My, Blanche! What need of chandeliers in here tonight? You quite outshine them all, my dear!"

Lady Blanche fingered her emeralds, and regarded him from beneath her long lashes. Could Sir D'Arcy, by any chance be daring to mock her? She always found it so hard to tell whether or not he was being serious.

She decided to accept his remark as a compliment. Gesturing toward his immaculate dark-green velvet evening coat, she declared with a smile, "So we both favor green this evening, D'Arcy. How interesting that our tastes are so often in harmony."

Lady Leamington, arrayed in an extraordinary creation of duck-egg blue and pink stripes, touched her niece's arm, and boomed, "Devilish tedious, I know, having to stand in line like this and receive. No doubt you're anxious for the *dancing* to begin, Blanche."

As she emphasized the word dancing, she cast a meaningful glance at Sir D'Arcy.

Lady Blanche averted her eyes. Really, it was too bad of Aunt Ottilia to be quite so obvious! Naturally, Blanche was longing for Sir D'Arcy to single her out for the honor of the first two dances. But he was very much his own man, and hardly likely to take kindly to heavy-weight hints dropped by Aunt Ottilia.

Smiling, Sir D'Arcy cast a glance toward the crowded anteroom. "I see there are many more guests ready to make their entrance, Blanche. They will no doubt claim your dutiful attention for some while yet. If you will excuse me, I shall take a stroll round the ballroom, to gather my strength for the fray of the cotillion."

Dashed, Blanche stood and watched him stride away. *Oh, what a fine figure of a man he was! And with such a fortune at his command! What a triumph it would be,* mused Blanche, *if he made an offer for my hand. And after all, why should he not find me an extremely attractive proposition? I come from a good family, I shall bring a respectable dowry. And I am far from ugly! I should make him an admirable wife. Besides it is not as if I am expecting him to fall passionately in love with me. Thank heavens, I have no truck with romantic nonsense such as that!*

No, it would be an excellent marriage of convenience. He is now in his early thirties. It is right that he should soon be married, and securing the family line with healthy sons and daughters. Naturally, I should do my duty by him in that respect. I should be an estimable wife and mother. But once the children were in the hands of nannies and tutors, oh, what a delightful life would lie ahead of me! I should have a handsome, rich husband. I should be mistress of large London house and a country estate. Of course, once we are married I shall ensure that he abandons this ridiculous whim to live in that Virginia Lodge place. It is far too small for a man in his position! Why he is so determined to purchase it I really cannot imagine. But there, until we are wed I had best keep those thoughts to myself. For the moment, I must allow him to believe that I fully support him in his quest to own the house.

Admittedly, it was excessively tedious having to endure those loathsome gallops with D'Arcy round the Lyme countryside, in search of that wretched standard. However, Blanche reasoned, it is all part of the price I have to pay to secure my objective of D'Arcy's ring on my finger.

Blanche had calculated that it was imperative for her to bring matters to a head with D'Arcy while they were both still resident in Lyme. She was well aware that once they both removed back to London, he would instantly become immersed in his own social circle and his own pursuits. He would be lost to her then. And, it had to be owned, there were in London a score of beautiful girls waiting to throw their caps at the handsome, eligible Sir D'Arcy.

Here in Lyme, thought Blanche, *I have a clear field. I am far and away the prettiest girl in the entire town.*

At least that had been her opinion, until that fateful day in the drive of Virginia Lodge when she had set eyes on Venetia Hamilton. Blanche had felt positively feverish with fury as she regarded the Hamilton girl's dazzling complexion, her fair, silken curls, the delicate face and those seemingly guileless blue eyes.

Blanche had disliked and distrusted her on sight. Oh, she had seemed innocent enough, the sweet and charming girl fresh down from Lincolnshire. But Blanche was too experienced a campaigner not to have observed the spark of interest in Sir D'Arcy's eye as he regarded the girl's graceful demeanor.

True, he had never in Blanche's hearing addressed

the Lincolnshire girl in a particularly affectionate fashion. *Yet it was strange,* mused Blanche, *the manner in which the Hamilton girl and Sir D'Arcy were so often to be seen in proximity. Why had she suddenly elected to walk up the drive of Virginia Lodge that day? Did she have prior intelligence that D'Arcy would be there? And what was the girl doing arriving at D'Arcy's house, seated beside him in his curricle?* Blanche had been livid over that incident. Had not D'Arcy promised faithfully to accompany her to the goldsmith's to advise her on selecting a new locket? Whilst they were there, Blanche had intended to draw his attention—in the most delicate, subtle manner of course—to the goldsmith's tray of wedding rings.

And then he had the gall to scuttle all her plans by arriving at his house escorting that weretched girl. And what a bedraggled state she was in, too! Blanche could not imagine what the pair of them had been doing . . . she closed her mind to all the fearful implicatons of the incident.

"Lord and Lady Duckan . . . Viscount Siddon . . . Sir Frederick and Lady Padlow . . ."

Standing at her Uncle Cedric's right hand, Blanche smiled, curtsied and murmured dutifully welcoming platitudes to the arriving guests. At the far end of the ballroom, the musicians were softly playing a medley of popular tunes. Blanche longed to turn her head and scan the brilliantly lit room for a sight of Sir D'Arcy. *Who was he conversing with? Was he looking at her? Oh,* she thought, *how I wish this interminable line of people would end, so the dancing may begin. Surely, Sir D'Arcy must ask me for the first two cotillions. I swear I shall scream with disappointment if he doesn't!*

"The Honourable Lucy Poynter and Miss Mary Poynter . . ."

Blanche was particularly gracious toward the Poynter girls—lumpy, pasty-faced creatures, dressed in a bilious shade of lime green. *There was definitely no danger of Sir D'Arcy requesting either of them to stand up with him for the first dance! And there was no danger either,* thought Blanche triumphantly, *of him seeking to dally with Venetia Hamilton. For she will be obliged to spend a quiet evening at home tonight, playing loo with her dear aunt!*

Yes, Blanche smiled, *I've spiked her guns all right! What good fortune that I happened to be in Millford's fitting room when that gossipy maid mentioned that Miss Venetia had no other ballgown with her in Lyme!*

Blanche felt not a pang of remorse or guilt at the way she had deliberately charged her horse at Tucker, and caused her to drop the dress box in the mud. *All is fair,* Blanche told herself, *in love and war. Admittedly, I am not in love with D'Arcy. But I intend to marry him. Therefore it follows that I must be at war with someone as infuriatingly pretty as Venetia Hamilton. And tonight, I think I can congratulate myself on scoring a notable victory over our lass from Lincolnshire!*

"The Earl and Countess of Brynton . . . Miss Hamilton . . . Miss Venetia Hamilton . . . "

The smile froze on Blanche's lips. It could not be true! Her ears were deceiving her. Surely the Hamilton girl had not managed to have that white silk dress cleaned in time for the ball! It seemed impossible!

Lady Leamington bellowed heartily, "Ah, Matilda! Glad to see more color in your cheeks! And here is dear Venetia. Cedric here has been longing to meet you. And I believe you are already acquainted with my niece, Lady Blanche Vaisey?"

Venetia dipped a curtsy to the florid faced earl, and received a roguish wink in return. Then she found herself face to face with Blanche.

The Lady Blanche felt as if she had been garroted. She could not believe her eyes. For here was Venetia Hamilton, standing before her in an elegantly simple blue silk ballgown, with a necklace of priceless sapphires glimmering round her slender throat.

Blanche thought she would choke. *Not only has this wretched girl made hay of my plans, and made an appearance at this ball, but it has to be owned . . . she also looks damnably, breathtakingly beautiful!*

"You're late!" Lord Leamington informed Aunt Matty. "Thought for a moment you weren't coming at all, didn't we Blanche?"

Blanche, ashen-faced, could only stutter, "Yes, indeed. That is . . . you are certainly amongst the last arrivals, Miss Hamilton. Er . . . Aunt Ottilia, would you care for me to go and request the musicians to strike up the first dance?"

Lady Leamington nodded vigorously. "That's right, Blanche! Let's get everybody moving! I've been standing here so long receiving, I've got pins and needles in my right foot."

"Stamp on it then!" ordered Lord Leamington. "Go on old girl! Give it a good whack on the floor."

"For heaven's sake, Cedric," rasped the Countess, "the first dance is to be a cotillion, not an uncouth morris dance."

Blanche meanwhile, had made her escape, and was giving the musicians instructions on which tune she favored for the cotillion. The orchestra, it appeared, had ideas of their own on the subject and a heated discussion was taking place, with Blanche declaring furiously, "Don't you dare argue with me! This ball is being given in my honor, so you will kindly play the tune I choose!"

Venetia was suddenly conscious of a tall, handsome man in dark green velvet making a courtly bow beside her.

"Miss Hamilton," said Sir D'Arcy, addressing Aunt Matty. "How delightful to make your acquaintance again. I hear you are now resident in Lyme?"

Aunt Matty blushed as she gazed up into his rugged face. "Why, Sir D'Arcy! This is indeed a pleasure. Yes, I removed from London to enjoy the pleasant sea air of Lyme. Oh! Allow me to introduce my niece, Venetia."

Venetia, who had been staring fixedly at a gilded rosette on the wall could not resist an impish smile as she dipped a curtsy, and observed in an archly social tone, "Sir D'Arcy! I am enchanted to meet you at last. I have heard a great deal about you!"

His gray eyes glimmered dangerously as he replied, "I observe, Miss Venetia, that you have clearly inherited the modestly charming demeanor of your aunt." He smiled at Aunt Matty. "I hope you will do me the honor of dancing the minuet with me later on, Miss Hamilton."

Aunt Matty's eyes sparkled. "Oh, I should be delighted, Sir D'Arcy."

He went on, "In the meantime, may I have your permission to escort your beautiful niece onto the floor for the first cotillion?"

Lady Leamington gasped. "But Blanche—" she blurted. Fortunately the rest of her sentence was strangled in a yelp of pain as Lord Leamington trod heavily on her foot.

"Yes, you run away and dance, Venetia," beamed Aunt Matty. "Oh, see, Ottilia, that nice Viscount Siddon has just approached Blanche for the cotillion. Aren't young people strange? Blanche does not look at all pleased to be singled out by such an eligible young man."

Blanche was staring furiously up the ballroom, her green eyes scorching into Sir D'Arcy as he led Venetia toward the first set of dancers.

My, thought Venetia, *poor Blanche looks ready to throw the chandeliers out of the window in rage that Sir D'Arcy has engaged me for the first cotillion! I have no doubt that he is an accomplished dancer. Although he is well built and muscular, he holds himself superbly. He moves, too, with grace and control, although at the moment he is walking a little fast for my liking.*

During their long progress down the ballroom, he had addressed not a word to her.

Venetia decided the time had come to break the silence. "Er, Sir D'Arcy," she uttered breathlessly, for he had a firm grip on her arm and she was almost having to run to keep up with him, "doesn't the ballroom look splendid tonight? I do so admire the silver and violet ribbons entwined through the balacony rails. And is that not a charming arrangement of spring flowers in the corner? I—why, Sir D'Arcy where are we going? Where are you leading me?"

Without a word, he strode on, his face set in grim, purposeful lines. They passed the first set of dancers, and the arrangement of fresh flowers in the corner. Then Venetia noticed a small door almost hidden behind a long damask curtain.

"Sir D'Arcy!" Venetia protested, as his hand reached out for the doorhandle. "What is this? Have you taken leave of your senses?"

He paid her no heed. He flung open the door, and hustled through into a cool courtyard, graced by stone urns filled with flowering shrubs. Still Sir D'Arcy did not pause. Roughly, he pulled Venetia across the cobbled courtyard, to the point where a limestone wall was illuminated by a coaching lamp hanging on a metal hook.

Sir D'Arcy swung Venetia round so her back was to the wall. He tilted her face up toward him, with the lamplight shining down on her flushed cheeks.

"Now," he said menacingly, "I believe you have some explaining to do, Venetia Hamilton!"

She stared up at the man towering over her. "On the contrary!" she flared, "It is you who owe me the explanation. How dare you pretend that you wished to dance with me, and then drag me out here into this courtyard. Why, we are quite alone! My poor Aunt Matty would be shocked at your ungentlemanly conduct!"

Sir D'Arcy laughed. "My, Venetia, you show a rare fighting spirit, I grant you that. *We are quite alone!*" He mocked her mercilessly. "That is rich indeed, coming from a lady who insists on roaming round the countryside totally unchaperoned, and who has been known to storm at anyone who might point out the foolishness of such an act!"

Venetia kept a firm hold on her temper, and her dignity. Glancing contemptuously at his hands, which were pinning her shoulders against the wall, she declared, "Sir D'Arcy, you are well aware that you are holding me here against my will. I must insist that you release me, and escort me back to the ballroom with no further delay!"

Again she was forced to endure his infuriating laugh. Then his tone became steely as he said, "Understand this, my golden-haired beauty. You are staying right where you are until you have given me a satisfactory explanation for your discourteous conduct!"

"What . . . what do you mean?" stammered Venetia.

"I am referring," said Sir D'Arcy icily, "to the day

134

you almost had the misfortune to drown. Clearly, in your mind the incident was so trivial you have totally forgotten it. Allow me to refresh your memory. We traveled in my curricle from the river to my house in Lyme where it was arranged that I would ask my housekeeper to provide you with dry clothes."

"Oh yes," interrupted Venetia, eager to justify her action in rushing off up the road after Tucker, "but you see—"

"Don't you dare interrupt me!" he thundered. "In order to ensure that you were properly looked after, and would not catch a chill, I made my self late for an appointment."

Yes, thought Venetia, scornfully. *An appointment with Lady Blanche Vaisey. She was anxious that you should accompany her to the goldsmith's.*

"Having put myself to considerable inconvenience on your account," he continued, "I found you had suddenly disappeared—gone skipping up the road without the courtesy of a word of explanation. Well, understand this, Venetia Hamilton," his hand was in her hair, keeping her face firmly tilted up toward him, "I am not the kind of man who will tolerate such high-handed behavior. Is that perfectly clear?"

Venetia's eyes blazed with indigation. That he, of all people, should presume to accuse her of arrogance! The irony of the situation would be amusing if only it involved a less infuriating man than Sir D'Arcy Rawnsley.

Frantically, Venetia tried to wriggle free from his grasp. But his strong hands held her firmly against the wall. *How dare he?* Her thoughts were furious. *Yes, I realize now that it was remiss of me to dash away from his curricle without explaining my reasons. But I was desperate. I thought the Virginia Lodge housekeeper had poisoned Aunt Matty!*

Had Sir D'Arcy approached me in a quiet, reasonable manner this evening, I should of course have expressed my apologies, and told him the cause of my hasty departure from his company that day after the river rescue. But instead of talking to me in a civilized fashion, he has chosen to drag me out here, pin me against this rough wall, and reprimand me in the most overbearing manner!

Venetia glared up at him, and declared with a defiant toss of her head. "Yes, Sir D'Arcy. I do owe you an explanation. But it is one I refuse to give under such duress. If you care to call on me one afternoon at Woodhouse Lodge, I may be prepared to spare you five minutes for a private conversation on the matter."

A gleam of admiration touched his gray eyes. "My, you're a proud minx and no mistake," he said grinning. Then he went on softly, "You owe me more than an explanation, Venetia. After all I did save you from a watery grave."

"It was always my impression," retorted Venetia, "that gentlemen who performed gallant deeds remained modestly silent about their actions."

He smiled and said, "But I have never been the quietly retiring type, Venetia."

Venetia took a deep breath and willed herself to look him straight in the eyes. She found it a curiously disturbing experience. "Very well," she said unsteadily, "Sir D'Arcy, please accept my profound thanks for your noble and timely action—"

Sir D'Arcy cleared his throat. "I fear you misunderstand me," he murmured. "I desire no pretty speeches from you. What would be more fitting, I think, is a physical expression of your gratitude."

Venetia blushed. She knew enough, now, of this man to realize when he was mocking her. It was his clear intention, at the moment, to make her feel skewered with embarrassment. How he would laugh at her struggles, her maidenly protests! And then, just at the last moment, he would release her, and tell her to run away back to the ballroom.

No, thought Venetia angrily. *You may be an experienced man of the world, Sir D'Arcy, but I'll teach you to regard me as a simple country lass from Lincolnshire. I may be unversed in sophisticated London ways, but that doesn't mean I'm fair game for rogues like you. You are probably unaware, Sir D'Arcy, but if there is one thing Boston folk are celebrated for, it's knowing when and how to seize the advantage!*

Sir D'Arcy was gazing down at her, a slight smile playing around his lips. Venetia said boldly, and coldly, "I gather Sir D'Arcy, that you require me to kiss you. Very well!"

Before he could make a move she reached up and in the space of one short second brushed her lips lightly against his.

Surprised, he dropped his hands from her shoulders, leaving her free. Venetia remained perfectly still, scorning the opportunity to flee into the Hall. She would not run away, she decided. She would stay and fight and defeat this arrogant man!

"Now, are you satisfied?" she enquired chillingly.

"Frankly, no," drawled the dark haired man. "I asked for a kiss, not a peck."

As he spoke, his arm reached out and encircled her slender waist. Frantically, Venetia strained against him, "Sir D'Arcy! May I remind you that I am a betrothed girl. I am promised to another man!"

"Well I trust you kiss him with more ardor than you just displayed toward me."

"Of course I do!" flared Venetia. "The crucial difference is, you see, that I love my fiancé—whereas I loathe you!"

"More fool you," he lashed back, "for falling for the obvious charms of a dissolute creature like Captain Dermot!"

Venetia raised her hand and struck him with all her might across the cheek. He did not flinch, though the resounding slap of the blow echoed round the courtyard.

Ventia stood her ground, though she was terrified that he would retaliate by knocking her to the cobbles. *But I could not allow him to blacken Drystan's name in such a dastardly manner!* she thought to herself. *It was only right and proper that I should defend the man I love!*

Instead of reacting violently, however, Sir D'Arcy took a pace back and stood for a moment with his head resting in his hand. When at last he spoke, his voice was grave and low.

"I beg your pardon, Venetia. I should not have spoken to you thus of your fiancé."

"I think," said Venetia with dignity, "the best course would be for us to return to the ball and forget that we were ever here together in this courtyard."

He nodded and, turning his head toward the house, listened for a moment. Then Sir D'Arcy remarked, "I believe the first cotillion is over. Shall we agree to forget our differences, and take our places for the second dance?"

"Very well," agreed Venetia. As she took his proffered arm, she was surprised to find that she was trembling.

As they slipped into the thronged ballroom and took their places in the set, Venetia cast an axious glance round, hoping they had not been missed. To her relief, the other guests seemed too engrossed with their dancing partners, or discussions of the decor, the dresses, the latest Lyme scandal, to have noticed the absence of Venetia Hamilton and Sir D'Arcy Rawnsley.

But one person in the ballroom had been acutely aware of their absence. As she danced the first cotillion with Viscount Siddon, a stiff smile had masked the fury she felt within. She had seen D'Arcy lead the Hamilton girl out into the courtyard. *What were they doing out there together?* Oh how Blanche longed to rush out and tear the pair of them assunder!

But instead she was forced to smile and make polite conversation with the Viscount. He was, admittedly, doing his best to be amusing. But Blanche was not in a laughing mood. A thousand curses on Venetia Hamilton. *It should be me,* fumed Blanche, *trysting romantically with D'Arcy in a deserted courtyard. I am, after all, a most suitable match for him. I am worldly, sophisticated, well-versed in the ways and needs of men. How foolish he is to indulge in a worthless flirtation with a fresh-faced country miss! If he married her, he'd be bored out of his mind within a week.*

What's worse, she would in all probability expect him to be faithful to her. There would be dreadful scenes, recriminations, accusations. Whereas I should not care a button whom he consorted with after we were married. His ring on my finger would be security enough for me. Oh why, why, can D'Arcy not see what is best for him?

And now the pair had reentered the ballroom. Blanche's green eyes ruthlessly examined every inch of Venetia's figure, her face, her hair. The flush on Venetia's cheeks, the curls in slight, though charming dissaray, the strange light in the cornflower blue eyes . . . no detail was too small to escape Blanche. *No,* she seethed, *D'Arcy has not merely been exchanging social pleasantries with our visitor from Lincolnshire. I would be wise to make it my business to ensure that she is removed from his sight at this ball as speedily as possible!*

On the other side of the ballroom, Venetia was mercifully unaware of Blanche's searing scrutiny. The second cotillion was under way, and as she had anticipated, Sir D'Arcy was proving an admirable partner. Gradually, lulled by the ritual of the steps, the lilting rhythm of the music, the furious pounding of Venetia's heart receded.

I have been in Leamington Hall for merely an hour, she thought, *yet what a dramatic sixty minutes these have proved to be!* She felt well satisfied with the outcome of her encounter with Sir D'Arcy. *It is honors even,* she decided. *At least I proved to him that I am no milk-and-water country lass, easily put to the blush at the hands of southern England's most eligible bachelor.*

Even so, Venetia reasoned, there was still one important thing which has been left unsaid during their tussle in the courtyard. She knew she could not rest until she had convinced herself that Sir D'Arcy had not really meant his vicious attack on her fiancé's character. Sir D'Arcy's cruel words had surely been spoken purely in anger and were not the result of true judgment.

Glancing up at him as they glided down the floor,

she murmured, "Sir D'Arcy, forgive me, but I feel I must raise with you the question of your unwarranted attack on my fiancé."

His face darkened. "My, Venetia. Do you demand blood? Have I not apologized?"

"Yes ... yes, indeed," stammered Venetia. "But I just wanted to be sure in my own mind that you do not really hold him in such low esteem."

"And why," he enquired laconically, "should my humble opinion matter so much to you?"

Why indeed? Venetia wondered in confusion. Nevertheless, she had begun this conversation. To abandon it now would only make her look foolish.

She replied with hauteur, "Naturally, as Captain Dermot is not here personally to defend himself, I feel it my duty as his fiancée to protect his interests. I cannot allow a slur on his good name to go unchallenged!"

"I adore your loyalty," responded Sir D'Arcy. But his voice was grim as he continued, "I have met Captain Dermot. I have formed my own opinion of him. And if you had been paying attention, Venetia, you would have noticed that I carefully phrased my apology: *I should not have spoken to you thus of your fiancé.* The operative word in that sentence is *you*. And that is my final declaration on the matter!"

Venetia opened her mouth to protest, but he quelled her with a frightening glance. And in glacial silence, they completed the final steps of the cotillion.

After supper, Lord Leamington escorted Venetia back into the ballroom. To her dismay she saw that he was leading her across to an arbor where Lady Leamington was in conversation with her niece. After her confrontation earlier in the evening with Sir D'Arcy, Venetia felt in no mood for a further verbal tussle with the green-eyed Lady Blanche.

But to her surprise, Lady Blanche was looking remarkably discomposed. The petulant expression marring her pretty face, had it appeared, been brought about by some abrasive remarks from the Countess.

"Ah, there you are Cedric," roared Lady Leamington, "come and lend me your support. I was just telling Blanche that she ought to take some riding lessons. She'll ruin my mare's mouth if she goes on tugging at the bridle the way she did this morning."

Lord Leamington nodded. "All young ladies should learn to feel at home on a horse. It's a first-rate accomplishment."

Lady Blanche tossed her red head. "With respect, Uncle, I must beg to differ. To my mind, the only proper way to travel is in the comfort of a carriage, not perched on the back of a galloping steed."

With her ruined white silk dress in mind, Venetia countered sweetly, "Horses do not spend their entire lives in an uncontrollable gallop, Lady Blanche. It is quite possible to restrain them to a gentle trot."

Eyes of green and eyes of blue met, held and challenged, blazing as fiercely as the emeralds and sapphires around the girls' throats. Lady Leamington, meanwhile, had momentarily lost the thread of the argument.

"Buckets!" she boomed, "whatever are all these buckets of sand and water doing around the ballroom? Cedric, did you order them to be placed here?"

Lord Leamington looked not at all put out. In fact his tone was quietly proud as he replied, "Calm down, Ottilia. Of course it was I who gave the instructions. I wanted the sand and water there as a fire precaution."

"Whatever are you twittering about?" demanded his wife. "We haven't had a fire at the Hall for over a hundred years. And then it was only in the laundry."

"Nevertheless," insisted the Count, "It's as well to be prepared. After all, Sir D'Arcy Rawnsley's country seat burnt down recently. And then there was the chimney fire at Woodhouse Lodge. One can't be too careful."

"But, Cedric, these buckets look so unsightly strewn around the ballroom like this! Surely there are more subtle methods of preventing fires?"

"Indeed there are, Aunt," said Lady Blanche. "When I was last at the Drury Lane Theater I was most impressed by the iron safety curtain and the reservoir of water maintained in case of fire."

Blanche looked smug, triumphantly establishing her position as an intimate of London society, in this gathering of country rustics.

Venetia, however, had spent a profitable morning reading the latest editions of the London newspapers. "I fear, Lady Blanche," she murmured, "that your approbation of the Drury Lane fire precautions was a little premature. Unfortunately the theater was burned to the ground four days ago."

"There you are! What did I tell you?" roared Lord Leamington. "Buckets are best, Ottilia. Now we must make sure there are enough stationed round the stables, my dear. Those grooms tend to be lax when they strike tinderboxes. Don't want any mishaps at the big hunt on Saturday."

"Well, I doubt if there's any danger of the stables being gutted by fire tonight," said Lady Leamington, glancing out of the long window, "just listen to that rain. It's positively sluicing down."

"Will you be riding to hounds on Saturday, Lady Leamington?" enquired Venetia.

"Try and stop me!" The Countess turned to Blanche. "You should come out and see us off my dear. It's quite a spectacular sight, I assure you."

Blanche wrinkled her nose. "I fear I shall be unable to attend, Aunt. I shall be quite at odds with all the boisterous high spirits, and I do so deplore the incessant barking of your hounds."

Lady Leamington's bosom heaved indignantly. "Hounds, Blanche," she hissed, "do not bark. They *speak!*"

"Not the same language as I, I fear," responded Blanche desperately. "I am sorry, Aunt, but I simply do not feel at home in the countryside. I am not an enthusiastic horsewoman, and I loathe all the creepy, crawly objects that scuttle in my path. When I was out at Virginia Lodge, for instance, I carelessly brushed against that horrid ivy, and at least a score of spiders ran up my dress. Oh it was disgusting!"

"That is an opinion you would do well to keep to yourself," counseled Lady Leamington nodding her head meaningfully toward Sir D'Arcy, who was approaching at the end of his minuet with Aunt Matty.

Lord Leamington mopped his brow. "Dashed hot in here. But I can't order the windows to be opened because of the rain. Venetia, do the decent thing and flag down a footman for some wine."

Venetia stopped the footman, and passed the parched Count a glass of claret. As he grasped the stem, Blanche idly raised a hand to fan her face. In so doing, she jogged her uncle's arm, and the claret tipped from the glass right down the front of Venetia's blue silk dress.

"Dash me!" exclaimed Lord Leamington. "I am monstrously sorry, Venetia! How careless of me!"

"It was not your fault, Lord Leamington," said Venetia quietly.

Blanche whirled round, her face a picture of regret. "Oh, Venetia, what a dreadful thing to happen! I fear the wine has stained your dress quite irreparably. Such a misfortune. Is there time, do you think, for you to hurry home and change into a fresh gown?"

As Venetia mopped at her dress with Lord Leamington's handkerchief, she reflected wryly that Blanche was perfectly well aware that she had no alternative ballgown hanging at Woodhouse Lodge. Feeling suddenly overcome by fatigue, Venetia wearily conceded defeat. *You have won, Blanche,* she thought sadly. *You have not only ruined two of my dresses but you have wrecked my evening as well.*

Eight

As if reading her thoughts, Aunt Matty touched Venetia's arm. "I think we had best go home, my dear."

Venetia felt wretched. "But aunt, I have no desire to spoil your evening. Why, there are hours of dancing ahead yet."

Aunt Matty shook her head. "Not for me, Venetia. Whilst I was minueting with Sir D'Arcy I slipped and turned my ankle. It is nothing serious, but the swelling is painful enough to prevent me dancing another step this evening. I will call at once, then, for the gig."

Lady Leamington frowned. *"Gig,* Matilda? But why did you not travel here in your carriage? The roads are rough and rutted round this neck of the woods. It seems insanity to me for you to attempt to drive a gig along them on a night such as this, especially as there's no moon."

Seeing Aunt Matty flush and begin to stammer with confusion, Venetia said quickly, "Regrettably, my aunt's carriage is at the coach yard, having a wheel repaired."

Fortunately, everyone in the party appeared to accept this explanation, and Venetia sensed her aunt's relief that she had not been forced to admit that she owned no carriage—because she could not afford one!

"Nevertheless," said Lord Leamington gruffly, "you'll have a dashed uncomfortable ride home in that gig, Matilda. Why, it's teeming down with rain. You'll both be soaked to the skin."

"Oh, dear," smirked Blanche. "How *very* unfortunate!"

At this point, an authoritative voice took command. "Naturally, there is no question of these two ladies riding home in an uncovered gig, *and* unescorted," declared Sir D'Arcy Rawnsley. "My carriage is at your disposal, ladies. And I shall travel with you, to ensure your personal safety."

Aunt Matty fluttered, and demurred. For her part, Venetia was horrified by Sir D'Arcy's suggestion. *Whenever he and I are in close proximity, we always seem to quarrel,* she thought. It is best by far that we avoid one another as much as humanly possible. Yet now it appears that we are to share the intimacy of a carriage!

There was no arguing with Sir D'Arcy. Within minutes, his magnificent carriage was at the door, and Venetia and her aunt had left the brilliance of the ballroom behind them. For Venetia, there was some slight consolation for her ruined evening in the memory of the outraged face of Lady Blanche Vaisey as Sir D'Arcy bade her a curt good night, and escorted the Hamilton ladies from the ball.

Venetia and Sir D'Arcy were obliged to wait in the large, drafty hall while Aunt Matty was waylaid in conversation by Lady Flynt. Sir D'Arcy leaned nonchalantly against the marble mantel, saying nothing. Unnerved by the lengthening silence, and Sir D'Arcy's infuriating composure, Venetia ventured the lighthearted remark,

"Well, Sir D'Arcy, it seems I must thank you once again for coming to my rescue! I am ever in your debt, it seems."

In reply, he drawled, "Are you sure you are not flattering yourself, Venetia? Has it not occurred to you that it is in fact your *aunt's* comfort and safety that I am seeking to ensure?"

Stung by what she considered to be a quite unwarranted rebuff, Venetia swept from the hall and entered the carriage. On the drive back to Woodhouse Lodge, she addressed not a word to Sir D'Arcy. He, however, appeared not to notice this, and devoted his time to encouraging Aunt Matty to recount some hilarious anecdotes about her first London season.

On their arrival at Woodhouse Lodge, Sir D'Arcy politely accompanied the ladies into the hall.

Venetia turned to him and said with a frosty smile, "My aunt and I are deeply grateful for your courtesy to us this evening, Sir D'Arcy. If you will excuse me, I will help my aunt upstairs, I think it important that she rests her poor ankle."

"Yes it is beginning to throb quite badly now. I should very much like to lie down," said Aunt Matty.

She expressed her thanks to Sir D'Arcy, and then allowed Venetia to take her arm and assist her upstairs. The faithful Tucker came hurrying out of Aunt Matty's apartments, and took immediate charge of her mistress.

"A cold compress is what that ankle needs," she declared. She sighed. "It's always the same with you, Miss Hamilton. You're as giddy as a young girl once you set foot on a dance floor. I suppose you turned the ankle while you were whirling round in a spirited country dance?"

"Not at all, Tucker," protested Aunt Matty, "I was engaged in a sedate minuet with that handsome Sir D'Arcy. But he kept making such amusing remarks about all the other dancers, that I was fair helpless with laughter, and that was what caused me to miss my footing." She turned to Venetia. "Sir D'Arcy is such a delightfully roguish companion, do you not agree?"

"I have known him such a short time, I have not yet formed an opinion of his character," said Venetia, trying to inject a note of faint boredom into her voice. She went on, "Now if you are quite sure there is nothing else I can do for you, Aunt, I will bid you good night."

As Venetia walked away, Aunt Matty looked perplexed. "How things have changed, Tucker, from my young days. When I was Venetia's age, I would have swooned with delight if such a dashing gentleman as Sir D'Arcy Rawnsley had so much as looked at me. But here's my niece, in the company of the most elegible bachelor she's ever likely to meet, and she chooses to regard him with total disdain! I confess I do not understand her at all."

"Mmm," grunted Tucker. "But she is an engaged girl, Miss."

"Oh yes!" fluttered Aunt Matty. "I really must try and remember that! I have not had the pleasure of meeting Miss Venetia's fiancé. But I cannot help wondering if he can possibly be as handsome, gallant, in every way as superior as Sir D'Arcy Rawsley?"

Although she herself does not yet realize it, that is precisely the question which is bothering Miss Venetia, thought Tucker sagely. But it was not her place to express such opinions. Instead, she hurried her mistress into her bedchamber, and set about making a cold compress.

Venetia, meanwhile, had slipped downstairs. Her mind was awhirl, and she knew it would be hours before she fell asleep. She intended to explore Aunt Matty's small library for a novel that would lull her gently into unconsciousness.

As she descended the stairs, she was suddenly bought up short. In a single, heart stopping moment, she realized that there was someone moving about in the Blue Saloon. Venetia stood gripping the stair rail, her knuckles white. It must be an intruder, she thought fearfully. Apart from Tucker, none of the other servants were required to wait up for Aunt Matty's return.

For a moment she stood hesitantly on the stairs, wondering what to do. But then her terror, her indecision, were strangely transformed into anger. *How dare he?* she raged. *How dare this person, this thief, choose Woodhouse Lodge for his sticky-fingered activities. When all around this area there are great houses owned by the titled and the wealthy ... Leamington Hall, Flynt Park ... Duckam Court ... Naturally, one would not wish on anyone the horror of a burglary. But it has to be admitted*

*that neither Lady Leamington, nor Lady Flynt nor Lady
Duckam would in any way miss a few stolen items of
silver, or a necklace or two.*

*But to Aunt Matty, a burglary would be a disaster.
She has a hard enough time as it is, just keeping up
appearances and making ends meet. To be robbed of her
precious few remaining valuables would be a shock from
which she would most likely never recover.*

The thought spurred Venetia into action. Running
lightly down into the hall, she seized the brass poker from
the hearth. Naturally, Aunt Matty could never afford to
have the hall fire lit. But the brass irons were always kept
there for the sake of appearances.

Venetia took a deep breath, tightened her grip on
the poker, then charged into the Blue Saloon.

"Stay perfectly still and you will not be hurt!" she
shouted, in what she fervently hoped was a menacing
tone.

With thudding heart, she gazed round the room. She
could not believe her eyes. The Blue Saloon was empty.

And yet, the lamp was lit near the window, illumi-
nating the one remaining blue silk curtain. The servants,
she reasoned, would never have done to bed without first
extinguishing all the lamps. And in any case, the Blue
Saloon is never used! It is unlikely that Aunt Matty lit
that lamp before we left for the ball. So who has been in
here? Who is still here?

A slight movement from behind the sofa attracted
her attention.

Boldly, she advanced toward it, brandishing the poker. "I know you're there!" she declared in ringing tones.
"Come out at once, whoever you are!"

There was a pause. Then slowly, from behind the
sofa, emerged the tall, muscular figure of Sir D'Arcy
Rawnsley. After her first shock of surprise and relief,
Venetia was overcome with rage.

How dastardly of Sir D'Arcy to have frightened her
so! And now he had the barefaced effrontery to stand
there laughing at her!

She said icily, "I am so glad you find the situation
amusing, Sir D'Arcy. It is a social convention, is it not,

that one always attempts to ensure the comfort and good humor of one's guests . . . even those who have patently overstayed their welcome."

To her chagrin, Sir D'Arcy seemed not at all put out by her sarcasm. "I beg your pardon for frightening you, Venetia," he laughed, "but you looked so magnificent marching purposefully in here clutching that poker. I simply could not resist diving behind the sofa, to lure you into believing that I was a genuine intruder."

Feeling somewhat foolish standing in the middle of the room clutching a brass poker, Venetia laid it gently in the grate and enquired gravely:

"Perhaps you would be so kind as to inform me what you were doing in this room in the first place? My aunt and I were under the impression that you had returned to the ball. Or do you make a habit of strolling, uninvited round the houses of unmarried ladies?"

"Oh dear," he said, drumming his fingers on the sofa back, "I can see you are quite determined to stay on your high horse. Very well. To explain. I was just about to take my leave, when I heard one of the window shutters banging in here. Realizing that the servants had retired for the night, I thought it would save trouble if I slipped into the room and secured the shutter. I had just completed my task when I glimpsed you striding across the hall, looking for all the world like a vengeful angel!"

As he spoke, Sir D'Arcy moved back a few paces and casually fingered the one remaining blue silk curtain. But Venetia knew that this was no meaningless gesture. How embarrassed, how humiliated she felt! Compelled to stand here before him in a blue silk dress that had obviously been fashioned from the absent curtains!

White faced, she stood immobile as he crossed the room and closed the doors.

"I think we must have a private talk," he declared, adding firmly, before she could protest, "and I will tolerate no female flutterings that it is not seemly for you to be alone with a man behind closed doors. You have already proved to me earlier this evening, Venetia, that you are a young lady with scant regard for convention."

A blush tinged Venetia's cheeks. She had no doubt

that he was referring to the bold manner in which she had reached up and kissed him, in the courtyard of Leamington Hall.

Yet, despite the commanding note in his voice, Venetia ascertained from the manner in which he was pacing the room, that Sir D'Arcy was considerably ill at ease. Well, she thought wryly, that makes a refreshing change!

He said at last: "I confess, Venetia, I find myself in unexpectedly delicate situation. You must forgive me if I sound blunt, even tactless. But it is important that we understand one another. If I couch my meaning in elegant phrases there is a danger that I may be misunderstood . . . and to my way of thinking there has been quite enough confusion already."

Venetia replied steadily, "You may speak plain with me, Sir D'Arcy. I should prefer it."

Sir D'Arcy stopped pacing the faced her. "It is about Virginia Lodge," he said. "I want it to be quite clear between us that I am deadly serious in my intention to own that house."

"I appreciate that this is not quite to the point," remarked Venetia, "but may I ask why you are so eager to purchase it? There are many other country houses for sale in the country. What makes Virginia Lodge so special in your eyes?"

He shrugged. "It is dashed difficult to put into words. There is an aura, a unique atmosphere about Virginia Lodge which instantly appealed to me. I suppose part of its enchantment lies in its tranquility—which not even the abrasive Miss Renshaw can dispel! As soon as I set eyes on the house, I felt drawn toward it. This may sound incredibly foolish and sentimental but it is the truth, it is as if it is my destiny to live there."

Venetia turned away, unable to utter a word. How uncanny that Sir D'Arcy's feelings toward Virginia Lodge exactly mirrored her own! But no, it was absurd to attach too much importance to what he had said. It was quite likely that a score of people could view Virginia Lodge and have exactly the same reaction. Virginia Lodge was, undoubtedly, an extremely attractive house. One would have to be completely lacking in soul not to appreciate its air of enchantment.

"What I desired to establish between us," went on Sir D'Arcy gravely, "is that the matter of buying the house is no game to me. I had believed it was a serious matter for you, too. Although we were rivals for Virginia Lodge, I was prepared to treat you with the honor and respect one always accords a worthy competitor. Now, however, I find that the quest for Lord March's standard is nothing more than an idle diversion for you."

"I fear I do not understand you," whispered Venetia. "An idle diversion?"

Sir D'Arcy looked extremely embarrassed. "Forgive me. But it is now glaringly obvious to me that even if you do find the standard, you have not the financial resources available to purchase Virginia Lodge."

He gazed at her dress . . . and at the blue silk curtain . . . and at her dress again.

Venetia sat down on the sofa, knowing not whether to laugh or cry. As she rested her head in her hands, she heard him murmur, "I had no wish, believe me, to cause you distress. It is not pleasant for me to speak thus. But I feel things must be clear between us, especially with regard to which one of us is to be the owner of Virginia Lodge."

Ventia was in a quandary. On the one hand, since he had been so fair and straight with her, she felt it was only courteous to repay the compliment by advising him that she was indeed as serious as he about Virginia Lodge. And, more important, that she did most certainly possess sufficient funds to purchase the house!

Yet if she told him this, he would still be curious about her blue silk curtain ballgown. And being an observant man, he could not have failed to notice the shabby furnishings of the Blue Saloon.

But if I tell him the truth about Aunt Matty's financial position, I shall be betraying a confidence, Venetia thought wretchedly. And yet, how I long to share my burden. I do so long for some intelligent advice on how to rescue my aunt from her pitiful state.

To her surprise, Venetia found that Sir D'Arcy was seating himself next to her on the sofa. His voice was low, and concerned. "Something is obviously troubling you," he murmured. "If I can be of any assistance, I hope you will feel free to put your trust in me."

Trust, mused Venetia. *Yes, that was the all important word.* She and Sir D'Arcy had clashed, quarreled, and fought. Even so, he was a man of integrity. A man who would never betray a confidence. A man she could trust. This Venetia knew instinctively.

Feeling deeply relieved, she took a deep breath, and began, "It all started when my aunt's maid mysteriously prevented me from entering her apartments one morning . . ."

Sir D'Acry listened attentively as Venetia told him how she had come to learn the truth about Aunt Matty's impoverished finances. Venetia explained too, why she had been compelled to make herself a ballgown from the curtains but she omitted all mention of Lady Blanche Vaisey from the episode when Tucker had dropped her original dress in the mud.

When she had finished her tale, Sir D'Arcy drew a hand across her forehead. "My, what an eventful life you've been leading, Venetia! But this is indeed distressing news about your aunt. I have a very high regard for her, you know."

"If only she would allow me to approach my father on her behalf." cried Venetia. "But she is so proud, so stubborn. Somehow, I must find a way to increase her fortune. But how?"

Sir D'Arcy shook his head. "It is an extremely difficult problem. I promise I will give it my earnest consideration. Somehow, there must be a solution." He regarded Venetia kindly. "This has been a terrible weight for you to have carried round by yourself. I am glad you have shared the burden with me."

"It is a relief," admitted Venetia.

"Rest assured," he said, "that my lips are sealed on the matter. But it is fortunate that I know the facts. If we are all in company together, I shall be on my guard to spare your aunt embarrassment from chance remarks—about why she does not own her own carriage, for instance."

Sir D'Arcy stood up. "It is growing late. I must take my leave."

Venetia accompanied him to the Blue Saloon doors, where he paused. "I am glad things are clear between us with regard to Virginia Lodge. It does seem absurd, however, that you and I should be such fierce rivals for the property. Is there no way I can persuade you to change your mind?"

"Assuredly not," replied Venetia firmly. "I am quite resolved that Virginia Lodge shall be the summer home of Captain Dermot and myself." She fixed Sir D'Arcy with a challenging stare. "However, I should be most impressed with your gallantry if you decided to withdraw your interest from Virginia Lodge."

He laughed. "Delighted though I should be to earn your approbation, I fear on this occasion you are doomed to remain disappointed in me. It is not just the house itself which fascinates me, I confess my curiosity is thoroughly aroused over the whereabouts of Lord March's standard. I shall never be able to rest until I have found it."

Venetia experienced a surge of relief at his words. It was obvious then, that he was still as mystified as she over where the standard might be hidden. She had feared that Sir D'Arcy had stumbled on some important clue. But evidently this was not so.

As they strolled into the hall, Venetia enquired casually, "I imagine you have many varied interests to fill your days. Are you able to devote much time to the search for the standard?"

Sir D'Arcy's gray eyes glimmered with amusement. "I will tell you plain, Venetia, that I am conducting a daily, and systematic search of the town and surrounding countryside of Lyme. Each day I cover a new section of ground. It may sound monotonous, but I believe that only a systematic approach will bring an answer to the problem."

"Oh, I disagree!" exclaimed Venetia vigorously. "I

could not possibly draw squares on a map and doggedly explore one section every day. Why, that kind of mathematical approach takes all the romance out of the situation. My method, Sir D'Arcy is quite the opposite from yours. I intend to find the standard using pure feminine intuition."

He bowed. "I wish you every success. May I ask in which direction your intuition is directing you tomorrow? It may be that I have already searched that area of Lyme, and could advise you against making a fruitless expedition."

"Certainly not, I have no intention of divulging my plans to you!" said Venetia hotly. "Besides, your search is most like not as thorough, or inventive as mine. Remember, it was a woman who hid that standard. It could be that it will take another woman to find it."

"Yes," said Sir D'Arcy with a mocking sigh, "you all have an innate understanding of the devious workings of the female mind. Now I must bid you adieu. I do hope your aunt is speedily recovered."

"Thank you," murmured Venetia. "I will pass on to her your best wishes."

Yet, still he lingered in the hall. An unfathomable expression gleamed in his eyes as he regarded the girl in blue, with her golden hair haloed in the soft lamplight.

"Did you really sit down this afternoon and make that dress?" he murmured. "That is rare determination and no mistake. I only hope your fiancé appreciates what a prize he has in you."

Venetia's face lit up at the mention of Drystan. "Tell me, Sir D'Arcy when did you meet Captain Dermot? Under what circumstances, at what place?"

Sir D'Arcy's mouth tightened. "I made his acquaintance in London," he said abruptly. "If you will excuse me, I would prefer not to discuss the matter further. Good night."

Turning on his heel, he flung his cloak over his shoulder and strode out into the night.

Venetia did not go straight up to bed. She stood in the hall, listening to the receding sound of the carriage wheels down the wet drive. In the quiet, lamplit hall, she could still detect in the air the faint, masculine aroma she had come to associate with Sir D'Arcy. It was as if he, too, were still with her, taunting, mocking, quarreling, sympathizing, laughing, caressing.

She leaned against the marble mantel, absently running her hand through her silken tresses. Caressing! That was a strange word to employ about Sir D'Arcy. And yet, there were times when most unexpectedly, he seemed to be caressing her, with his eyes, and his deep attractive voice. It was not, of course, that he had ever uttered romantic words to her. But occasionally, when he was making the most ordinary remark, there was a note in his voice, a sudden gleam in his eyes which Venetia knew were intended specially for her.

Venetia was suddenly aware that the lamp was flickering. The marble felt cold on her back. How long had she been standing here, in a daze of dreams and fanciful notions?

She shook her head. Less of this, Venetia, she instructed herself. Remember, you are engaged to Drystan. *It is he whom you love. Admittedly, Sir D'Arcy Rawnsley is an extremely attractive man. But he is also an experienced man. It is child's play for him to exert his charm over a young impressionable girl from Lincolnshire . . . in the hope, no doubt, of blunting her determination over Virginia Lodge.*

Venetia smiled as she walked upstairs to bed. *Yes,* she thought fervently, *thank heavens I have the wit to see through you, Sir D'Arcy! In future, never must I allow myself to forget that we are deadly rivals!*

At the top of the stairs, Venetia turned right toward her bedchamber. At the opposite end of the corridor, Tucker hovered in the shadows. Shamelessly she had eavesdropped on Venetia's conversation with Sir D'Arcy in the hall. Yet whereas Venetia went to bed feeling confused by the night's events—and Sir D'Arcy's obvious power over her—when Tucker retired, it was with a rare smile of satisfaction on her face.

During the last few days of April, there was no possibility of either Sir D'Arcy or Venetia being able to search for the standard. For the rain which had started on the night of Lady Leamington's ball continued to fall. Relentlessly, it sleeted down, until the soft green hills were blotted out and the sea turned a dull slate gray.

During this time, Venetia devoted herself to the care of her aunt. The turned ankle was infuriatingly slow to mend, and sprightly Aunt Matty did not take kindly to being confined for so long to bed and couch.

"Really, Venetia," she protested, as her niece made her comfortable on the drawing room sofa, "If this continues much longer I shall turn into one of those pale, languid creatures who treat a single shaft of sunlight like a missive from the very devil himself. Oh the hateful sun! It will discolor my complexion! It will bring forth hateful freckles! Oh, the shock is so great I must lie down and be cosseted for at least the next week!"

Venetia laughed. Seating herself at the harpsichord, she selected some cheerful tunes with which to entertain her aunt.

"Your ankle is well on the mend, Aunt," Venetia said, "and as for this dismal weather, it is the first of May on Monday, you know. I am convinced the sun will shine for us then."

"Oh I must be on my feet by Monday," declared Aunt Matty with unaccustomed vigor. "It is absolutely imperative!"

Venetia smiled as her hands flew over the keys. How pleasant that she and Aunt Matty were evidently so in accord in their eager anticipation of the first of May. *Undoubtedly,* mused Venetia, *May is one of the most delightful months of the year. The weather is growing warm, the leaves are coming into full leaf, the trees are laden with blossom and oh, there is such a spirit of optimism abroad in the air!*

This year, Venetia looked forward to May with special enthusiasm. For blazing within her was a burning conviction that this was to be the month in which she finally unearthed the elusive standard of Lord John March.

After Lady Leamington's ball, she had steadfastly refused to tell Sir D'Arcy which area she intended to

157

search next. But she had already made up her mind to concentrate her efforts on the seashore. After all, Lady March had been born and bred in Lyme. The sight and sound of the sea would have been part of the fabric of her life. And had not Lady Leamington mentioned (in tones of considerable bewilderment) that Lady March had amused herself by collecting pretty beach stones, and arranging them artistically in bottles? Surely, reasoned Venetia, when the time came for her to conceal the standard, she would quite naturally have been drawn towards her favorite haunts by the sea.

As it fell out, Venetia and Aunt Matty were not disappointed in their hopes for the first day of May. Overnight, the rain clouds cleared, and May Day dawned fresh and bright, with a strong sun shining on the rain-rinsed slate roofs of Lyme.

As Aunt Matty hobbled into the breakfast parlor, Venetia cried anxiously, "Now, Aunt, are you quite sure it is wise for you to be putting your weight on that ankle? You must give it time to heal."

"I was determined to be on my feet on the first of May and I have succeeded," announced Aunt Matty defiantly.

"Isn't it a glorious day!" exulted Venetia. "I confess I am longing to escape from the house. Would you care to accompany me on a stroll along the seashore, Aunt? You never know, we may find all sorts of treasure which has been washed ashore during the heavy rains!"

Aunt Matty smiled at her niece's healthy exuberance. "No, Venetia, I believe I shall be quite content here, puttering gently round the garden. You go ahead and enjoy yourself down by the sea. You will be quite safe as long as you stay on the Cobb, or the main beach. But don't wander any further than the bay, will you? I hear the tide comes in monstrous fast, and the current is treacherous."

"Fear not," Venetia reassured her, smiling. "And I shall not be away long, so you will have no cause to grow anxious on my behalf."

"Oh, now you must not return early on my account," insisted Aunt Matty. "I know how it is when one reaches the seashore. There are so many fascinating things to see, somehow the hours just slip away. You make the most of the sunshine, my dear. Take the gig. I shall not be requiring it today."

Feeling highly delighted with life, Venetia tied the deep mauve ribbons of her new bonnet, and set off in the gig towards Lyme. She stopped only once, when she spied some wood violets peeping shyly out from beneath some leaves. Within minutes, the violets were adorning her straw bonnet. In her pale lilac dress and pelisse, Venetia attracted many admiring glances as she swept through Lyme. But she was oblivious to them all. Her sights were set on the sea, and examining the bay where Lady March had walked so often, collecting her sea stones.

Venetia took the gig down to the Cobb, the picturesque old harbor which lay to the west of the town. For a while, she strolled along the old gray Cobb wall, which stretched out into the sea, enjoying the tang of the salty air, and the fresh sea breeze.

As Aunt Matty had predicted, there was much to catch Venetia's attention. The nearby boatyard was a hive of activity as the fishermen attended to their crab and lobster pots. Venetia spied old Ben Jack, who was busy tarring his boat. She gave him a friendly wave, remembering how they had sat up at his folly and shared a slice of his delicious homemade bread.

That was the day, recalled Venetia, *when I looked down into the valley on Virginia Lodge, and knew for sure that it must be mine. Oh, I must find that standard before Sir D'Arcy! I could not bear to see anyone else living at the house—and I should be especially infuriated if its new master was Sir D'Arcy Rawnsley. How superior he would feel. He would probably have the gall to invite me to his first ball at Virginia Lodge just to rub salt into the wound!*

Well, resolved Venetia, *it shall not happen that way! For I shall be mistress of that house, and Drystan shall be its master. And I shall never invite Sir D'Arcy there. Once Drystan and I are married I shall never want to set eyes on Sir D'Arcy again. Of that I am convinced!*

In her reticule, Venetia had tucked her last letter

from Drystan. Athough she knew the lines by heart, she was longing to read them again, just for the pleasure of gazing on the bold handwriting of her beloved. But, for the moment, Venetia sternly refused to allow herself such a luxury. *There will be time enough later in the day for you to peruse Drystan's letter once more,* she told herself. *In the meantime, there is work to be done!*

Walking briskly, Venetia left the Cobb and made her way down onto the wide shingled crescent of the bay. Turning her back on the gloomy gray cliffs which rose sharply from the beach, Venetia faced the sparkling blue sea, which was dotted here and there with the billowing white of sailing boats.

The tide was out, revealing a stretch of golden sand below the shingle line. Everywhere along the bay there was movement and rhythm. A few intrepid souls were venturing into the chill water. Their shrieks of laughter echoed above the haunting cry of the curlews circling overhead. Waves lapped gently at Venetia's feet, and tiny crabs scuttled for the safety of their rock pools.

Above the sand line, the damp pebbles gleamed in the sun. Venetia knelt, and allowed them to run through her slender fingers. Most were of a dull, grayish-brown shade, but here and there she was able to pick out a treasure. A pretty blue stone, then one of almost pearly whiteness . . . a perfectly smooth, terra-cotta circle . . . than a long, spiky green stone, the color of grass.

Yes, mused Venetia, *I am beginning to understand their attraction for Lady March. They would indeed look pretty, placed in an interestingly shaped glass bottle, and covered with water to maintain their luster. It is fascinating, too, the way one can ascertain from the shape of the stone how long it has been near the sea. The sharper-edged varieties are clearly fairly new. For as time goes by the force of the sea will knock off the rough edges, and make the stones smooth to the touch.*

Venetia walked the length of the bay, and examined every cranny and recess in the tall forbidding cliffs. Vaguely formed in her mind was the notion that the standard would probably be wrapped in a protective oilcloth, and jammed into a narrow hollow in the rocks. That is what she was looking for.

But as the hours went by, Venetia's spirits began to droop. Her stockings were torn to shreds from scrambling over rocks, and her fingers ached from so much contact with rough stone. *And it is all for nothing,* thought Venetia with a sigh. *For unless Lady March was singularly athletic, and actually climbed half way up these cliffs to hide the standard, then I am absolute convinced that she did not conceal it anywhere here at sea level.*

Venetia sat down on a dry rock. She dipped her handkerchief in the sea, wrung it out and held it for a moment over her burning forehead.

Suddenly she smiled. *Oh Drystan,* she thought, *if you could see me now, with my fingers bleeding, my stockings torn and my hair in such windblown disarray!*

She had never seen Drystan looking anything less than impeccable. How dashing and bold he had looked in his hussar's scarlet uniform!

It occurred to Venetia then, with a stab of surprise, that the uniform was in fact the main thing she could remember about Drystan. But what of his face? His eyes? His expression? What could she recall of them?

Frantically, she searched her mind. His eyes of course were blue. His hair was fair. Yet however much she tried, she found it impossible to visualize his exact features. It was a hard and chilling fact. But it had to be accepted that the face of the man Venetia loved remained only a blur to her.

Venetia shook her head impatiently, shaking her hair to allow the keen wind to blow through her curls. *It is absurd for me to worry so much about Drystan's physical attributes,* she decided. *After all, it is his nature and his character which are all-important.*

To underline this point, she took his letter from her reticule. She would, she knew, gain comfort and reassurance from his loving words, his tenderly expressed hopes for their future.

Often in the future, Venetia was to look back on what happened next, and certain events which followed.

She was to wonder by what strange quirk of fate she should happen to be sitting on that stretch of beach when the accident occurred.

It was as if the wind suddenly took on a willful, demon-like form. One moment, she was sitting quietly reading Dystan's letter. The next, the wind howled round her, and snatched the pages from her trembling fingers.

With a cry of alarm, Venetia jumped up from the rock and chased along the shingled area, her hands stretched up in an attempt to seize back the letter. But the pages danced tantalizingly before her in the air, until at last, propelled by a strong gust, they blew up into the somber heights of Ware Cliffs.

Venetia stood on the beach, tears of despair stinging her cheeks. The cliffs were high, craggy, and dangerous. Even a strong man would think twice before venturing up there.

And even if I did nerve myself for the ascent, thought Venetia despairingly, *most likely the wind would by then have blown Drystan's letter even further away—perhaps even out to sea. Oh, how cruel life is to me at the moment. To rob me of the one possession I treasured above all others! What have I done to deserve this?*

Slowly, Venetia walked back toward the Cobb. The sights and sounds of the beach held no pleasure for her now. She closed her ears against the peals of laughter from the people bathing. The gently insistent lapping of the waves merely irritated her. And to Venetia's ears, the cry of the circling curlews held a mocking note.

You cannot remember, they seemed to say, *what your own fiancé looks like! And now you have lost the last link with him which you possessed. He has given you no portrait, no lock of hair, no ring. Soon you will begin to wonder if he ever existed at all.*

No, thought Venetia resolutely as she marched toward her gig. *I must not fall prey to such despairing thoughts. Drystan loves me, of that I am convinced. And any day now, I am sure to receive another letter from him. Perhaps it will contain news of his forthcoming leave. Oh how wonderful that would be!*

Venetia gathered up the reins, and set off at a cracking pace back to Woodhouse Lodge. A mile away from her aunt's house, she was passing the bakery when she spied a plump, dark-haired girl struggling along the road with a basket of bread.

"Would you like a lift back to Virginia Lodge, Mollie?" Venetia called. "That basket looks dreadfully heavy."

Gratefully, the parlormaid climbed into the gig. "Thank you ever so much, miss. It never fails to amaze me the way a simple thing like bread can weigh such a ton."

"Mmm. Perhaps it is not very good bread, then," commented Venetia, turning the gig in the direction of Virginia Lodge.

"That's exactly what Lord March used to say when he was alive," said Mollie. "He'd make the most fearful ruckus if a slice of bakery bread appeared on his plate."

Venetia was pleased that Mollie had introduced the subject of Lord John March. "Tell me," she said, "do you remember much about the standard which used to fly from Virginia Lodge? Can you advise me what it looked like?"

Mollie wrinkled her nose. "It was a tattered old thing. I should think at one time it must have been gold colored, but by the time I came into service at the Lodge it was all faded. And it had Lord March's coat of arms embroidered on it, in red and black silks." She turned to wave at a passing milkmaid, and said casually, "But of course, the standard didn't fly from the flagpole all the time."

"You mean it was only hoisted when Lord John was in residence?"

Mollie shook her head. "No, miss. Oddly enough, it was always Lady March who flew the flag. She would never even let any of the footmen do it for her. She used to climb up—there's a small ledge on the roof—and hoist the flag herself."

"How very strange," murmured Venetia. "And where was Lord March during this flag-raising episode?"

"I don't know, miss. As I said before, Miss Renshaw

163

never let me have very much to do with the master and mistress. And all the staff were very close-lipped. If Miss Renshaw found that you'd been asking questions, she'd most like box your ears."

"Yes, I can well imagine," said Venetia dryly, guiding the pony through the Virginia Lodge gates. "How are you getting along with Miss Renshaw, Mollie?"

"What annoys me," said Mollie indignantly, "is that she affects to be a great stickler for the rules. All the staff have their allotted jobs, and if you take on someone else's duties, there's hell to pay from Miss Renshaw. But she's not averse to taking advantage of people when it suits her."

"In what manner?" smiled Venetia.

"She knows full well that on my half day off I always visit my mother in the village. So what do I get? 'Oh Mollie, while you're there, kindly pick up a dozen loaves from the bakery . . . three pounds of butter and some cream from the dairy' . . . so it goes on. And when Lady March was alive it was even worse, because she was always wanting those glass bottles she put her stones in. Every other week you'd find me staggering out of the glass blower's with yet another collection of containers."

"She must have been a diligent gatherer of stones to require so many display bottles," mused Venetia.

"You'd think so. But the odd thing is," said Mollie, jumping down from the gig and hauling the basket after her, "that there's no sign of those stone-filled bottles anywhere in the house now. And to think how I nearly broke my back carrying them to the house for her." She smiled at Venetia. "Thank you very much for the ride, miss."

"Not at all. It was a pleasure," said Venetia sincerely. She liked the dark-eyed parlormaid. And was it not always delightful to have the opportunity to see Virginia Lodge again?

Venetia was in a thoughtful mood as she drove back down the drive. *Perhaps,* she concluded, *my outing has not been so fruitless after all. True, my expedition to the seashore was nothing short of a disaster. I did not find the standard hidden there. And worse, I had the misfortune to lose Drystan's letter.*

Yet my chance meeting with Mollie has certainly given me interesting new intelligence to ponder over. The standard, it seems, was always raised by Lady March, herself. Strange behavior indeed. Yet from what others have told me of her, Lady March was not noted for her eccentric behavior. One could well imagine Lady Leamington thrusting her footman aside and clambering up onto the roof of Leamington Hall to hoist a flag. But the meek and mild Lady March? It seems quite out of character. And where was Lord John when his wife was engaged in the standard-raising? Surely he could not have been in residence?

Venetia's mind raced. Could it be that Lady March employed the standard as some sort of signal? But for whom? A lover perhaps? No, the idea was preposterous. All the people Venetia had spoken to confirmed that Lord and Lady March were a devoted couple. Indeed, the whole point of Lady March's complicated will, and the quest for the standard, was that as she had been divinely happy at Virginia Lodge she wished the new owner to perpetuate that atmosphere of contentment.

If only, thought Venetia, *I could discover more about the character of the mysterious Lady March. I am strongly of the opinion that she was not the bland, unassuming lady most people assumed her to be. There was clearly a darker, more secretive side to her nature. Yet because she so rarely ventured into society, there appears to be no one living in Lyme who can give me more information about her.*

No one, that is, except the housekeeper, Miss Renshaw. She it is who clearly holds the key to the whole affair. But her lips are firmly sealed. She has made that abundantly clear! Yet it is interesting that Lady March should put so much trust in her housekeeper. Miss Renshaw admitted that she knew where the standard was hidden. I wonder what happened then at Virginia Lodge to inspire such a bond between mistress and servant?

As she bowled up the drive of Woodhouse Lodge,

Venetia shook her head in total bewilderment. *Yes,* she thought, *I have learned many new fascinating facts today. But none of them have brought me an inch further to finding the standard. My one consolation, however, is that I am sure Sir D'Arcy Rawnsley is ignorant of all I have gleaned today. He is welcome to his methodical, foot-by-foot, exploration of Lyme! I shall continue to approach the search in my own, individual manner. For I am convinced that eventually, all the pieces of my puzzle will fall into place, and it will become blindingly obvious to me where that faded standard is hidden.*

As Venetia drew up outside the Woodhouse Lodge front door, Tucker came rushing out to greet her. Her face was as pale as the cap set awry on her tousled white hair.

"Oh Miss Venetia! Thank heavens you are come. The most dreadful thing has happened!"

Venetia's heart seemed to miss a beat. "Has something befallen Aunt Matty?" she demanded. "Tell me quickly, Tucker!"

"Yes, it is indeed your poor aunt," cried the distraught maid. "Oh dear. I hardly know how to tell you. She's—Miss Hamilton has been abducted!"

Nine

"*Abducted?*" screamed Venetia.

She was so shocked she almost fell out of the gig. Was this some kind of jest? Was Tucker deranged? Who on earth would want to abduct dear sweet Aunt Matty, a lady of no fortune, and in the middle years of her life?

Tucker gripped the side of the gig, and said earnestly, "I know it sounds absurd, miss, but I speak the truth."

Sensing that the maid was on the verge of hysteria and panic, Venetia forced herself to speak in a quiet, controlled tone, "Calm yourself, Tucker. Tell me quickly, and quietly, what happened."

"She didn't want you to know," blurted Tucker. "Your aunt was so worried, you see, about the desperate state of her fiances, that she . . . well . . . oh dear . . . you will be so angry."

Venetia was so agitated she felt she would throttle Tucker if the maid did not get to the point, "Tucker," she said firmly, "I promise you I will not be angry! But how

167

are we to save my aunt if you do not tell me exactly what has occurred?"

Reaching into her pocket, Tucker handed Venetia a crumpled newspaper cutting. "Your aunt sent a reply to that," whispered the maid.

Venetian smoothed open the paper, and realized that it was an advertisment from the *Morning Chronicle.* Swiftly, her amazed blue eyes scanned the lines:

> *Respectable female of good breeding required in matrimony by wealthy widower. Applicants must be healthy, meek, and skilled in all feminine accomplishments. A lady of mature years would not be met with disfavor providing her pedigree was impeccable. Replies in confidence to Mr. P. Robinson, Linton House, Oxford.*

"*Impeccable pedigree,* indeed!" exploded Venetia. "Anyone would think he was searching for a new gun dog, not a wife! And you're seriously telling me that Aunt Matty answered this outrageous advertisement?"

Tucker nodded miserably. "It just goes to show how worried she was, trying to live on such a reduced income."

"I had not realized her situation was this bad," murmured Venetia, in distress.

"She was anxious that you should not be bothered with her problems," explained Tucker. "So she answered the advertisement, and received a reply from Mr. Robinson. It transpired that he was a retired draper."

"*A draper!* Aunt Matty, the sister of Sir Peter Hamilton of Boston Park, is contemplating marrying into trade!"

"At least he was a successful draper, miss," said Tucker apologetically. "In his letter he gave details of his house, and annual income. Miss Hamilton thought he sounded a man of substance and so she wrote and asked him to visit her here, so they could discuss the final arrangements for the marriage."

Venetia raised a hand to her brow. "So that was why she was so determined to be up and walking by the first of May. She was expecting Mr. Robinson to call. No wonder she told me not to hurry back from my walk along the beach!"

Tucker wrung her hands. "The tragic thing is that having invited Mr. Robinson to Lyme, Miss Hamilton underwent a change of heart."

"You mean she came to her senses," muttered Venetia.

"As Mr. Robinson's carriage rolled up the drive, Miss Hamilton was waiting in the drawing room, quite determined to tell him that she had made a grave error of judgment, that she had brought him here on a false errand."

"So what happened between them? You say he abducted my aunt?" cried Venetia.

"I was not, of course, present at the interview between them," said Tucker. "But I was hovering in the hall, in case Miss Hamilton should call. The next thing I knew, he came striding out, dragging poor Miss Hamilton with him!"

"But did you not try to stop them!" demanded Venetia in horror.

"That I did, Miss! I flew at him, kicking and screaming blue murder. But he was a powerful man. He pushed me into the china room and locked the door. By the time cook heard my screams and came to let me out, the scoundrel had bundled Miss Hamilton into the carriage and made off with her."

"But this is dreadful!" exclaimed Venetia. "Whatever are we to do? They could be well on the road to London by now."

Tucker shook her head. "No, miss. It's worse than that. I heard him tell Miss Hamilton that he had a special license and they were to be married without delay in Lyme!"

Venetia's eyes blazed with fury. "Then I shall go after them, posthaste. At any cost, this marriage must be stopped! I shall relish the opportunity of giving this Robinson person a tongue lashing he'll not forget for many a day."

Tucker seized the pony's bridle. "Wait a moment,

Miss Venetia. Your intentions are for the best, I know. But I should warn you that this Mr. Robinson is a monstrous huge fellow. Strong as an ox, the bruises he left on my arm will testify to that."

"I am not afraid of the bullying creature!" declared Venetia stoutly. "I shall have right on my side, and anger lending me stregth. He shall not daunt me!"

"Nevertheless," insisted Tucker, "I fear he will soon overmaster someone as slender as you, Miss Venetia. Remember, he had the power to hold Miss Hamilton in one hand and throw me into the china room with the other. What is to stop him from locking you in a cupboard, too? Then all would be lost for Miss Hamilton."

Reluctantly, Venetia was forced to see the sense of the maid's words. "Then what are we to do, Tucker? Time is running short. He already has a head start. We *must* act, and quickly!"

A faint blush tinged Tucker's cheeks. "It seems to me that we must enlist the help of a strong man. We must fight brute force with masculine strength."

"Yes, yes, that is the answer," agreed Venetia. She cast desperately around for an available male. "There is the gardener . . . oh but he is a doddery creature. Perhaps that footman would be more suitable."

"No, you misunderstand me." said Tucker. "It must be a man who is not only physically strong, but who is capable, by his noble hearing and presence, to overwhelm Mr. Robinson."

Light was beginning to dawn for Venetia. "No doubt you have such a paragon in mind, Tucker," she commented dryly.

"Sir D'Arcy Rawnsley, miss. He would willingly dash to Miss Hamilton's aid. I am convinced of it."

Venetia wasted no more time in argument. Cracking her whip she set forth at a furious pace for Sir D'Arcy's house in Lyme.

Tucker is right, of course, thought Venetia as the gig careered along the winding lanes. *Sir D'Arcy is the obvious choice. He not only holds Aunt Matty in high esteem, but he is also the only person outside the household who is aware of her distressed financial position. He will understand at once what drove her to answer that scandalous advertisement. And he will move heaven and earth to remove Aunt Matty from Mr. Robinson's clutches.*

And yet how I wish I were not compelled to turn once more to Sir D'Arcy for help! Every time we meet, I leave him feeling strangely unsettled. This is only, of course, because of our rivalry over Virginia Lodge. But how much easier it would be if we could merely maintain a distant antagonism. It is bad enough for two opponents to be required to meet socially, as we do. But how much worse is it for me now to find myself begging once more for his help and protection?

But no doubt Sir D'Arcy would justify the situation by declaring that he was not helping you, Venetia, but Aunt Matty, she reassured herself. The gig screeched to a halt outside Sir D'Arcy's bay-windowed house. Venetia jumped down, and flung herself at the front door.

It was opened by a footman. To her dismay, he informed her that Sir D'Arcy was not at home.

Venetia's heart sank. *Please,* she prayed fervently, *don't let him be out roaming the countryside in search of the standard. It could be hours before he returns!*

In reply to her fevered enquires, the footman ventured the information that Sir D'Arcy would probably be found at the nearby Assembly Rooms.

As the roads were so congested, Venetia left the gig, and ran the steep length of Broad Street to the imposing Assembly Rooms. On the dais, the band was playing a medley of popular tunes. Below the musicians, the cream of Lyme society promenaded, and admired the extensive views of the sea.

The hurried arrival of the pretty girl with violets in her bonnet provoked a ripple of interested speculation.

"There's a charmer for you! What a dazzling sparkle in her eyes!"

"But she appears to have been *running* Hubert! How unseemly."

Oblivious to the buzz of remarks, Venetia fought her way through the throng, almost sobbing with relief as she espied the athletic figure of Sir D'Arcy reposing on a window seat. He was poring over a large map. Lady

Blanche Vaisey, looking beautifully bored, reclined languidly beside him.

She raised an eyebrow as Venetia rushed toward them, and said, "My, D'Arcy. From Miss Hamilton's distrait appearance I do believe the very building must be on fire."

Sir D'Arcy took one look at Venetia's anxious face and leaped to his feet. "What is wrong, Venetia?" he demanded, seizing her trembling hands in his.

She paused for breath, gaining immeasurable comfort from the strength and authority of his presence.

"Sir D'Arcy, I must speak to you most urgently. And privately." Her eyes flickered toward the suddenly alert form of Lady Blanche.

"Of course," said Sir D'Arcy. He turned to the green-eyed girl and said abruptly, "Blanche, would you kindly excuse me for a moment."

Instantly, Blanche arose and declared in arctic tones, "Please feel free to take my seat, Miss Hamilton. I was about to vacate it any any case. I see that Viscount Siddon has just arrived to take me for a ride in his new carriage."

She swept across the room and greeted Viscount Siddon with her most dazzling smile. If he was surprised that his unexpected encounter with the Lady Blanche should be the occasion of such warmth and vivacity on her part, he had the good breeding not to show it. Within a few minutes, he held out his arm and with the greatest of pleasure escorted her to his new carriage. Unfortunately, the look of triumph betstowed by Lady Blanche on the couple on the window seat was completely lost on them. They were too deep in earnest discussion to be aware of anyone else in the Assembly Rooms.

"So," muttered Sir D'Arcy angrily, "this wretched draper, having made his fortune, is now seeking to elevate his status in the world by marrying into a well-bred family."

"He is obviously a dastardly opportunist," remarked Venetia, "for he must have been only too well aware there are in this country hundreds of gentlewomen who have fallen on hard times. He sought to take advantage of their poverty, by offering them a home, and a secure future."

"No doubt many such advertisements are genuine," said Sir D'Arcy. "A lonely widower searching for a companion. There is no harm in that. But from what you have told me, this Robinson fellow is a thorough scoundrel." He stood up. "Come, Venetia, let us go and rout him out!"

As Sir D'Arcy took her arm and hurried her to the door, Venetia protested anxiously, "But Sir D'Arcy, how are we to know where to find them? Lyme is a small town sure enough, but must contain a hundred hiding places for Mr. Robinson and my poor aunt."

"I am acting on the assumption that Robinson is a stranger in Lyme," said Sir D'Arcy, striding so fast up Broad Street that Venetia was compelled to run to keep up with him. "He will, therefore, have made straight for the principal inn, which is the White Lion. It is a hostelry which rents rooms to travelers, so would be ideal for his purpose."

"Oh dear," murmured Venetia as Sir D'Arcy marched into the coaching yard of the White Lion. "I hope we are not too late."

The yard was bustling with carriages, hostlers, departing visitors, and stableboys. Sir D'Arcy scrutinized the carriages for a moment, and then demanded of Venetia, "What color did Tucker say Robinson's carriage was painted?"

"Dark blue," replied Venetia. "And Tucker was very scornful. Because in the place on the door where those who are entitled have their coat of arms emblazoned, Mr. Robinson had a silver motif, comprised of two R's, back-to-back, encircled by laurel leaves."

Sir D'Arcy rolled his fine eyes. "Just the kind of pretension I would have expected from one so crass as he." Then Sir D'Arcy gave a start, and exclaimed triumphantly, "Ah! Look, Venetia, over there in the corner. What do you see?"

There it was. A dark-blue coach, with the silver R crest on the doors.

"So they are here!" cried Venetia with relief. "But

Sir D'Arcy, we must hurry. See, the boy is harnessing up the horses. It seems likely that Mr. Robinson will very soon be making his departure for the church!"

Sir D'Arcy turned on his heel and marched into the inn. The main room was pervaded with a sour smell of ale. Dirty tankards lay strewn on the chipped tables, and Venetia noticed with distaste that the sawdust on the floor apparently had not been changed for weeks.

The innkeeper hurried forward. He took one glance at the fine clothes, the elegant air of the couple standing before him, and instantly favored them with his most ingratiating smile.

"It is indeed a pleasure, sir, to welcome you and your lady to my humble hostelry. May I offer you refreshment? A hot luncheon, perhaps, or some of our special spiced wine?"

Sir D'Arcy regarded the platters of half finished, greasy food littering the tables, and said with distaste, "Thank you, no. I should be glad if you would merely answer a simple enquiry. You have a person named Robinson staying here. In which room will I find him?"

A sly expression crossed the innkeeper's face. "Well now, that's confidential information, see? I mean, I can't just go telling all and sundry who's staying here, can I? My guests wouldn't like it. I have my reputation to consider, you know."

Venetia felt like hitting the grinning dolt. *Don't you realize,* she wanted to scream, *that my aunt is in danger of being carried off and wed by an out-and-out common rogue? How dare you stand there prevaricating, when time is so precious if we are to save Aunt Matty?*

Sir D'Arcy, however, had reached into his coat, and with a weary sigh pressed a coin into the man's grimy hand. "Will this appease your conscience?"

"Oh yes, sir. Thank you very much, sir. Always a pleasure to have a true gentleman at the White Lion."

"Which room?" demanded Sir D'Arcy, in a menacing tone.

"Room eight, sir!"

As Sir D'Arcy made for the stairs, Venetia hurried after him, declaring breathlessly, "You will be careful, Sir

174

D'Arcy? Tucker said Mr. Robinson was extremely strong."

"I should not be at all surprised," replied Sir D'Arcy acidly, as he marched down the dusty corridor, "all those years spent heaving bales of cloth about would naturally have given him powerful muscles."

Outside the door of room eight he listened intently for a moment. Then he whispered to Venetia, "All is well. They are both in there. Now Venetia, for the duration that we are in that room, I want you to agree with everything I say. However preposterous or outlandish my remarks, for heavens sake don't contradict me, or my plan will be ruined. Is that quite understood?"

"Yes ... of course," stammered Venetia nervously, wondering what on earth Sir D'Arcy had in mind. *Whatever had she committed herself to?*

But there was no time for further speculation. Sir D'Arcy had raised his fist and was hammering mightily on the door of room eight.

"Open this door at once!" demanded Sir D'Arcy. "Miss Hamilton! Are you unharmed?"

Aunt Matty's attempt at a reply was swiftly muffled. Then a man growled from the other side of the door, "Who the devil are you? How dare you come disturbing my peace?"

"My name is Sir D'Arcy Rawnsley! And I'll disturb more than your peace when I get my hands on you. Now open this door this instant, or you'll rue the day you ever set foot in Lyme!"

Venetia held her breath as she waited for Mr. Robinson's reply. "I don't care if you're the Prince of Wales himself, a gentleman's entitled to his privacy. Now take yourself off, before I call out the law to you!"

My, what effrontery, thought Venetia.

She took a pace back as Sir D'Arcy thundered furiously, "How dare you call yourself a gentleman! Persons who bear that name do not, I assure you, abduct defenseless women from their homes and force them into matrimony! And as for calling out the law, it is you, Robinson, who deserves to be flung into gaol, not I!"

A spitting sound was heard from the other side of

the door. "Pah! You are clearly some young blood crazing for a fight. You have your facts all awry. I am not compelling this lady to marry me. She is coming to the altar of her own free will. Is that not right, Miss Hamilton?"

Venetia pressed her ear against the wood, and heard her aunt quaver, "Yes!"

Sir D'Arcy muttered, "Clearly, the scoundrel is twisting her arm most cruelly." He raised his voice and shouted, "I am weary of this playacting, Robinson. I shall count from ten. If you do not unlock the door, I shall break it down!"

Venetia paled. It was obvious to her, as it must be to the odious Mr. Robinson, that the door was made of solid oak. Admittedly, Sir D'Arcy was a powerful man, but could even he break down an oak door with his bare hands?"

The same thought had obviously occurred to Mr. Robinson. "Go to the devil, Rawnsley!" he taunted. "I shall not be intimidated by the likes of you. You may be a big fish in this part of the world, but let me assure you I am regarded as a man of considerable substance in Oxford."

Sir D'Arcy ignored him. He began counting. "Ten, nine, eight——"

"I refuse to be cowed!"

"Five, four, three——"

"I assure you, you are making a grave error——"

"Two, one, zero!"

Sir D'Arcy turned to Venetia and ordered, "Stand back!"

Wide eyed, Venetia flattened herself against the wall as Sir D'Arcy charged, shoulder first, toward the door. As his well-muscled shoulder smashed against the oak, Venetia heard what was to her at that moment the sweetest sound in all the world—the sound of splintering wood.

Sir D'Arcy stepped back a few paces, then launched himself once more into the attack. As he struck the door with a mighty force, the middle section fell clean away. Peering past him into the room, Venetia gasped with relief as she saw Aunt Matty, ashen faced with terror, sitting on a hard chair.

Grim faced, Sir D'Arcy strode into the room. Venetia pushed past him, and ran to embrace her trembling aunt.

"Aunt Matty! Oh, I am so relieved to find you!"

"My dear, it is like a miracle seeing you and Sir D'Arcy here! I really thought I was done for!"

As the two women embraced, Sir D'Arcy was directing the full force of his attention to Mr. Robinson. The draper was a man almost six feet tall, heavily built, with a fleshy face and balding head.

He gazed up at the steel-eyed Sir D'Arcy, and began to bluster. "Now look here, Rawnsley! This is all a mistake. I am not marrying Miss Hamilton against her will. I have a signed contract between us!"

"That is perfectly true," quavered Aunt Matty. "I did write and agree to marry him."

Triumphantly, Mr. Robinson waved Aunt Matty's letter aloft. "There! You see! Read it, read! It's all there in black and white."

Sir D'Arcy took the letter. Scornfully, he tore it into four pieces and threw them at Mr. Robinson's feet.

"That letter does not constitute a contract, and you know it!" he accused.

Mr. Robinson puffed out his chest and attempted to reassert himself. "Now, just one moment," he blustered. "Exactly who are you, sir, that you presume to burst in here and speak on Miss Hamilton's behalf?"

The dark-haired man stood with arms akimbo. He said icily, "How regrettable that your memory has become addled by the excitement of the occasion. I believe I have already informed you that my name is Sir D'Arcy Rawnsley."

"Yes, yes," snapped Mr. Robinson impatiently, "I know how you are called, but what is not clear, is by what right you are attempting to intervene for Miss Hamilton. She is, after all, an independent woman. She is quite capable of making her own decisions. Of her own free will, she wrote agreeing to my suggestion of marriage—"

"My aunt was under extreme duress when she composed that letter," flared Venetia. "As you well know, when you arrived at Woodhouse Lodge, my aunt explained that she had been in error. That she could not marry you."

Mr. Robinson favored the two ladies with an indulgent smile. "Oh, but surely we all understand that Miss Hamilton was merely enjoying a little last minute playacting. She wished only that I should spend more time in wooing her."

"But you dragged my aunt in the most unceremonious manner, out of the house and into your carriage!" protested Venetia. "Some wooing!"

Sir D'Arcy once more took command. "Let me make it quite plain to you, Robinson," he said, his voice cracking like a whiplash, "that Miss Hamilton does not, under any circumstances whatsoever, desire to marry you."

"But you still have not informed me," Mr. Robinson said, glaring, "on what authority you speak for the lady. You do not bear the same name, so clearly you are not a blood relative. For all I know, you could be some casual acquaintance, dragged in off the street by the young lady here, to try and persuade Miss Hamilton to change her mind."

At this, Aunt Matty looked up. "Oh, you must not speak of Sir D'Arcy in such a fashion. Why, he is—"

"I am not a blood relative of Miss Hamilton's," interrupted Sir D'Arcy firmly. He drew himself up to his full height of six-feet-two, "But I have the honor to be the future husband of her niece."

As Venetia choked, and Aunt Matty blushed with amazement, Sir D'Arcy continued blithely, "As Miss Hamilton has not male relatives resident in Lyme, I do not think it unreasonable for her niece's fiancé to step forward and speak on her behalf."

Mr. Robinson was not an easy man to convince. He turned to Venetia and demanded, "Is this true? Is he your fiancé?"

This was the moment Venetia had been dreading.

Now she understood why Sir D'Arcy had instructed her to agree with everything he said . . . however outlandish. Well, thought Venetia, he could hardly have hit on a more preposterous scheme than this one!

However, she was determined, for Aunt Matty's sake, to play her part well. First she raised her blue eyes in a look of pure adoration at Sir D'Arcy. Then she dropped them again, and murmured with a maidenly blush, "Oh yes. We are soon to be married!"

Such was the perfection of her demeanor—the modestly downcast eyes, the tremor in the voice—that now it was Sir D'Arcy's turn to glance hurriedly away, lest the laughter in his eyes belie him.

Behind her calm exterior, the newly betrothed lady was seething. She had caught that glimmer of amusement in Sir D'Arcy's eyes. *He has done this deliberately,* she raged, *to mock and humiliate me! He is enjoying every moment of this ridiculous charade. If it weren't for Aunt Matty, I'd rush across and strike him hard on his arrogant cheek.*

Mr. Robinson, meanwhile, had taken a pace back, toward the door. Sir D'Arcy was quick to follow up his advantage. "Yes," he said coldly, "I should effect a hasty departure, Robinson. Before I throw you out!"

Without another word, the draper from Oxford backed from the room, and ran away down the corridor.

Aunt Matty slumped in her chair with a moan of relief. "Oh, what an odious man! How could I have been so foolish?" Tearfully, she gazed up at Sir D'Arcy. "How can I ever thank you for your timely intervention?"

Sir D'Arcy bowed. "Depend upon it. I am always at your service, ma'am."

Venetia took her aunt's hand, and explained hurriedly, "I took the liberty of advising Sir D'Arcy of your situation, aunt."

"I am glad," smiled Aunt Matty. "I know I can rely on your discretion, Sir D'Arcy, and truly today, I should have been lost without you."

"May I suggest," said Sir D'Arcy, "that we remove

to the more salubrious surroundings of my house. I am sure I speak for us all when I say I have seen enough of the interior of the White Lion to last me many a day."

As he escorted the ladies through the door, Aunt Matty echoed Venetia's thoughts as she remarked, "My, Sir D'Arcy. I confess I was utterly overcome with admiration at the manner in which you smashed through this solid oak door!"

Sir D'Arcy smiled. "Much though I am tempted to bask in your esteem, Miss Hamilton, honesty compels me to point out that the door is not, in fact, made of solid wood. I took one look at that sly landlord downstairs and immediately suspected that he would never lay out money for solid doors, when a cheaper veneer would suffice."

"Why yes!" cried Venetia, examining the splintering door. "See, the inside is fashioned of plain deal. And a thin layer of oak has been stuck on top. How very ingenious!"

"And how clever of you to have noticed, Sir D'Arcy," remarked Aunt Matty.

They proceeded downstairs, and waited in the courtyard while Sir D'Arcy had a few quiet words with the landlord. Within a quarter of an hour, the party was safely installed in Sir D'Arcy's spacious drawing room, where he insisted on pouring Aunt Matty a reviving glass of brandy.

During the course of their discussion, it was agreed that Sir D'Arcy would introduce Aunt Matty to his financial advisers in London, with a view to finding a hopeful solution to her monetary problems.

"Oh Sir D'Arcy, whatever should I do without you?" murmured Aunt Matty, adding with a twinkle in her eye, "You seem to have an answer to everything. And we are soon, I gather, to welcome you into the family? How delightful!"

Venetia, furious at her aunt's mischievous remark, said hastily and firmly, "Now you know full well, Aunt, that Sir D'Arcy was not serious when he spoke of our forthcoming marriage. That was said merely to cod Mr. Robinson. I need hardly remind you both that I am, in fact, betrothed to Captain Dermot."

"Ah yes," said Sir D'Arcy, leaning back in his leather chair and crossing his long legs. "No doubt you receive the most tender letters from France every single day?"

"I only wish it were so," blurted Aunt Matty. "It is my humble opinion that Captain Dermot is an exceedingly lax correspondent."

Stung, Venetia returned vehemently, "My fiancé, you will recall, is not a gentleman of leisure, idling his days away in a round of idle pleasures. He is in a foreign land, endangering his life in the defense of our country!"

"Oh well spoken!" applauded Sir D'Arcy.

Sensing the sudden tension in the air, Aunt Matty rose to her feet. "We must take our leave of you, Sir D'Arcy. My maid will be wondering what has become of me."

As he escorted them into the hall, Venetia could not resist a final barb. "I am surprised, Sir D'Arcy, that having demonstrated your superior strength in smashing down the door, you did not immediately hurl Mr. Robinson from the window. It would have saved us all the bother of standing arguing with the wretched man."

"I assure you, my immediate instinct was indeed to knock the impudent fellow senseless. But for the sake of your aunt, I deemed it better to vanquish him with words instead of blows. Imagine the scandal if the fellow had come hurtling out of the window onto the cobbles below. Within minutes he would have blurted out the whole story and the entire town would have been agog with the scandal. That would not have served Miss Hamilton's best interests at all."

Aunt Matty shuddered. "Oh, I should have been compelled to quit Lyme immediately." She started. "But Sir D'Arcy, what about the landlord at the White Lion? How are we to ensure his silence? He is bound to be angry about the broken door, and he saw me enter with Mr. Robinson."

"Fear not," Sir D'Arcy reassured her. "He and I have had a few words on the subject and come to a mutual agreement. His lips are sealed."

Venetia wondered how many sovereigns had

changed hands to ensure the landlord's silence. *Oh dear,* she thought. *As each day passes we seem to become deeper and deeper in debt to Sir D'Arcy!*

Venetia and Aunt Matty were unable immediately to drive away in their gig, because the magnificent maroon carriage belonging to Viscount Siddon was blocking the road.

Venetia observed with interest as Lady Blanche Vaisey leaned from the carriage and waved imperiously at Sir D'Arcy. He strode across and addressed the pair.

"Afternoon, Siddon. That's a finely matched pair of grays out front. I'd be interested to see how they compare for speed with mine."

The Viscount smiled. "We'll arrange a race some day. The loser stands the winner to the best dinner in Lyme."

"Done!" Sir D'Arcy turned to the red-haired girl seated beside the young Viscount. "May I assist you to descend, Blanche. If you recall, you expressed an interest in accompanying me for a walk along the seashore."

Lady Blanche fluttered her hands most prettily. "Oh I must beg to be excused Sir D'Arcy. I am hardly dressed for walking. And the Viscount and I have been enjoying such a pleasant ride. I confess I am reluctant to curtail it."

Sir D'Arcy took a step back. "As you wish," he said curtly.

The maroon carriage continued its slow descent down steep Broad Street. Venetia cracked her whip, and she and Aunt Matty began their journey home.

Venetia's eyes sparkled as they left the town behind them. *So, the Lady Blanche was campaigning to heighten Sir D'Arcy's interest in her by making him jealous! How amusing it had been to see him snubbed. And how even more furious he would be when, after an exhausting afternoon combing the bay, he discovered that Lord John's standard was nowhere to be found there!*

Ten

Dear Miss Venetia Hamilton,
I should be most grateful if you would call at
Virginia Lodge at any time which suits your
convenience. I have some information on a mat-
ter of mutual interest which may prove useful
to you.

The note was written in bold, spiky handwriting. It was
signed, *Emily Renshaw.*

Understandably, Venetia was in a fever of impatience, and longed to rush immediately to Virginia Lodge.
Information on a matter of mutual interest . . . Miss Renshaw must be referring to Lord March's standard. Was
she, perhaps, prepared now to divulge more details about
its whereabouts?

With the note in her hand, Venetia paced up and
down the small library at Woodhouse Lodge as she considered the matter. *Yes, she decided, Miss Renshaw must
be referring to the flag. There is certainly no other subject
of mutual interest between her and me.*

But consumed with curiosity though she was, Venetia decided not to visit Virginia Lodge that day. First, there was Aunt Matty to be considered. She was still extremely shaken after her ordeal with the dreadful Mr. Robinson.

It would be remiss of me to leave her side for a few days yet, thought Venetia. *Not only is she far from calm. But I must ensure that she has no other bizarre schemes in mind for increasing her fortune.*

Now she had had time to consider the matter, Venetia felt quite stunned at her aunt's initiative in answering Mr. Robinson's advertisement. Why, the entire Hamilton family had always regarded Aunt Matty as a sweet, mild little creature who wouldn't say boo to a goose.

It seems we have all underestimated her, mused Venetia. *Beneath that meek exterior there is a woman of determination. Admittedly, it was rash and foolhardy of her to have answered that advertisement. But it took courage, too. We must respect Aunt Matty for that. At the same time, I only hope we have seen an end of her wild schemes. And to think, my dear Mama writes from Lincolnshire saying she hopes I am not findng Dorset too dull, and Aunt Matty's company too unexciting!*

Venetia tucked Miss Renshaw's note into her reticule. *Apart from the fact that Aunt Matty needs my attention, I am determined not to give Miss Renshaw the satisfaction of seeing me come skittering up to the Lodge two minutes after receiving her letter. It would not, I think, be seemly for me to be in haste to answer the summons of a mere housekeeper. Especially a woman who has made it her business to be thoroughly objectionable.*

No, Miss Renshaw, cruelly hard though it may be, I am determined to curb my impatience over what you have to tell me. I shall play the waiting game!

Consequently, it was a full four days later that Venetia set forth for Virginia Lodge. Her spirits were high. She had established to her own satisfaction that Aunt Matty was fully restored to health. And Venetia's eagle eye had been able to detect in her aunt's demeanor no sign that she was hatching any further devious plots to secure her financial future.

In deference to the lovely spring weather, Venetia was wearing one of her favorite ensembles: a white muslin dress, sprigged with leaf green. Over this she wore a green pelisse, and on her golden curls was a matching riding hat, with three white ostrich feathers jauntily blowing in the breeze. With the May blossoms just coming into bloom, and the hedgerows bursting into leaf, Venetia felt that her dress fully complemented the beauty of the day.

The last time I wore this particular ensemble, she mused, *was the very first time I visited Virginia Lodge. On that particular occasion, Miss Renshaw was absent and I was able to wander round the house by myself.*

Instantly, a vision of the enchanting rose bedchamber flashed into her mind. She saw herself lying on the bed, with Sir D'Arcy Rawnsley standing over her. And her mouth was still warm from the passion of his kiss.

Furious with herself for dwelling on such a shameful incident, Venetia rounded the gig between the open lodge gates and sped at a cracking pace up the drive. Outside the front door, a surly looking groom took the reins and assisted Venetia to dismount.

To her surprise the door was not opened by the smiling Mollie. Instead, a pudding-faced maid ushered her in and muttered that Miss Renshaw was in the morning room.

In her somber black dress, the gaunt housekeeper looked quite out of place in the light, golden surroundings of the elegant morning room. Miss Renshaw arose from the carved chair at the writing table, and summoned a passable imitation of a smile.

"Ah, Miss Venetia. How kind of you to call."

"I trust I find you in good health, Miss Renshaw," said Venetia politely.

Miss Renshaw stood erect, her bony hands, as ever, playing with the keys at her waist. "Oh yes indeed. *I* am never ill. I have seen too much sickness in this house—"

She broke off, and opened the morning room's

french window. "No doubt my note has aroused your curiosity. You will be wondering what it is I have to tell you."

Naturally, Venetia was burning to know! But at the same time, she was resolved not to give the housekeeper the satisfaction of realizing the extent of her anxiety. Above all, Venetia was determined that the crucial word standard should fall first from Miss Renshaw's lips, not her own.

Accordingly, Venetia said in a flat, faintly disinterested voice, "Your note was certainly of interest to me, Miss Renshaw."

The housekeeper smiled. "It occurred to me, that if it does come to pass that you become mistress of Virginia Lodge, then I shall not be here to advise you on certain matters. I have made up my mind, you see, that when the next owner of Virginia Lodge takes up residence, I shall retire, and go and live with my sister in Bath."

To conceal her relief at this statement, Venetia affected to brush a wayward strand of hair from her face. That, at least, was one problem solved! Venetia was quite sure that Miss Renshaw was a ruthlessly efficient housekeeper. *But never would I have her in my employ,* decided Venetia. *There is something chilling about the woman. I would never feel easy with her living under my roof.*

Miss Renshaw led the way into the garden. "You have viewed the interior of the house Miss Venetia, but I realized I should be failing in my duty if I neglected to show you the garden, also."

"The garden?" echoed Venetia in disbelief.

Miss Renshaw smiled. "Why yes, I have heard tell that your aunt is passionately interested in flower and plant life. I assumed that you would have inherited her green fingers. I thought it would be a good notion if I gave you a little tour of the garden, and pointed out which plants and shrubs will be in bloom in each season."

"That is indeed most thoughtful of you, Miss Renshaw," murmured Venetia. She felt thoroughly bewildered. Surely the housekeeper was not merely concerned that Venetia should be familiar with all the species in the garden? It must be that her words held a deeper meaning.

I must listen carefully, Venetia resolved, *so I am alert to any clue, any reference, however, faint, to Lord March's standard, and where it may be hidden.*

Accordingly, as they strolled down the well-tended paths, Venetia listened intently as Miss Renshaw explained that when the tulips in the middle border had died away they would be replaced with lilies. Meanwhile, in the opposite bed, she would see a magnificent midsummer display of roses and lavender.

"The fire thorn looks nothing at this time of year," went on Miss Renshaw, "but in late summer it is ablaze with red berries. As is the whitebeam in the corner. The scarlet fruit looks quite spectacular against the downy leaves."

She turned the corner and led the way up to the kitchen garden. "This has always been my particular domain," she smiled. "Especially the herb garden, see how healthy and vigorous they look."

Venetia cast her eyes over the sweetly scented bay laurel, rosemary, thyme, mint, parsley . . . yes, every variety of herb was represented here. But what, thought Venetia furiously, has all this to do with the standard? Try as I might, I have been able to discover no clues in Miss Renshaw's horticultural lecture. Could it be that I have been brought here on a fool's errand? Is the housekeeper enjoying a private joke at my expense?

As they reentered the house and proceeded down the hall, Venetia said with dignity, "I greatly appreciate your kindness in showing me the garden, Miss Renshaw. Although on reflection, it occurs to me that it would be quite possible for one of the gardeners to point out the flowers and shrubs to the new owner. Or Mollie, perhaps, may be of help, since she has been in service here for some years."

Miss Renshaw paused at the front door. "Oh, the gardeners we have here are a dozy crowd, Miss Venetia. They can never remember the proper names of the plants.

And as for Mollie, she is no longer in service at Virginia Lodge." She opened the door. "Ah, the groom has turned your gig. I will bid you good day, then, Miss Venetia."

"Good day, Miss Renshaw," replied Venetia coldly. As she seated herself in the gig she wondered whether a meaningful glance flickered between the surly groom and the gaunt housekeeper?

She drove off down the drive with her head held high, though inwardly she was seething. *I have been duped,* she thought, *I feel it in my bones.—"I thought it would be a good notion if I give you a tour of the garden."—Indeed! Miss Renshaw may possess a witch's interest in growing herbs, but that is the extent of her concern for gardens. People who truly love flowers and plants are like my Aunt Matty—they have a sensitivity of spirit, a true gentleness of nature which is glaringly lacking in Emily Renshaw!*

And what is this about Mollie no longer being employed at Virginia Lodge? I believe this is a matter which bears further investigation, for she and Miss Renshaw were ever at daggers drawn.

Remembering that Mollie had told her her mother lived near the village bakery, Venetia stopped there and made some enquiries of the florid-faced baker. A few minutes later, she drew up outside a small, thatched cottage. A gray-haired woman sat spinning in the porch, while a brown-haired girl busied herself clearing weeds from the flagstone path.

Mollie looked up with a start as Venetia hailed her from the gig. Joyfully, she ran forward, wiping her grimy hands on her blue smock. "Oh, Miss Venetia, how good to see you! But you must excuse the state I'm in! I look a sight, I'm sure."

Venetia smiled. "Miss Renshaw has just taken me on a tour of the Virginia Lodge gardens, Mollie. And I was surprised to learn that you are no longer working there."

Mollie shrugged, and said bitterly, "She dismissed me."

"But why, Mollie?"

The girl would not meet Venetia's eyes. "It doesn't matter now. You know how she was always picking on me, always finding fault for nothing at all."

Venetia took hold of her arm. "Mollie, it is most important that I known why you were dismissed. Please trust me, and tell me the reason."

Mollie made a pattern in the dusty road with the toe of her boot. "It was that day I had all that bread to carry, and you gave me a ride up to the house in your gig," she blurted. "Miss Renshaw saw. She was livid. She smacked me round the face and told me I was never to speak to you again."

"Oh how dreadful," sighed Venetia.

Mollie grinned. "It wasn't that bad, miss. I was so angry at her hitting me, I just saw red. I lashed out and kicked her on the shin, good and hard. My, did she yell! Then she told me to pack my bags and go. I wasn't sorry, to own the truth. Virginia Lodge is a beautiful house. It was lovely working there when Lord and Lady March were alive. But with Miss Renshaw in charge, it's like all the rooms were painted black. Do you know what I mean, miss?"

"Yes, Venetia said and smiled. "I do understand, but Mollie, I feel most responsible for your dismissal. Have you another post to go to?"

"There's a lot of work at this time of year, miss. As the London season draws to a close, all the fashionable ladies and gentlemen will be coming to the country, and they'll need good maids. Don't you fret, miss. I'm young, and healthy. My mama and I won't starve."

Despite Mollie's cheerful attitude, Venetia was well aware that come the autumn as Lyme emptied of its visitors, Mollie might find it difficult to secure a position in a respectable house. Especially as Miss Renshaw would be most unlikely to furnish her with a reference.

She said earnestly to the girl, "Mollie, I am quite determined that before the summer is out, I shall be the new mistress of Virginia Lodge. And when that day comes, I give you my word that you shall be the first to be offered a position in my household."

Mollie beamed. "Oh, miss. I'd like that!"

Venetia pressed a silver coin into her hand. "It is a pact, then!"

Mollie stood back to allow the gig to pass. "Thank you, miss. And good luck!"

Good luck, thought Venetia, *is exactly what I do need! For it has to be faced that in practical terms, I am no further to finding the standard than I was a month ago, when I first set eyes on Virginia Lodge. Oh, to be sure, I am now in possession of all manner of strange facts which may or may not be meaningful. Did Lady March fly the standard as some kind of signal? And if so to whom, and why? Was it Lady March to whom Miss Renshaw was referring when she remarked, "I have seen too much sickness in this house"?*

What, then, had ailed Lady March?

It occurs to me, mused Venetia, *that there are two mysteries intertwined here. And that before I can determine where the standard is hidden, I shall be required to solve the riddle of Lady March's strange illness.*

Instead of driving home, or into Lyme, Venetia turned the gig onto what was known as the Sidmouth Road, the main carriage link to Sidmouth and Exeter. She drove toward Lyme for about a quarter of a mile, then veered right onto a narrow track which led to Ware Commons. This was the thickly wooded area above the steep cliffs that rose up from the beach. Venetia intended to take the gig as far as she could, then take a gentle walk along a path that led through the trees. It was always so peaceful up here, with glimpses of the blue sea sparkling through the trees, the wind whispering in the branches, the wrens hopping among the brambles. Surely, she reasoned, in such a tranquil setting she should be able to clear her mind, and concentrate her throughts on where that standard might be.

But Venetia was not destined to enjoy her solitary walk that morning. As she drove the gig down the rutted cart track, one of the wheels struck a sharp piece of flint. Normally, this would have been of no consequence, but it happened that on this particular occasion, the wheel was already loose.

Before Venetia realized what was happening, the gig was out of control. The wheel spun off, the gig lurched off the path toward a clump of elder trees. As the gig overturned, the scream died in Venetia's throat. She was aware of being pitched forward, and a sickening blow on her head. After that there was nothing but darkness.

The narrow track along which Venetia had driven was very rarely frequented by the people of Lyme, and had anyone chanced to be strolling that way, their attention would probably have been directed toward the glimpses of the sea occasionally visible through the gaps in the trees and undergrowth.

There was nothing to make the walker look right through the trees to a spot where a gig lay overturned, half hidden by shrubs and brambles, and where a fair-haired girl lay crumpled on the moss, her eyes closed, as if in sleep—or death.

One person, however, was in the habit of treading the path at the top of the cliffs. He was Ben Jack, the fisherman. Once a week, he walked to the dairy on the far side of Ware Commons and presented the dairyman with two choice mackerel. In return, he was given half a pound of butter, and a pound of cheese. It was an arrangement which greatly suited the wiry fisherman. He was looking forward to a tasty supper tonight: a handful of plump sprats, cooked in his iron pan over the range, followed by his home-baked bread, with a thick layer of creamy butter and a wedge of good sharp cheese.

Ben Jack smacked his lips in anticipation. Then he stopped for a moment, as high above he heard the distinctive drilling of a woodpecker. His eyes narrowed as he searched amongst the trees for the bird. Some said that a woodpecker only bored into rotten trees—that the sign of a tree in good health was if the woodpecker left it alone. It irritated Ben that he had never been able to get close enough to observe the bird in action, and test the theory for himself.

Ben was quietly proud of his knowledge of the ways of animals and birds. Already, in a muddy stretch of the path, lower down, he had observed the tracks of a fox.

And, he thought, there's been some sort of scuffle here this morning. Some poor creature's come to a sticky end, by the looks of it.

His keen eye had spotted two white feathers lying crushed in the path. Bending, he picked them up and blew the dust off them, curious to determine from which bird they came.

But as he gazed on the feathers, a low whistle escaped from his dry lips. For he realized that these soft, snowy feathers had fallen from no ordinary English bird. They were ostrich. Costly, first-quality ostrich feathers.

Ben Jack frowned. The last time he'd seen ostrich as fine as this was in a lady's hat. He remembered quite clearly. It was the day that pretty Miss Venetia Hamilton had stopped by at the folly to take bread with him. She was wearing a fancy green hat, with three white ostrich feathers sticking out at a jaunty angle.

The fisherman shook his head, and walked on. He tucked the two feathers into his pocket and would have dismissed the incident from his mind had not another incongruous object caught his eye. It was a riding whip. And it was dangling from the branches of a thorn tree.

Ben Jack wasted no more time, but plunged into the undergrowth.

Ten minutes later, he burst in on the startled dairyman and shouted, "Quick, bring your trap up to the cliff path. There's a young lady lying up there. She's had an accident. She's still breathing, but she's pale as the milk in that churn."

The dairyman glared. "I can't waste my time on dilly girls who go adventuring in the woods. I've got eight churns of milk waiting to be delivered to Leamington Hall."

"Let Lady Leamington wait for her milk!" snapped Ben Jack. "Knowing that lady, she'd most like rather drink ale, in any case. And it's not some common serving wench who's come to grief on the clifftop. 'Tis Miss Venetia Hamilton. Now bring round the trap. And send your girl with word to Miss Hamilton at Woodhouse Lodge that she must call the physician, with all possible haste. From the pallor of Miss Venetia's poor face, I'd say any delay in getting her medical attention could be fatal!"

At first, it was as if the voices were coming from a long distance away. The muffled words reached her in waves, advancing and receding, a tide over which she had no control.

Gradually, however, Venetia was able to establish that one voice was considerably more strident than the other. Both voices were female. But one had an almost masculine authority to it.

"Ottilia, I beg you not to interfere! Venetia has been gravely ill. It is essential that she lie in quiet and darkness!"

"Stuff and nonsense, Matilda!" boomed the stentorian voice. "I don't hold with all this creeping about and speaking in hushed tones."

"I would remind you that Venetia is my niece not yours. It is I who am responsibile for her welfare. It is too vexing of you, Ottilia, to come striding into Venetia's bedchamber in this uncouth manner, and start issuing orders for her convalescence. I repeat, I am in charge, not you!"

"My dear Matilda, there is no cause to come over all senstive. The plain fact is that I am more acquainted than you with the treatment for Venetia's ailment. She has had a fall, don't you see?"

"There is no need to treat me like a half-wit. Obviously, she has had the misfortune to fall from the gig. I am not disputing that. What I am saying—"

"The point is, Matilda, that I have had scores of falls from a horse. Terrifying the first time, of course, but after a while you grow used to it. Now in my experience, for the first day or so all you want to do is lie in a darkened room with a cold compress over your eyes."

"Which is precisely—"

"But after a few days, to mollycoddle the patient is merely encouraging her to put on self-indulgent airs. Besides, this bedchamber is positively unhealthy, Matilda. We must fling back the curtains, and open the windows to admit the bracing fresh air!"

"Ottilia are you quite mad? Why, it has not stopped raining for the past three days. We cannot possibly allow all that dreadful damp air to pervade poor Venetia's bedchamber."

"I fear, Matilda, that your anxiety over your niece has caused your vision to become seriously impaired. See! Regard!" There was a screech as the curtains were pulled along the brass pole. "That yellow object burning in the sky, Matilda, is known as the sun—spelled, S-U-N."

Venetia stifled a giggle as she opened her eyes and observed Lady Leamington and Aunt Matty standing on either side of the window, glaring furiously at one another.

"Really, Ottilia," said Aunt Matty in a quiet, dignified voice, "I feel this sarcasm is quite uncalled for. I must insist that you leave this room, and this house, forthwith!"

Realizing that she was, unwittingly, about to be the cause of a serious rift between the two ladies, Venetia decided that it would be timely for her to utter a gentle moan. Instantly, Aunt Matty and Lady Leamington rushed to her side.

"Venetia!" exclaimed Aunt Matty. "Are you feeling better? Oh, I cannot tell you what a relief it is to see your lovely blue eyes open!"

Lady Leamington boomed the answer to Venetia's unspoken question. "Three whole days you've been lying here. I must confess when I first set eyes on you I thought it would be kinder to have you shot."

"Really, Ottilia! Venetia is not a horse, to be put out of her misery!" Aunt Matty leaned over the bed, and said tenderly, "How are you feeling, Venetia? Does your head hurt?"

"Nasty crack you gave it on that elder tree," rasped Lady Leamington. "Luckily, its above your hairline, otherwise your face would be a sorry sight."

Venetia lay back on the pillows and smiled. "My head is throbbing a little. But it is nothing serious, I am sure. I must confess, though, that my main feeling is one of ravenous hunger!"

The ladies burst into relieved laughter. "Now I know

you are truly on the mend," smiled Aunt Matty. "I will give instructions to the cook forthwith."

While Aunt Matty was out of the room, Venetia told Lady Leamington all she could remember of her fatal ride along the clifftop track . . . "Quite suddenly, the gig appeared to be completely out of control. We were hurtling through the trees. Then we hit something . . . an old tree stump I think . . . and the gig began to overturn. I remember being thrown clear. But then—nothing."

"You hit the elder tree and were knocked unconscious," said Lady Leamington. "Fortunately old Ben Jack was passing that way, and had the wit to organize an efficient rescue party."

"But I knew something was wrong even before the dairyman's daughter came with the news," said Aunt Matty, reentering the bedchamber. "I looked out of the window and saw the gig pony happily grazing on the lawn! Oh, it gave me such a fright, I imagined the most terrible things. It was almost a relief when the girl came and told me you were unconscious, but alive!"

There was a tap on the door, and a beaming Tucker entered bearing a tray laden with nourishing chicken broth, cold meats and fruit. Also neatly stacked on the tray was a pile of engraved calling cards.

"Half the country has been at the house, enquiring after you, Miss Venetia," said Tucker, setting the tray on the bed. "And Sir D'Arcy Rawnsley has called three times!"

"Don't I know it!" exploded Lady Leamington. "My niece Blanche is beside herself with fury."

"But why?" enquired Venetia, lifting a spoonful of the delicious broth to her lips.

Lady Leamington sat down heavily on the window seat and declared in exasperated tones, "Oh, it had been arranged that Sir D'Arcy would call for her, and take her to watch some race which had been organized between his grays and those of Viscount Siddon. Blanche spent two hours fussing over her toilette in readiness for the outing, and then Sir D'Arcy's footman arrived with a note explaining that you had had a fall, and he was waiting on you at Woodhouse Lodge."

"Oh dear," murmured Venetia.

"I must confess," thundered Lady Leamington, "I have never before been able to detect any family likeness between Blanche and myself. But on this occasion she acted with all the foolhardy forthrightness that I am prone to. I freely admit, I am apt quite often to put my foot in it with my blunt, frank manners. And Blanche, it seems, has inherited this unfortunate characteristic."

"Why, what did she do?" queried Aunt Matty.

"She leaped onto one of my horses, and intercepted Sir D'Arcy on his way here to Woodhouse Lodge."

"My, how rash!" exclaimed Aunt Matty, tying back Venetia's damask bedcurtains.

"Especially so, when you recall that Blanche rides a horse as if she were mounted on a camel," snorted Lady Leamington. "Accordingly, the beast gave her an extremely uncomfortable ride which did little to improve her temper. Thus when she did at last encounter Sir D'Arcy she was in a tearing rage."

Venetia was beginning to feel considerably restored. "What happened then, between Sir D'Arcy and Lady Blanche?" she ventured. Knowing Sir D'Arcy, she knew he must have been highly diverted by the spectacle of a distraught, red-faced Blanche advancing toward him on a bucking, foaming horse!

Lady Lemanington shrugged. "I am not, of course, privy to the details of their conversation. But Blanche is planning to quit Lyme within the week. And Viscount Siddon is to escort her back to London!"

"It is probably for the best," murmured Aunt Matty tactfully, removing Venetia's empty soup bowl and placing it on a side table. "Blanche never seemed really at home in a country setting such as this."

Lady Leamington said gruffly, "Well, I must take my leave. I'm glad to see you on the mend, Venetia. Now if you'll take my advice you won't lie around in bed for too long. Movement and fresh air—that's the answer!"

"Thank you, Ottilia," said Aunt Matty stiffly, holding open the door.

When Lady Leamington had departed, Aunt Matty sank onto Venetia's bed and muttered indignantly, "Really, Ottilia seems to regard everyone as no more than prize horseflesh. I'm only surprised she didn't march in here bearing a nosebag and saddle soap!"

"She means well," smiled Venetia. Then her face clouded. "But Aunt Matty, I feel so guilty about your gig! Is it quite beyond repair?"

"I am afraid so."

Venetia sank back on her pillows with a cry of despair. "This is dreadful. You must allow me, Aunt, to make full recompense. I cannot allow you to remain for long without a means of transport."

Aunt Matty patted her hand. "Now you are not to fret, Venetia. Everything has been taken care of. As soon as he heard of the accident, Sir D'Arcy very kindly had one of his own gigs sent up, with instructions that I am to keep it on permanent loan. Naturally, I protested, but he insisted that as he rarely has occasion to use it, I would be doing him a service by making use of it."

Then, observing that Venetia's lids were drooping, Aunt Matty removed the tray, tiptoed to the window and drew the curtains. The sun had disappeared behind the clouds, and it was beginning to rain again.

Within another forty-eight hours Venetia was feeling perfectly fit once more. Aunt Matty, however, was still concerned about her and insisted that her niece should rest on the drawing room sofa. Realizing that her aunt's solicitude was kindly meant, Venetia complied with her wishes, although in truth she was longing to escape from the house and enjoy a long walk through the lush combes around Lyme.

But Venetia was forced to put all thoughts of a walk from her mind, as outside the rain poured incessantly down. And meanwhile, there were important duties for her to fulfill. First she wrote a note to Ben Jack, thanking him for his prompt action in rescuing her from the clifftop. She would, she determined, call on him at the folly at the earliest opportunity.

Then there was the letter which must be sent posthaste to her parents. Aunt Matty had, naturally, written to them immediately after the accident, and Venetia was anxious to reassure them that she was fully recovered. On no account, she emphasized, must they worry about her, as she was in the best of hands at Woodhouse Lodge.

Venetia was deeply disappointed that there was still no letter from Drystan. It was now over a month since he had written!

For an entire morning Venetia lay on the sofa, torturing herself with wild imaginings of Drystan lying slain on some foreign field ... of him returning home, and his ship overturned and wrecked in a storm ... of the mail coach held up by highwaymen, and his precious letter cast carelessly aside in the mud as the blackguards searched feverishly through the mail for packets containing banknotes ...

Observing her niece's drawn and distant expression, Aunt Matty was highly relieved when a visitor arrived to provide a diversion.

"Why Venetia, here is Sir D'Arcy Rawnsley come to call on you." She smiled as Tucker ushered the dark-haired genteman into the drawing room. After a few minutes conversaton, Aunt Matty arose. "Pray excuse me, Sir D'Arcy. It is Tucker's brithday, tomorrow, and I must go into Lyme and select a present for her."

As the doors closed behind her aunt, Venetia raised an eyebrow and commented wryly, "My, Sir D'Arcy. You have indeed inspired my aunt's trust. Normally she would never dream of leaving me unchaperoned in the company of an unmarried gentleman!"

Sir D'Arcy smiled, and sat down in the chair opposite her. "I am happy to say that your aunt and I have recently established an excellent rapport."

"I heard you have called every day. I was under the impression you had come to see me!" laughed Venetia.

"So I did. But as you were for so long in a world of your own, I had the opportunity to converse with Miss Hamilton. We had some fascinating discussions. She was especially amusing about the years of her youth, when she came out."

Venetia nodded. "I have come to the conclusion that Aunt Matty is one of those ladies whose mild exterior conceals a very wickedly observant eye." Venetia sat up straight on the sofa, and continued, "But I hope your calls here to enquire after my health have not been distracting you from your methodical search for the standard? May I ask how much of the map you have now explored, and crossed off?"

"I have no intention of telling you," he said, stretching his long legs. "I assume however, that the standard was the reason you were up on Ware Commons when you had your accident. You had some idea in your mind where it might be. How in pursuit, you were driving your gig at a recklessly furious pace along that track—"

"I was not!" cried Venetia indignantly. "I am a most responsible driver!"

Sir D'Arcy raised his gray eyes to heaven. "My experience advises me otherwise," he murmured.

Venetia flushed. "Very well, I admit that on the occasion of our first meeting I was driving very fast down that lane. But I assure you, up on Ware Commons, I had restrained the pony to a trot. I was deep in thought, you see, as I had just had an extremely puzzling encounter with Miss Renshaw—"

"Miss Renshaw!" exclaimed Sir D'Arcy, leaning forward. "What was this? What did she say?"

Venetia raised a hand. "Since we are in competition for Virginia Lodge, Sir D'Arcy, I have no intention of telling you what passed between Miss Renshaw and myself."

Sir D'Arcy stood up. For a moment it seemed as if he would stride across to the sofa and shake Venetia. But controlling himself, he leaned against the mantel and said gravely, "Venetia, this could be very serious, I beg you, lay all past rivalry between us aside for a moment, and relate to me your conversation with the housekeeper."

Something in his tone compelled Venetia to obey. Quickly, she told him of Miss Renshaw's note, her visit to Virginia Lodge, and the ensuing mysterious tour round the garden.

"From her note, I had assumed it was a matter of some urgency she wished to discuss with me. Naturally, I was hoping the standard would feature in our conversation." Venetia spread her hands helplessly, "Perhaps I was being extremely stupid. But I could detect nothing in her words about the plants and shrubs which had any bearing on the question of where Lord John's standard is hidden."

Sir D'Arcy stood lost in thought, drumming his fingers on the mantel. "I do not trust that woman," he murmured, almost to himself. Then he turned to Venetia, and said courteously, "I am glad to find you fully recovered."

She replied, in a tone which matched his, "I deeply appreciate your concern."

A mocking smile flickered in his eyes. "How civil we are to one another today, Venetia! No doubt it is this endless rain, dampening our customary fire."

Venetia laughed. "Be not deceived, Sir D'Arcy. I still intended to be mistress of Virginia Lodge."

He paused at the door, looked her straight in the eyes, and declared, "And I, Venetia, fully intend to be its master!"

It was only as she watched the rain battering down on the roof of his splendid carriage as he drove away that Venetia sat up with a sudden start. The rain! Aunt Matty had said she intended driving into Lyme. But she would never have taken out an uncovered gig in this appalling weather!

Venetia crept into the hall, and listened. Sure enough, from the top of the stairs, she heard her aunt's voice murmuring something to Tucker.

Perplexed, Venetia returned to the drawing room sofa. Why had Aunt Matty gones to such lengths to ensure that her niece had a private conversation with Sir D'Arcy? It was all most bewildering.

Unconsciously, Venetia found her eyes drawn to the mantel, visualizing the dark-haired man as he had stood there deep in thought over her encounter with Miss Renshaw. She remembered how he had raised a hand to the back of his neck, and his gold signet ring had flashed for a second in blindingly brilliant reflection in the mirror.

How strange, mused Venetia, that one small incident like that should blaze so in her memory.

Then she paused in the middle of the drawing room. Aghast, she whirled round, and stared once more at the area above the mantel. No, her memory had not played her false. Hanging over the fireplace was a gilt framed oval mirror.

But before her accident, there was no mirror there, thought Venetia in a state of total alarm. Instead, there was a portrait, of a young girl with luminous eyes ... the portrait of a girl hopelessly in love.

The color drained from Venetia's face as she realized the truth. The Reynolds portait, Aunt Matty's most treasured possession, had disappeared!

Eleven

Before Venetia could rush upstairs and question her aunt on the matter, the lady herself entered the room. Misinterpreting the cause of Venetia's anguished expression, Aunt Matty fussed with the lace collar of her dress and declared nervously, "I . . . I was all dressed ready to go out, Venetia, when I saw that it was still raining. Foolish of me not to have realized before. However, I will go into Lyme first thing tomorrow and choose a gift for Tucker's birthday."

Her voice trailed away. Venetia was staring pointedly at the oval mirror above the mantel.

"Where is it?" whispered Venetia. "The portrait which Charles Maitland commissioned Mr. Reynolds to paint of you?"

Aunt Matty affected a careless laugh. "Oh that! Why, I have sent it to be cleaned. After that unfortunate chimney fire in the Blue Saloon, the smoke blew all through the house, and I realized the other day how grimy that portrait had become. So whilst you were lying upstairs, I had it taken into the picture restorers in

Lyme. They are extremely busy at this time of year, so I fear it will take them some time to clean the painting, but I'm sure it will be returned in a much improved condition."

Venetia turned, and held out her hands to her aunt, "Dearest Aunt Matty. Will you not have faith in me? I know you too well not to realize when you are speaking less than the truth."

Aunt Matty lowered her eyes. Two telltale spots of pink had appeared on her cheeks. She sank down on the sofa, and buried her head in her hands. "Oh, Venetia," she sobbed, "I am so wretchedly unhappy!"

Venetia ran to the sofa, and held her aunt in her arms. "Dear sweet, Aunt Matty. Please tell me what has happened. You know I only desire to help, in any way I can." She pressed a handkerchief into Aunt Matty's trembling fingers.

At last, Aunt Matty gained sufficient control of herself to explain, "I am still so worried about my financial position, Venetia. Oh, I know Sir D'Arcy has kindly offered the services of his bankers, but all that is going to take time. And to be frank, I need money quite desperately. I have been racking my brains for a solution."

Venetia cried in despair, "But Aunt, if only you would allow me to loan you some funds . . . at least until you have had the opportunity to discuss the matter with Sir D'Arcy's advisers."

"You should know by now that I am a stubborn, independent woman," smiled Aunt Matty through her tears. "I was so determined to find my own way out of the wood. My first thought was that I might open a little shop in Lyme."

"Oh no!" moan Venetia.

Aunt Matty said defensively, "It is not such a wild notion. After all, your modiste Miss Millford makes an excellent living with her little business. I hoped it might be possible for me to set up as a milliner."

"Aunt Matty! Not only do you know nothing about organizing a business, but you are hardly the most skilled needlewoman in the world."

Aunt Matty shook her head sadly. "That is what

finally deterred me from the scheme. As you so rightly point out, I am hopelessly inept at sewing so much as a straight seam, let alone styling an entire bonnet! And even if I employed a needlewoman to do the work for me, I should never be able to muster much business sense."

"No," agreed Venetia, with a smile. "Knowing your kind nature, Aunt, you would end up giving away all your stock and making no profit at all."

"So," sighed Aunt Matty, "I realized that to raise some funds, there was only one solution." Her voice broke. "I decided to sell the Reynolds."

Venetia paled. "Sell? Aunt, you cannot be serious!"

"Believe me, I am in deadly earnest," replied Aunt Matty sadly.

Venetia sat speechless with horror. The portrait, she knew, was her aunt's most prized possession. Not because it had been painted by the celebrated Joshua Reynolds, and was therefore worth a vast amount of money. But more importantly, because it was her one remaining link with Charles Maitland, the man she had loved and had planned to elope with.

No other man had ever taken his place in Aunt Matty's heart. Since her parents' death, she had lived alone, with only her memories to sustain her. How often must she have sat and gazed on that portrait of herself as a young girl, and remembered how she and Charles walked in the garden near Mr. Reynolds's studio—in those all too brief sunlit hours when they pledged their love, and planned their future together.

A future that was never to be. For Aunt Matty's father had foiled the elopement telling Charles that his daughter was engaged to marry another man. And as if that tragedy were not enough for her to bear, she was now compelled to sell the portrait. Why, thought Venetia in anguish, it must almost be like parting with half of her soul!

Venetia turned to her aunt and murmured urgently, "Aunt Matty, I do not understand. There is a piece missing in this puzzle. I appreciate that your financial position is giving grave cause for concern, but why this sudden haste to sell the portrait? Surely you could have waited a little longer, until Sir D'Arcy's advisers have examined your accounts. He is confident, you know, that they will arrive at a solution to your problems."

Aunt Matty bit her lip, and murmured vaguely, "It is all so complicated, Venetia. I would really rather not discuss the matter further. You will simply have to take my word for it that it is essential for the portrait to be sold."

Venetia's mind raced. Why was her aunt suddenly so desperate for extra funds? What additional expense has she unexpectedly incurred that necessitated the sale of the Reynolds?

Then inspiration struck Venetia like chilling stabs of chipped ice.

"The gig!" she whispered. "You need the money to buy a new gig."

"Nonsense!" asserted Aunt Matty, her hands fluttering nervously. "You know full well that Sir D'Arcy has kindly put up his vehicle at our disposal."

"But you are afraid that all Lyme will know it is his gig," said Venetia slowly. "After a while, people will begin to wonder why you have not bought a new one of your own. Tongues will begin to wag—"

Venetia looked deep into her aunt's brown eyes and knew she had stumbled on the truth. Her aunt was a courageous woman, and a proud one. She would die rather than have it be known in Lyme that Matilda Hamilton had fallen on such hard times that she could not afford to replace the gig her niece had smashed.

For a moment, Venetia felt infuriated with her aunt. "It was my fault the old gig was wrecked, Aunt Matty, I insist on paying for a new one. There is no cause for you to go to such drastic lengths as selling the Reynolds!"

Aunt Matty shook her head. "It is not as if you willfully overturned the gig, Venetia. It was purely an accident. These things happen. It could easily have been me—or Tucker—who was driving and who had the mishap. No, I would not dream of allowing you, my niece and a guest under my roof, to pay for damage to my property."

Venetia realized that the time had come when she

must take charge of the situation. "Aunt Matty, I shall listen to no more argument. I shall write out a banker's order immediately for payment of a new gig. And you must send word into Lyme first thing tomorrow to whoever has the Reynolds that there has been a mistake. You must tell them that the picture is not for sale, and must be returned immediately." She paused. "Just who have you sold the portrait to, aunt?"

"I don't know," sighed Aunt Matty, "I could not bear to undertake a direct transaction myself. So I sent it to the auction rooms."

Venetia's spirits rose. She was beginning to see a glimmer of hope. "And do you know when the auction is to take place?"

"Yes," whispered her aunt. "It is taking place now, this very afternoon. So you see, my dear, I am afraid—"

But she was talking to an empty room. Venetia had gone.

To the Woodhouse Lodge groom, it seemed as if the whole world had suddenly gone mad. He had been enjoying a quiet nap in the tack room by the stables. Then the door was wrenched open, and there stood Miss Venetia, a pelisse flung round her shoulders, a shawl round her hair, ordering him to harness the pony to the gig.

He opened his mouth to point out to the lady that the rain was still teaming and the gig was uncovered. But one look at Miss Venetia's determined face sent him scurrying across the yard to do her bidding.

Meanwhile, Miss Hamilton came running from the house, seized hold of her niece's arm, and tried to drag her away from the gig. For a full minute the two ladies stood in the driving rain, the one tugging at the other. Miss Hamilton pleaded, remonstrated, ordered. But the young woman was in no mood to listen. Finally, she seized her aunt by the shoulders, pushed her back into the house, jumped into the gig, and set off down the sodden drive.

Mercifully, within a few minutes the rain lessened to a mild drizzle. But Venetia was oblivious to the state of the elements. Had she been driving through the worst snowstorm of the year she would have been quite unaware of it.

Pounding round her brain was the sole, fervent prayer: Please let me not be too late! Please let that picture not yet be sold!

However much it costs, she resolved, I shall buy it back for Aunt Matty. I shall never be able to rest until I see it hanging once more in its rightful place above the mantel in her drawing room.

As she began the steep descent into Lyme, Venetia reflected that she could, of course, have brought Aunt Matty with her and persuaded her to withdraw the portrait from the auction.

But in my aunt's present stubborn mood, she would never have agreed to that. Naturally, I have to admire her determination to solve her own financial problems. But I cannot stand by and allow her to sell the Reynolds. For I know only too well that what she would gain in sovereigns, would never recompense her for the loss of that which she holds most dear.

The fact that she had never in her life attended an auction did not for one moment deter Venetia. There was certainly no time for her to feel nervous or apprehensive about bidding against those more experienced in this field. Indeed, she felt surprisingly undaunted by the prospect. For she had often found that when she was driven by a white heat of anger or determination, the blazing importance of her mission overcame all her fears. Once in the auction room, and within sight of the portrait, she knew instinctively that she would know what to do, and how to act.

Broad Street's cobbles glistened in the gentle rain. Venetia hastened down from the gig, tethered the pony and gave her a quick hug.

"I'm sorry we had to rush so," she whispered. "But it is important!"

The pony whinnied softly, as if she understood. She flicked her tail, and watched her young mistress run lightly down the road, and disappear between the portals of Messrs. Sowerby and Sons, Evaluers and Auctioneers.

At the door to the auction rooms, Venetia almost

collided with an extremely distinguished looking admiral. Gallantly, he stood aside and held open the door for Venetia. Smiling her thanks, she received a brief impression of a rugged, handsome face beneath the tricorn hat, and a strong broad figure wearing to perfection the gold-frogged dark-blue frock coat.

"If you are looking for this afternoon's auction," he said, in a deep, kindly voice, "It is being held in the room at the end of the corridor."

"I am most grateful to you," murmured Venetia, and hurriedly made her way into the main auction room.

As she entered, she felt almost overwhelmed by the noise and confusion. At least a hundred people were present, wandering from stand to stand, examining the objects which still remained to be auctioned. The auctioneer, a robust apple-cheeked man, stood on a dais at the end of the room. He was engaged in a distinctly acrimonious discussion with Lady Leamington about a small porcelain horse which was soon to come under the hammer.

"You cannot possibly allege that that pathetic object is meant to represent a horse!" boomed Lady Leamington. "Why, just look at the way it is standing, with both front legs forward and both back legs stretched out behind. Have you ever seen a horse position himself in such an absurd manner?"

"With respect, Lady Leamington, you are missing the point," argued the auctioneer, his cheeks beginning to glow an even brighter red. "It is only meant to be a stylized representation of a horse. The beauty of the piece lies in the quality of the porcelain, the—"

"Poppycock!" thundered Lady Leamington. "I am beginning to entertain serious doubts about your ability to conduct this auction, young man. I shall speak to your father, Mr. Sowerby, about you!"

"I regret, my lady, that such an interesting exchange will have to be deferred yet awhile. I fear my father passed on many years ago."

"Oh dear," murmured a bored voice behind Venetia. "It will be an age before the auction is allowed to continue. My aunt has got her teeth firmly into that wretched

Sowerby and she'll not let him go until she's drawn blood."

Turning round, Venetia came face to face with Lady Blanche Vaisey, escored by Viscount Siddon.

"Why, it is Miss Venetia Hamilton from Lincolnshire," drawled Lady Blanche. "I do hope you are fully restored to health. We have all, I assure you, been waiting with bated breath for news of your recovery."

Venetia ignored her sarcastic tone. She was too absorbed in studying the items for sale, which were heaped on stands and tables round the side of the auction room. Such a variety of objects met her eye . . . colorful japanned urns, a mahogany library wheelbarrow, ornate gilt sugar vases, tables, chairs, ormolu clocks . . . yet, nowhere could she see the portrait of the young Matilda Hamilton.

Blanche, meanwhile, had turned to Viscount Siddon, and was exclaiming loudly, "I declare, I really cannot decide between the silver muffineers and that set of Chelsea bonbonnières." She fluttered her eyelashes at the Viscount and glancing to see if Venetia was listening, she continued, "I am quite overcome by the excitement of the occasion. To think that as soon as we arrive back in London, we shall be accouncing our engagement to the world!"

"Hush, my dear," remonstrated the Viscount. "You know it would not be seemly for the event to become public knowledge before I have had the opportunity to seek an interview with your papa."

Blanche patted his hand. "Of course you are right. I will do my best to curb my tongue. Ah, it appears that my aunt has finished baiting Mr. Sowerby. The auction is about the recommence."

Venetia's heart sank at the sight of Lady Leamington in full sail toward her. The Countess was the last person she wished to encounter this afternoon. For once Lady Leamington discovered the purpose of Venetia's visit to the auction, she would inevitably insist on taking charge of the bidding for the portrait and the whole episode would be all round Lyme within hours.

Determined to save her aunt from such an embarrassing consequence, Venetia touched Viscount Siddon on the arm and enquired desperately, "Please, could you advise me? Have you noticed anywhere in the room a Reynolds portrait of a young girl in a light blue dress?"

The Viscount pondered for a moment. "Mmm . . . a rather fine Reynolds as I recall. A fine delicacy of touch, which admirably suited the subject. And it was in an oval rosewood frame. Very beautiful indeed."

Venetia's heart seemed to stop. *"Was?"* she faltered.

"At Sowerby's, the paintings are always the first things to be auctioned," said the Viscount. "That Reynolds was sold over an hour ago. There was some fierce bidding, too, as I recall."

"This is most important," said Venetia urgently, "Please can you try and remember who was the successful bidder for that portrait?"

Perplexed, the Viscount scratched his head. "Dashed if I can, Miss Venetia. I was busy examining these muffineers at the time. I'm so sorry."

Venetia closed her eyes, swamped with disappointment. She had failed. Some nameless, faceless person had bought Aunt Matty's portrait. It would hang in an unknown house and anonymous people would look at it and ponder, idly: *what a lovely young girl. I wonder who she was?*

And meanwhile, thought Venetia sadly, Aunt Matty will cry herself to sleep because she has lost that last precious link with the man she loved.

Wearily, Venetia threw her shawl round her shoulders, and prepared to go home. Then, quite unexpectedly, she heard Blanche drawl, "An admiral. The gentleman who bought that portrait was an admiral."

"Oh Lady Blanche! Are you sure?" cried Venetia.

The red-haired girl nodded. "I remember remarking most particularly that he was a singularly handsome man," she glanced at Viscount Siddon and continued hurriedly, "handsome I mean, bearing in mind his age. He was of course, no longer young—"

Venetia realized there was no time to lose. She rushed to the Broad Street doors of the auction rooms and enquired breathlessly of the porter.

"Do you recall an admiral leaving here about half an hour ago? We almost collided in the doorway. Can you tell me in which direction he went?"

Fortunately for Venetia, the porter was a man with almost forty years experience behind him. He had learned how to be quietly, meticulously observant of all the ladies and gentlemen who passed before him. He replied, "Gray hair? Gold ostrich feathers in tricorn? Immaculate white stock round neck? Stranger in Lyme?"

"How do you know he was a stranger?" queried Venetia.

"Because he was obliged to ask me the way to the Assembly Rooms," announced the porter with a triumphant smile.

The smile was lost on Venetia. Already she had picked up her skirts and was running, in the most unladylike fashion, down the length of Broad Street.

Although the Assembly Room was crowded, the admiral was easy to find. He was sitting near one of the windows, enjoying a dish of tea and tapping his foot in time to the music of the orchestra. Venetia rushed up and flung herself into the seat opposite him.

If he was surprised at her unceremonious arrival, he had the breeding and maturity not to show it. Instead, he raised his right hand to his forehead in gentle salute, and commented, "I confess, I find your eagerness to claim the seat opposite me most flattering. Am I singled out for any special reason, or are you running away from someone?"

At any other time, Venetia would have appreciated, and responded to, his dry humor. But on this occasion, she was in deadly earnest. Indicating the large package by his side, she gasped, "Admiral. I believe you have just bought a Reynolds portrait from the Sowerby auction rooms. I have come here to tell you that whatever you paid for that portrait, I will top it by fifty guineas."

Understandably amazed, the admiral leaned back in his chair. "My dear, much though it grieves me to disappoint a lady as lovely as yourself, I fear I cannot entertain such a transaction."

"One hundred guineas!" cried Venetia. Then, as the

gray-haired admiral again shook his head, she exclaimed, "One hundred and fifty! Two hundred! Name your price! Admiral, I beg you to sell me that portrait."

Her blue eyes fixed him with an imploring stare. She whispered, "It is not for me, it is for my aunt. That portrait means more to her than anything else in the whole world. Allow me to buy it back for her, and you will be rewarded with the knowledge that you have saved a dear kind lady from overwhelming feelings of anguish and desolation."

The Admiral looked somewhat shaken at the fervor in Venetia's appeal. For a while he was silent. Then he steepled his hands together and said gravely, "You have, I assure you young lady, struck me to the heart. Pray do not regard me as unfeeling when I repeat that I cannot, under any circumstances, let that portrait go. You see, it means a great deal to me, too."

Venetia's eyes filled with tears. To be so near to achieving her mission, and then to see success slipping from her grasp!

Full of concern, the admiral gazed on the fair-haired girl, noting the damp shawl, her mud spattered pelisse, the shadows of fatigue under her lovely blue eyes.

He motioned to a footman. "Kindly bring some tea for the young lady. And would you be so good as to speak to my valet who is waiting outside. Tell him I have been delayed, and will not be requiring my carriage for another half hour."

"Yes, sir," bowed the footman. "May I enquire who the valet has the honor of serving, sir?"

"Maitland," said the man in the tricorn hat. "Admiral Sir Charles Maitland."

A name so carelessly uttered. Yet it had the effect of banishing, as if by magic, the strain and exhaustion from Venetia's face.

"M-Maitland!" she stuttered, her eyes luminous, her hands clenched. Hardly daring to hope, she breathed, "And was your father named Sir William Maitland?"

"He was indeed," said the Admiral in surprise. "You are acquainted with my family?"

"Only indirectly," said Venetia in a rush. "You see, my name is Venetia Hamilton. I am the niece of one Matilda Hamilton. I believe the name is familiar to you."

Now it was the Admiral's turn to blanche. "Am I dreaming?" he murmured. "Can this really be true? Your aunt. She lives nearby?"

Venetia nodded. "At Woodhouse Lodge, just outside the town."

"And is she . . . has she . . . does she live alone?"

Venetia smiled. Here was a man accustomed to commanding men, and ships and naval strategies. Yet he could not bring himself to utter the question that so clearly tormented him.

Venetia said gently. "Yes, she lives alone, Sir Charles. My aunt Matilda has never married."

He let out a long breath. "Thank God," he murmured. Then he frowned. "But wait. Are you positive that she is not, in fact, a widow? She was engaged once, I know to Lord Wilston. Her father told me himself."

Yes, thought Venetia, *that night you planned to elope with Aunt Matty.* She explained hurriedly. "Her father told you that in order to thwart your plans to wed my aunt. She was distressed beyond words when she discovered what had happened. But she had no opportunity to tell you the truth of the matter, for she learned that you had quit Norfolk and joined the navy."

The Admiral sighed heavily. "I knew she was the only woman I could give my heart to. When I was, as I thought, rejected by Matilda, I turned my back on romance and marriage, and made the navy my whole life. I spurned England, too, preferring to spend even my leaves from the navy in foreign climes."

"Then what happy accident brought you to Lyme, and to the auction rooms today?" enquired Venetia.

"Unfortunately, on my last voyage we encountered heavy gales, and one of my captains was washed overboard. He drowned, poor chap. He'd served with me for many years and was one of my best men. I felt it my duty to call on his family in Lyme, and offer my deepest condolences. Then it came on to rain, and I took shelter in the auction rooms. I was wandering round, looking at this piece and that of the goods for sale. And then I came upon Matilda's portrait. I simply could not believe my eyes."

Enthralled, Venetia sipped her tea, imagining the conflict of emotions that must have gripped the Admiral as he stood transfixed, staring at the portrait of the woman he loved, and believed he had lost.

"I couldn't fathom why the portrait was up for auction," went on Sir Charles, rubbing his weather-beaten face. "At first I thought that Matilda, having been married all these years to Lord Wilston, had finally decided to discard unwanted memories of her youth. Then, with a terrible blow, it occurred to me that she might have died, and her family was clearing the house. But one thing I did know for sure. That whatever the cost, I had to own that painting."

Venetia smiled. "It is fortunate that I did not arrive an hour earlier at Sowerby's. Else we should have found ourselves bidding in fierce opposition. For I, too, was determined to buy the Reynolds!"

The handsome gray-haired man leaned forward. "But why did you harbor such a burning desire to have the portrait? And why was it up for sale?"

Venetia decided that she had monopolized the Admiral's attention for quite long enough. She finished her tea, and said, "I do believe these are questions which would be best answered by my aunt herself. Will you accompany me back to Woodhouse Lodge, Sir Charles?"

He murmured earnestly. "It has been a long time. Do you sincerely believe your aunt would still be pleased to receive me?"

"I am sure," smiled Venetia, "that nothing in the whole world would delight her more."

So it was that Venetia left the Assembly Rooms on the arm of the distinguished Admiral Sir Charles Maitland. She led the way home in the gig, and Sir Charles followed in his carriage, with the portrait of Matilda Hamilton tucked protectively under his arm.

As they entered the hall of Woodhouse Lodge, Tucker came hurrying down the stairs. "Oh Miss Venetia, thank heavens you are home. Miss Hamilton has been in such distress after you rushed off like that in the rain. She is waiting for you in the drawing room. I—"

The blood drained from Tucker's face as she regarded the well-built man quietly handing his hat and gloves to the footman. "Why . . . it cannot be . . . oh, is it really you, sir?"

The Admiral smiled as Tucker sank into a curtsy. "No, you are not seeing a ghost, Tucker. I am happy to see you here. You have been with Miss Hamilton for all these years?"

"Yes sir," whispered Tucker. "I would never dream of leaving Miss Hamilton. Oh, I'm sure she will faint right away when she sets eyes on you."

In which case, thought Venetia, *I am sure the Admiral will be delighted to revive her with a kiss!* She moved to the drawing room doors, and motioned to the Admiral to remain in the hall for a moment.

As she stepped into the room, a harassed Aunt Matty arose from the sofa. "Venetia! I have been so worried! I was so afraid you would catch a chill going out in that pouring rain, and then I should have felt so responsible!"

Smiling, Venetia raised a hand. "I am perfectly well. I assure you, Aunt. And it is not a chill I have brought back from Lyme. But a visitor, Aunt Matty, for you."

Venetia stood aside, and Sir Charles Maitland strode into the room. For as long as she lived, Venetia knew she would never forget the expression of surprise, wonder, and pure happiness that flooded her aunt's face.

"Charles!" cried Aunt Matty, her voice breaking. "Oh, Charles!"

Then as her aunt held out her arms to the man she had not seen for twenty-five years, Venetia withdrew into the hall, and tactfully closed the drawing room doors behind her.

Dinner at Woodhouse Lodge that night was a joyous, festive affair. While Aunt Matty and the Admiral were engaged in their private reunion, Venetia and Tucker whirled into action. They raided the cellar for the last remaining bottles of Aunt Matty's vintage claret and port.

216

And they called for the cook, and arranged for her to prepare a celebration feast of trout, and leg of mutton served with walnuts and melted butter.

Venetia herself attended to the table decoration, with her aunt's favorite delicate anemones set against a cloud of pale-blue forget-me-nots.

When they were gathered round the candlelit table, Sir Charles raised his glass. "We must drink a toast to you, Venetia. For had it not been for you, my dear, I should never have found my beloved Matilda again."

Aunt Matty's eyes were brimming with joyful tears. "Oh Venetia, you must be the first to know. Charles is insisting that we marry without delay!"

"I am delighted for you both!" exclaimed Venetia, rising to kiss first her aunt, and then the Admiral. "I know you will be blissfully happy."

"Matilda has told me everything," said the Admiral. "I was utterly appalled when I heard of her distressing financial circumstances. But all that is in the past, now. You shall dispose of this house, Matilda, and come and take up residence at my family seat in Norfolk."

"Oh, my parents will be delighted," cried Venetia. "You will be able to visit them in nearby Boston whilst the Admiral is away at sea."

The Admiral waved a dismissive hand. "No, no. I intend to retire from the navy. I only entered the service in the first place to give my life some purpose after I lost Matilda. But now we're together again, I don't intend to be parted from her for a single day. There's been so much time lost already."

Aunt Matty gave a happy sigh. "How fortunate that when I quit London, I decided to come and live in Lyme. Otherwise we would probably never have met again, Charles."

"And why did you choose Lyme?" enquired Sir Charles, sipping his claret. "For the bracing sea air, I suppose?"

"Not especially," said Aunt Matty. "It was simply that I had enjoyed many amiable visits to the area, to the house of my good friend, Lady March."

There was a clatter as Venetia dropped her knife.

"You—you have stayed at Virginia Lodge, Aunt? But why did you never tell me?"

Aunt Matty regarded her niece's anguished expression with surprise. "Why, you never asked me! And somehow, the matter never seemed to arise in our conversations."

Sir Charles looked thoughtful. "I seem to recall a Lord March at some of the London balls we attended, Matilda. Didn't he marry a quiet, pretty, dark-haired girl?"

"That was Georgina," nodded Aunt Matty. "We came out together. Then after she married Lord John, we kept in touch, and I occasionally came down to Virginia Lodge to visit her. It's a charming house. But, of course sadly, both Lord John and Georgina have passed on now."

"Yet they were happy together?" enquired Sir Charles.

"Oh yes," said Aunt Matty, "except for those odd days when poor Georgina was not well, not quite herself."

Venetia laid down her napkin, her curiosity thoroughly aroused. "What do you mean, Aunt?" Her heart was pounding. Was she at last to learn the truth about Lady March's strange, eccentric ways?

"Well," said Aunt Matty slowly, "it was all kept very quiet at the time. But I suppose there is no harm in talking about it now. The fact is that Georgina was prone to sudden, quite inexplicable rages. It was as if she were a woman possessed. She'd become wild-eyed and throw the china at the walls."

"The china!" exclaimed Venetia. So that was why Miss Renshaw had been so reluctant to allow anyone near the Virginia Lodge china room!

"Oh yes," said Aunt Matty, "nearly all the priceless Sèvres and Dresden was smashed. And she was fond of arranging pretty sea stones in glass bottles. But when she had one of her strange days, I fear she'd vent her fury on the bottles."

Venetia sat back in her chair. At last all the pieces were beginning to fit! She murmured, "And when Lady

218

March was so unwell, did she send Lord John out of the house until she was recovered?"

"She did indeed," said Aunt Matty. "She hated him to see her in such a condition. And she knew that before the day was out, she would be recovered. No, the only person allowed near her at such times was the housekeeper. Miss Renshaw had a clever way with herbs, and would brew her mistress up some mysterious herb tea which never failed to calm her."

"Dashed situation," said the Admiral. "Can't help feeling sorry for Lord March, being banished from his own house. Where the devil did he go?"

"He was happy enough, sitting up at the top of his folly, looking out to sea," replied Aunt Matty. "And he could see Virginia Lodge from there, too. He knew when it was safe to go home, because Georgina would raise the family standard from the flagpole, as a sign that she was fully recovered."

Venetia pushed aside her plate, and enquired urgently, "Are you referring to Jack's folly, Aunt? I thought it was called that because Ben Jack, the fisherman, lives there?"

Aunt Matty shook her head, "No, it is known as Jack's folly because it was built for Lord John when he was a boy. I understand that in those days he was called Master Jack by everyone roundabout Lyme."

Venetia could hardly contain her excitement. Of course! Jack was a common enough nickname for anyone called John. Why had she not thought of that before?

She sipped her wine, smiling as a tide of elation flooded through her. Thanks to Aunt Matty, she was sure now where the standard was hidden. It must be concealed somewhere within the folly. It was the obvious place.

And to think, when I sat up there talking to Ben the fisherman, I was nearer to the standard than I have been in the whole month since! Oh, what a happy day I shall have tomorrow. I shall enjoy a leisurely breakfast with my aunt. Then I shall take the gig, and drive very slowly up to the folly on Dragon's Hill. There will be no need to rush: I shall take my leisure, and savor every moment of

219

the end of my quest. Why, if all goes well and Mr. Plumb,
the attorney, is quick to draw up the relevant documents,
by tomorrow evening I could well hold the deeds to
Virginia Lodge in my hands!

The Admiral drained his glass, and said reflectively,
"Strange business, this mysterious illness of Lady
March's. Could her physician do nothing to help her?"

"He confessed himself baffled," said Aunt Matty.
"For most of the time she was the quietest, most mild-
natured of women. Then quite out of the blue, she'd
complain that her head felt as if it were splitting open,
and this was always a sign that a rage was due to descend
upon her. But I tend to agree with Sir D'Arcy Rawnsley
on the matter. He feels that there is probably some simple
cause for it, which in years to come will become clear to
medical practitioners."

Venetia gripped her glass, her voice almost hoarse
with horror, "Sir D'Arcy? You have discussed this matter
with him?"

"Why yes," Aunt Matty said, smiling. "I think I
mentioned to you, whilst you were recovering from your
accident, Sir D'Arcy and I enjoyed the most amiable
conversations. He was amused by my anecdotes of my
first London season. I happened to mention Lady
March's name in that context, and he appeared most
interested in her."

"I can well imagine," Venetia said dryly. "And you
told him all about Lord John, and the folly, and the
standard?"

"Of course," replied Aunt Matty. "Why, Venetia,
whatever is the matter? You have turned deathly pale.
Oh, Charles, I do believe she is going to faint!"

Twelve

He knew! Thanks to Aunt Matty, Sir D'Arcy had been aware for days of the probable hiding place of the standard.

This unwelcome intelligence beat a merciless tattoo in Venetia's head as she drove up Dragon's Hill the following morning. It was fortunate that Aunt Matty, exchausted by the exciting events of the previous evening, had asked for a breakfast tray to be sent up to her bedchamber. She was thus not present to witness the unseemly spectacle of her niece cramming two slices of toast into her pretty mouth, gulping down some tea, and bolting for the stables.

The climb up Dragon's Hill seemed interminable. *Please,* prayed Venetia as Jack's folly came in sight, *please let Lady Luck be on my side.* There was, after all, just a slim chance that Sir D'Arcy might not have considered the folly a suitable place of concealment for the standard. Or perhaps he had not yet had the time or opportunity to make the journey up Dragon's Hill to make the search.

I am clutching to straws, Venetia admitted. *In all probability, Sir D'Arcy is in Mr. Plumb's chambers at this very moment, smiling as he receives the deeds of Virginia Lodge.*

Tears of sadness and frustration sprang to Venetia's eyes. It pained her beyond measure to think that the house she had set her heart on was not to be hers. That all these weeks of searching, and raised hopes and false alarms, had all been for nothing.

As the gig reached the top of the hill, Venetia could not resist turning to gaze on the stone-built house which nestled in the valley below. How lovely it looked, with the sun glinting on the windowpanes, and the green ivy trellising the walls. A wistful smile touched Venetia's lips as she regarded the Virginia Lodge gardens. So often, she had imagined herself strolling down the lavender-bordered paths, pausing to cut a rose here, a frond of honeysuckle there.

But it seems that is not to be, Venetia reasoned. *For I am sure that immediately after his conversation with my aunt, Sir D'Arcy will have wasted no time in coming up here to claim the standard.*

As she tethered her pony, Venetia was relieved to see that there was no sign of Sir D'Arcy's magnificent gray. *That at least is one consolation,* thought Venetia wryly. *How dreadfully embarrassing if we had both arrived here at the same time, and then engaged in an undignified tug of war over the standard!*

As Venetia approached the tall, limestone folly, the door opened and Ben Jack came out to welcome her. Venetia greeted him warmly and immediately expressed her thanks for the manner in which he had come to her rescue up on the cliffs.

"It was lucky you happened to be wearing that pretty green hat with the ostrich feathers in it," he told Venetia. "Seeing them lying in the path was what first alerted me."

Venetia shuddered at the memory. "Well as you can see, Ben, I'm wearing lavender today. I am convinced I shall never to able to bring myself to wear a green hat ever again. It is clearly unlucky for me."

Ben Jack smiled. "It's good to see you fully recovered, miss. Would you care to step inside for a moment? I'm just in the middle of mixing up some dough for a fresh batch of bread."

Venetia followed him into a neat, spotlessly clean kitchen. All the pots and pans hung in orderly rows on the walls, the plates were tidily stacked in the rack, and even the two brooms stood like sentries on either side of the door.

Ben Jack observed her curious glance, and observed with a grin, "I like to keep everything shipshape, Miss Venetia."

She watched as he began to knead the dough, and then enquired, "I believe the late Lord March maintained that your bread was the best in all the county?"

Ben Jack nodded. "He did that. He wouldn't have no truck with that bakery in the village. Whenever he came up here, he never left without taking a loaf or two away with him."

"When he came here to the folly, how did he pass his time?"

"Well, he'd pass the time of day here with me for a while. Then he'd disappear upstairs. It's just the first two stories that I use, you see, Lord March kept the top floor for himself. Sometimes he'd be up there for hours."

"May I see the top floor?" ventured Venetia.

"Of course," said Ben Jack. "Just open that door along from the range, and you'll find some stairs. Keep climbing till you can't go no further. You'll excuse me not escorting you up but I've got a great deal on my hands just at the moment." Laughing, he waved his doughy fingers at her.

Venetia's throat was dry, her heart thudding with excitement as she ran up the curved staircase. At last the end of her quest was in sight! Every instinct told her that this was without doubt where Lady March had hidden the standard. This lonely room at the top of the folly had been her husband's private domain. Here he had patiently waited, until she raised the standard as a signal that she was well again, waiting at the Lodge to receive him into her arms.

The door at the top of the stairs lay ajar. With trembling fingers, Venetia pushed it open. Would the standard still be here? Or had Sir D'Arcy forestalled her, and seized the prize for himself?

Stepping inside, Venetia found herself in a light, airy, sparsely furnished room. There was a chair, and table. On the latter rested an old telescope, directed toward the window which commanded a magnificent view of Lyme Bay, and the blue sea beyond.

The second window, which looked out on the valley, and Virginia Lodge, was obscured by a thin curtain. At least, a curtain is what it appeared to be at first sight.

Venetia suddenly stopped in her tracks, unable to tear her eyes away from the rectangle of faded, golden material. Then she rushed across the room and swept it from the rail.

Her face was radiant with joy as she knelt on the floor and handled the soft fabric, her fingers running over the red and black embroidery of the March family crest.

"I've found it!" she exulted. By some miraculous stroke of luck, Sir D'Arcy did not come here before me. Perhaps he misunderstood Aunt Matty when she chattered on to him about Lord March and the folly. Or it could be that he simply wasn't paying attention! Whatever the reason, it has lost him Virginia Lodge. For there can be no doubt that this is the true March standard. And the house, the house of my dreams, is mine!

Not totally yours, Venetia, advised the voice of reason. Have you forgotten that you will be sharing it with Drystan, your husband-to-be?

Slowly, Venetia stood up. Drystan. Her fiancé. The man in whose company she was destined to spend the rest of her life.

She could not understand why she felt so chilled at the prospect. Why was her heart not fluttering with happiness? She should be dancing with joy at the thought that she and Drystan would now be able to start their married life in the tranquil atmosphere of lovely Virginia Lodge.

But far from feeling transported with delight, Venetia felt strangely heavy-hearted. Confused, she carefully rolled up the precious standard, and tucked it under her arm as she began to descend the stairs.

I am merely suffering from a feeling of anticlimax, she told herself. For all these weeks, I have thought of practically nothing else but finding the standard and claiming Virginia Lodge for my own. Naturally, if Drystan were here to share the victory with me, I should be overcome with elation. But he is not here. And it is over a month since I received a letter from him.

She shook her head, bewildered and disappointed. Why, *why* has he not written?

Leaving the folly, she found Ben Jack outside, sweeping the path that circled the building. Seeing his eyes flicker toward the bundle under her arm, Venetia explained.

"Don't worry, Ben. It is quite in order for me to take this . . . this piece of cloth."

He nodded and remarked. "Strange the sudden amount of interest there's been in that tatty old thing."

Aghast, Venetia whispered. "What do you mean, Ben? Has someone else been up here asking you about it?"

Ben Jack leaned on his broom, and said carelessly, "Why, only two days ago a very well-dressed gentleman was here, asking to see Lord March's room. Up he went, same as you did, and came out with that cloth under his arm. Then he did a very rum thing. He paced about here for a while, deep in thought. And he turned on his heel, went back up the stairs and came down emptyhanded. Now what do you make of that, Miss?"

Venetia felt as if she had been struck a violent blow. For a dizzying moment, the folly, Ben, the sea, and the valley seemed to spin around her.

When at last the world steadied, Venetia found Ben Jack regarding her anxiously. "Are you sure you're all right to drive that gig, Miss? You've come over all pale."

Venetia hastily assured him that she was perfectly well, and as he assisted her into the gig she repeated her warm thanks for rescuing her when she lay unconscious up on the cliffs. As she drove away, she turned to smile and wave to the friendly fisherman.

But as the pony delicately picked her way down steep Dragon's Hill, the smile died on Venetia's lips. Beside her on the seat lay the faded gold standard.

"Why?" she whispered to herself. Why had Sir D'Arcy returned the standard to the folly? He had seemed so deadly earnest in his desire to own Virginia Lodge. For weeks we have vied with one another in the quest for the standard. Yet when victory lay within his grasp, Sir D'Arcy turned away, and left the prize for me. Why?

But deep in her heart, Venetia already knew the reason. She had known it when she stood outside the folly, with the standard in her hands, and the world had seemed to spin around her. Suddenly, whenever she thought of Sir D'Arcy, or pictured his face, or imagined his voice, it was as if a strange current sparked through her, making her blood race and her heart beat faster.

Venetia was in such an agitated state, she nearly dropped the reins. With an effort of will, she forced herself to control her emotions.

I need to think she realized. *But in my present confused state of mind, if I allow my thoughts to wander I shall surely crash the gig. And if it were to be discovered that I had had two accidents within one week, my aunt would begin to wonder if it were safe for me to be allowed out alone!*

As if directed by some remote, primitive instinct, Venetia found herself driving toward the Cobb. *Yes,* she thought, *here is the solution, I shall walk by the seashore and allow the salt wind to clear my head of the strange fancies which seem to possess it.*

She left the gig at the Cobb, and with the standard tucked under her arm, she began to walk along the beach. There must have been a storm far out to sea, she realized, for the waves were choppy and crested with foam. Even so, further along the bay, there were a few intrepid souls bathing.

How ironic, thought Venetia, *that the last time I walked here, the wind snatched Drystan's letter from my fingers, and whirled it away over the cliffs. How bereft I*

226

felt! Yet now my heart is troubled once more because—it has to be faced—I am suddenly unsure of my love for him.

Unsure? Venetia's honest nature would not allow her the luxury of such an evasive word. Venetia turned her face to the sea, lifting her head so the wind blew through her lovely hair.

"I do not love Drystan," she said boldly. "I love—"

But she could not bring herself to voice the person. To breathe the name which had suddenly come to mean so much to her. Wracked with anguish, she continued her walk, her boots crunching on the wet shingle.

Why did I not realize before? How could I have been so blind? But I imagined us to be rivals, and therefore, enemies. Ironically, it was Virginia Lodge itself which confused the issue. Had he and I met under normal social conditions, perhaps I should not have regarded him with such disfavor.

And, thought Venetia, *what are his true feelings toward me?*

She blushed. She need not have posed the question, for she knew the answer. She had known from the moment Ben Jack told her how Sir D'Arcy had gallantly returned the standard to the folly.

Oh, how I long to go to him now! How willingly should I surrender to his embrace!

A wave washed over Venetia's boot and the shock of cold water jolted her back to reality. *Have you forgotten,* said the chilling voice of Venetia's conscience, *that you are an engaged girl? How could you conjure such unseemly thoughts? Your fiancé is in a foreign land, bravely fighting for his country. When he returns home from battle, he will expect to find his future wife waiting with her arms outstretched toward him. Are you to deny him that? Are you about to join the ranks of fickle women whose love is unable to stand the test of parting, and who then run off with another man, leaving the gallant hussar with nothing but a brief note of farewell?*

No! protested Venetia. *I am not fickle. I have tried with all my will to remain faithful to Drystan. I did not*

*invite Sir D'Arcy's affections. I did not realize my heart,
my emotions, were under siege from him. But now I find
I am his captive. And I am glad! So very glad!*

But what am I to do about Drystan, pondered Venetia. *I have given him my word that we shall marry. When
my battle-weary fiancé returns home, how am I to tell
him that my affections now lie elsewhere? Why, I despise
women who have not the stamina to wait, loyally and
faithfully, when their men are parted from them. In my
own eyes, I shall look so shabby! And equally, how can I
give myself to Sir D'Arcy with my dreadful treatment of
Drystan on my conscience? Why the happier I am with
Sir D'Arcy, the guiltier I shall feel about my discarded
fiancé.*

Venetia was well aware that there were scores of
girls of her acquaintance who cheerfully became engaged
to a different gentleman every month of the season. Accepting proposals was no more than a game to them.
They spared no more thought for last month's fiancé than
they did to a last year's favorite bonnet.

But it is not in my nature to love lightly, mused
Venetia. *When I give my heart, I truly mean it to be
forever. So it was when Drystan proposed to me. I believed myself to be deeply in love with him. But looking
back, I fear I was more in love with the romance of the
situation. The dashing hussar in his bold scarlet uniform.
Our whirlwind romance. We were the talk of Boston.
Everywhere we went, heads turned, the people remarked.
How we reveled in it all! My mistake, however, was to
confuse that blaze of breathless excitement with love. The
two are not the same at all. I know that now.*

*What I feel for D'Arcy is quite a different emotion. I
suppose because it is not a sudden thing. It has been
growing within me for some time, although I was too
foolish to realize what was happening. Of course, I should
have understood that day in the Rose Room at Virginia
Lodge, when I opened my eyes and found he had kissed
me. Did Drystan's kisses ever arouse such fires in me? No,
never!*

But again, because of our rivalry over Virginia

Lodge, I mistook the fire of passion for the fire of anger. I should have remembered that hate is often very akin to love! Yet if you had told me then that I would fall hopelessly in love with Sir D'Arcy Rawnsley, I would have laughed until the tears streamed down my cheeks.

It was a laugh, at that moment, which startled Venetia out of her reverie. She paused to watch as three ladies emerged from the bathing machines and descended the steps to test the water.

My, shivered Venetia, that water looks monstrously cold to me! How brave the girls are even to dream of bathing!

The three girls evidently shared Venetia's opinion. After much giggling, and dipping of toes into the water, they began to ascend the steps of the machine. But at the door, with his back to Venetia, stood a fair-haired man in shirt and breeches. Laughing, he seized hold of the plainest girl, and pushed her into the water. Outraged, she screamed in horror as the cold water lapped round her shoulders.

The man seemed quite impervious to her cries. He urged the other two back up the steps. As they ran toward him, he embraced the first, and kissed her. Meanwhile with his spare hand he drew the other girl close, and squeezed her ample derriere.

Horror-struck, Venetia stood as if rooted to the beach. She was quite unable to tear her eyes away from the scene on the bathing hut. Not so much because she was affronted by the appalling behavior of the man. That was bad enough, to be sure, but what made the whole episode totally shocking to Venetia was that the fair-haired man was someone she recognized.

"Drystan!" The name shot accusingly from Venetia's frozen lips.

The sound carried over the water. The fair-haired man disentangled himself from the excesses of his embrace, and glanced towards the beach. The person he saw standing there caused him to turn pale. Hurriedly, he pushed the two girls into the bathhouse. The third girl was heaving her dripping wet form up the steps. He ignored her. Cupping his hands, he called, "Venetia! My dearest! Do not judge me too hastily! We must talk. Wait!"

But Venetia, suddenly sickened, had turned on her heel. Blindly, she ran towards the cliff steps and began to climb. She had no thought for her destination. Her one driving desire was to escape from the sight and sound of the man who had once meant everything in the world to her.

Captain Drystan Dermot was not accustomed to watching women walk disdainfully away from him.

Dash it all, he fumed, as he reached for his red coat, *Venetia is displaying a distinctly unbecoming naïveté. How was I to know she would choose just this moment to stroll along the beach. And what the devil is she doing in Lyme in the first place? I imagined her to be safe at home in Lincolnshire, not spying on me in Lyme!*

By the time he was properly dressed, the bathing machine had been hauled back onto the beach, and his lady companions properly placated, Venetia was almost out of sight. Captain Dermot's blue eyes narrowed as he gazed on the craggy heights of Ware Cliffs. Yes, there she was, the minx! He could just make out a flash of lavender-colored muslin nearing the top of the cliff steps.

The hussar waste no more time, but set off in hot pursuit. Finally, he caught up with his fiancée on the narrow path which ran along the clifftop.

"Venetia!" he cried, striding towards her, "Why did you run away from me? Are you not glad to see your betrothed once more?"

Furiously, she whirled round to face him. "Yes, I should have been pleased to see you, Captain Dermot. Had you paid me the courtesy of notifying me of your arrival from France. And had I not discovered you cavorting in the most unseemly manner with not one lady, but three!"

Laughing, he seized her by the shoulders. "Come now, Venetia! You are not going to allow a bit of harmless fun come between us? To own the truth, I came to

Lyme for a spot of relaxation before taking on the responsibilities of marriage. I know you're not a London sophisticate, Venetia, but surely even you can't condemn me for wanting to sow a few last wild oats?"

Venetia regarded him coldly, "I should have thought, Captain Dermot, that after so long an absence from your fiancée, your first thought would have been to reunite yourself with her. Instead, you stand before me, babbling on about wild oats!" She went on angrily, "And why have you not written to me? I have received just one letter from you since you went away!"

The severity of her tone sobered him. Hastily he changed tack. "I am mighty sorry you have not received my letters. I wrote to you every day, truly I did. But I fear the mails between France and England are dreadfully unreliable."

Venetia looked him straight in his eyes. He could not hold her glance, but looked shiftily away. Desperately, he stammered, "I did mean to write every night, Venetia, I swear it! But the battles were so hard, so strenuous. At the end of the day I collapsed, exhausted, into my tent. All my strength had been used in the fight to save my country from invasion."

"Do I look that much of a simpleton!" flared Venetia, her blue eyes blazing. "You are lying, Captain Dermot! It is plain to me now that at the end of your fighting day you were more than happy to be comforted by the soothing words and caresses of the camp women. Do you dare to deny it!"

"How dare you make such an accustation!" he blustered. "It is you I love, Venetia! You whom I intend to marry."

Venetia said quietly, "No, Captain. You must consider our engagement at an end. We shall never be wed. It was all a mistake from beginning to end."

She turned away from him. But he seized her arm, and pulled her back along the path.

"Is this your parents' doing?" he stormed. "They were against me from the start."

"I should have listened to them," replied Venetia

breathlessly as he dragged her along with him. "They were right. We should never have become engaged. We are not suited."

She cried out as the Captain pulled her through the thicket of thorn bushes and brambles, tearing her stocking and the hem of her dress.

"Captain Dermot . . . Drystan!" she protested. "You are acting like a man possessed. Where are you taking me? What—"

The words died in her throat as she found herself gazing down, down, down at the terrifying drop to the foaming sea below. Drystan had brought her to the very edge of Ware Clifffs!

Gripping her arm tightly, he hissed, "You will marry me, Venetia! Give me your solemn promise, now, that our engagement is not broken. Say you will be my bride!"

Despite her rising panic, Venetia had not lost her courage. She whispered, "Have you ever truly loved me, Drystan?"

He laughed. "Come, Venetia. Let us not play childish games with one another. You are a beautiful girl. You are rich. You belong to a highly respected family. Whereas I have had the misfortune to see most of my family fortune swallowed up in gambling debts. I need a wealthy wife, Venetia. I need you!"

"No!" she screamed, writhing desperately in his steely grasp. "Do with me what you will, Drystan. I shall never agree to marry you. I do not love you!"

"For the last time, Venetia, will you marry me!" he demanded.

"I will not!" she cried. "I could never marry a man I do not love!"

"Venetia! Do you think I can allow it to become common intelligence that you have spurned me? No, my dear, my pride will not permit that! I shall have to force you to marry me!"

"You are crazed!" gasped Venetia as she felt his strong hands grasping her slender shoulders. She closed her eyes against the shock of terror, and the frightening might of the waves lashing against the rocks so far below.

232

Desperately, she tried to kick against him. But he was too powerful. Venetia felt a sudden, frightening choking sensation. But instead of losing consciousness, she found herself pulled back with a violence that caused her to stumble, and fall among the sharp brambles.

But the pain of the thorns was instantly forgotten as she heard a furious voice declare.

"You blackguard, Dermot! Take that! And that, and that!"

Venetia could hardly believe it. But opening her eyes, she saw that it was—by some miracle—Sir D'Arcy Rawnsley who was setting about giving Captain Dermot the milling of his life.

The Captain's easy smile and charming demeanor had completely disappeared. Indeed, his face was scarcely visible at all under the streaks of blood. The hussar was, in fact, putting up a creditable fight, but he was no match for the athletic Sir D'Arcy. For five minutes the two men grappled on the cliff edge, first one gaining the advantage, then the other. But at last, Sir D'Arcy delivered a mighty right hook, which sent his opponent hurtling, unconscious, into a thorn bush.

Sir D'Arcy dusted himself down, and strode across to the path, where a wide-eyed Venetia was waiting.

"You are unharmed, Venetia?" he enquired, in a low, tender voice.

She felt unaccountably shy. It was impossible to meet his eyes. "Yes," she murmured. "I am unharmed—thanks to you. But how did you happen to be here on the cliffs, just at my hour of need?"

He took her arm, and escorted her along the path. "I came up to examine the wrecked gig in which you had your accident," he said. "It had been impossible for me to make an inspection before, because of all the rain. But today I took a careful look at the wreckage. And I cannot be a hundred per cent sure, but I have a strong suspicion that the wheel of the gig had been tampered with."

Venetia gasped. "But by whom?"

"If I remember correctly, you had just called at Virginia Lodge," Sir D'Arcy reminded her.

"And spent a mystifying half hour with Miss Renshaw whilst she gave me a lecture on the local flora," exclaimed Venetia. "Do you imagine that she gave instructions for the wheel to be loosened?"

"Naturally, I have no proof," said Sir D'Arcy slowly. "But it is important for us to remember that, for all her faults, Miss Renshaw was totally loyal of Lady March. She was terrified that during your search for the standard, you would also stumble across the truth about Lady March's strange illness. I believe that this put her into such a fever of agitation that she became almost deranged, and in a totally unbalanced state of mind, she arranged the accident to your gig."

"Poor Miss Renshaw," breathed Venetia thoughtfully. "How terrible that such devotion to her mistress's memory should have whirled her into a nightmare situation such as this. What will become of her now?"

Sir D'Arcy replied reassuringly, "I understand that she is quitting Lyme, and going to live with her sister in Bath. She will be well cared for there. I am sure that in a few months she will be fully restored to health, with the drama of the standard just a mercifully distant memory."

"The standard!" cried Venetia. "I had it in my hands when Drystan dragged me to to cliff edge. But where is it now? Oh, surely I couldn't have dropped it over the cliff into the sea?"

Sir D'Arcy laid a restraining hand on her arm. "Calm yourself, Venetia. Look!"

He pointed to the bend in the path. There, hanging over a branch, the faded gold glinting proudly in the sunlight, was Lord March's standard.

"You dropped it on the path," Sir D'Arcy said with a smile. "Whilst I was examining the gig, I heard a scream. I dashed out of the wood, and there lying on the ground before me, was the standard. It told me that it was you who had screamed. You who were in danger."

Venetia gazed up at him, her blue eyes soft and luminous. "Is it chance, or destiny which has decreed that you will always be on hand to come to my rescue? How is it that you are always there, just when I need you?"

He took her by the shoulders, and swung her round

to face him. "Does my presence displease you?" he murmured.

"No," she whispered. "Quite the reverse!"

Suddenly, all words seemed superfluous between them. Sir D'Arcy swept the trembling girl into his arms, and kissed her with a warmth and passion that took her breath away. He paused for a moment, and tenderly traced the delicate line of her face with his hand. And then he kissed her again, with a savage, demanding intensity that kindled a raging fire within her, and she clung to him, almost dizzy in her desire for him.

"I love you," he whispered, holding her close. "I have adored you for all the time I have known you. Oh, how it pained me to hear that you were enamored of a man I knew to be a liar and a dissolute gambler!"

"I was thoroughly deceived by Drystan," Venetia murmured sadly. "I knew nothing of his gambling debts. I believed he truly loved me. But it was my fortune he cared for. Why, he thought so little of me, he did not even trouble to write and advise me of his forthcoming leave. Imagining me to be safely at home in Boston, he came to Lyme, with the intention of disporting himself with the loose women of the town." Then she gazed up at Sir D'Arcy and said, with a challenging light in her blue eyes, "Even so, you yourself were not completely unattached. All Lyme imagined there to be an involvement between the Lady Blanche and yourself."

"At the risk of sounding ungallant," replied Sir D'Arcy wryly, "that was a rumor fostered entirely by the lady herself. It was only finally scotched on the day of your accident. I was riding hell for leather for Woodhouse Lodge to enquire after you, when Lady Blanche appeared over the hill, precariously seated on an angry bucking horse. When she learned of my destination, she informed me in the most haughty tones that she felt unable to recommend to her father that he accept my offer of her hand in marriage."

Venetia gasped. "And how did you reply?"

"I fear I was obliged to advise the lady that such a conversation with her father would only leave the old gentleman severely confused. For I had no intention of asking her to marry me. My heart, you see, was pledged to another."

Venetia blushed. Then she raised a hand to her head. "Oh, but I have forgotten to tell you! Aunt Matty is to be married, to her childhood sweetheart! He is an admiral now, and such a charming man."

"I know," smiled Sir D'Arcy. "The admiral made the acquaintance of Lady Leamington in the Assembly Rooms this morning. The Countess's voice being somewhat resemblant of a foghorn, the news was all round Lyme within the hour. But I am delighted for your aunt. It solves so many problems for her."

"And they are so deeply in love," said Venetia. "They are to be married without delay."

Sir D'Arcy ran his fingers through her hair. "I am afraid it will take us a little longer to tie the knot. First, you must take me to meet your parents."

"Yes, we must be wed in the family church in Boston." Venetia sighed happily. She closed her eyes, visualizing her handsome bridegroom standing beside her in the church. She would wear her new white silk gown, with the gold embroidered fleurs-de-lis, decided Venetia. "And then we shall return to Lyme, shall we not, to spend the rest of the summer in Virginia Lodge?"

Sir D'Arcy drew her close to him. "I shall carry you over the threshold," he told her, "And up the stairs, along the corridor to the Rose Room. And there I shall lay you down, and kiss you . . . and then we shall truly be rivals no more."

"Yes!" Venetia laughed. "The contest is over. Love is the victor." She closed her eyes, and willingly surrendered to his loving embrace.

YOUR WARNER LIBRARY OF REGENCY ROMANCE

THE FIVE-MINUTE MARRIAGE
by Joan Aiken   *(84-682, $1.75)*

LADY BLUE
by Zabrina Faire   *(94-056, $1.75)*

PHILIPPA
by Katherine Talbot   *(84-664, $1.75)*

AGENT OF LOVE
by Jillian Kearny   *(94-003, $1.75)*

ACCESSORY TO LOVE
by Maureen Wakefield   *(84-790, $1.75)*

THE MIDNIGHT MATCH
by Zabrina Faire   *(94-057, $1.75)*

THE ROMANY REBEL
by Zabrina Faire   *(94-206, $1.75)*

ENCHANTING JENNY
by Zabrina Faire   *(94-103, $1.75)*

THE SEVENTH SUITOR
by Laura Matthews   *(94-340, $1.75)*

THE SMILE OF A STRANGER
by Joan Aiken   *(94-144, $1.75)*

GWENDELINE
by Jane Ashford   *(94-247, $1.75)*

THE WICKED COUSIN
by Zabrina Faire   *(94-104, $1.75)*

THE PINK PHAETON
by Juliana Davison   *(94-270, $1.75)*

OUTSTANDING READING
FROM WARNER BOOKS

PASSION STAR   (91-498, $2.50)
by *Julia Grice*

The sapphire was called the Passion Star. It was stone-mined by
men and polished to brilliance—but to Adrienne McGill the six-
spurred Passion Star was both magic charm and mystic curse. It
transported her out of the slums of Glasgow to training and star-
dom on the stage. But the girl with the radiantly pale blonde hair
had stolen the treasure in the throes of rape. Now she must pay
for her deed with her heart . . .

AMERICAN ROYAL   (81-827, $2.50)
by *Anne Rudeen*

They had loved each other once . . . but with a youthful passion
that consumed them; now Selena, more beautiful than ever, was
a rich widow whose husband nearly had become President of the
United States. And Hank was now a racing car magnate who had
agreed, without knowing his parentage, to let Selena's son Blair
race for him. For a race that may be the beginning or the end.

THE BEACH CLUB   (91-616, $2.50)
by *Claire Howard*

Have fun in the sun with . . . Laurie: a smouldering redhead
whose husband, down from the city only on weekends, brings
along a teenage babysitter bursting out of her bikini and out of
bounds; B. J.: sharp-tongued rich girl who trapped her husband
into marriage and herself into a swinging scene; Sandy: the loving
wife whose husband has so much love in him it just overflows—
to other women; and Jan: the plain girl whose husband lost interest in her as soon as her father took him into the business. It's
hot in the sun and getting hotter for the four couples exposing
bodies, secrets and passions under the umbrellas at THE BEACH
CLUB.

CARVER'S KINGDOM   (81-201, $2.50)
by *Frederick Nolan*

Sarah Hutchinson, married to an irresponsible wanderer when
Theo Carver, the merchant adventurer, first met her, loved her
and lost her. Sarah Hutchinson, who irrevocably changed the lives
of the ruthless brothers who had wrestled riches and power from
expanding America . . . the men of CARVER'S KINGDOM.

ROMANCE...ADVENTURE... DANGER...

THIS TOWERING PASSION
by Valerie Sherwood
(81-486, $2.50)

500 pages of sweet romance and savage adventure set against the violent tapestry of Cromwellian England, with a magnificent heroine whose beauty and ingenuity captivates every man who sees her, from the king of the land to the dashing young rakehell whose destiny is love!

THIS LOVING TORMENT
by Valerie Sherwood
(95-745, $2.75)

Born in poverty in the aftermath of the Great London Fire, Charity Woodstock grew up to set the men of three continents ablaze with passion! The bestselling sensation of the year, boasting 1.3 million copies in print after just one month, to make it the fastest-selling historical romance in Warner Books history!

THESE GOLDEN PLEASURES
by Valerie Sherwood
(95-744, $2.75)

From the stately mansions of the east to the freezing hell of the Klondike, beautiful Rosanne Rossiter went after what she wanted —and got it all! By the author of the phenomenally successful THIS LOVING TORMENT.

LOVE'S TENDER FURY
by Jennifer Wilde
(81-909, $2.50)

The turbulent story of an English beauty—sold at auction like a slave—who scandalized the New World by enslaving her masters. She would conquer them all—only if she could subdue the hot unruly passions of the heart! The 2 Million Copy Bestseller that brought fame to the author of DARE TO LOVE.

DARE TO LOVE
by Jennifer Wilde
(81-826, $2.50)

Who dared to love Elena Lopez? She was the Queen of desire and the slave of passion, traveling the world—London, Paris, San Francisco—and taking love where she found it! Elena Lopez— the tantalizing, beautiful moth—dancing out of the shadows, warmed, lured and consumed by the heart's devouring flame.

LILIANE
by Annabel Erwin
(91-219, $2.50)

The bestselling romantic novel of a beautiful, vulnerable woman torn between two brothers, played against the colorful background of plantation life in Colonial America.

AURIELLE
by Annabel Erwin
(91-126, $2.50)

The tempestuous new historical romance 4 million Annabel Erwin fans have been waiting for. Join AURIELLE, the scullery maid with the pride of a Queen as she escapes to America to make her dreams of nobility come true.